The battle was brief but fierce.

Magics lit the air in a rainbow spectrum of colors. Their spells had no effect against the Incarnates directly—the unwavering hope and faith required for such conjuring was solely the province of the young, and such had not described them for a long, long time—but they could still launch projectiles and manipulate the environment to inflict injury upon their enemies. They even managed to down a few of the demons, staying well clear of the smoke funnels that rose from their putrid bodies.

Then the delicate well of artcraft ran dry for each of them, their conduits to the Upper shriveling like parched beanstalk within their minds, and the few remaining Olders sank to their knees in the ruins of their village and surrendered.

A large black Andalusian trotted through the ranks of the Incarnate battalion, ridden by a demon who wore thick leather armor tipped with wickedly sharp metal spires along the shoulders, torso and arms. Its gloves and boots were well-made, the former sporting bony, six-cupit long hooks that curved over the fingers: the poisonous claws of a barcun. Beneath the brown plates, the rest of its body was covered in form-fitting, tightly-woven black burlap meant to keep the afternoon sun off its sensitive flesh. A bronze helm sat upon its head, one with twisted horns growing from the sides like the roots of a tree. This Incarnate was far better dressed than the others, some sort of commander in whatever passed for their army's structure.

Tash might be physically blind, but he could see well enough through his conduit's eye, even with his artcraft so depleted. He wondered if the demon that killed his son had looked as resplendent as this one, in those fruitless wars fought so many centuries ago. By now, his boy—once a corporal in the United States Marine Corp, when such an outfit existed—was no more than dust moldering on an ancient battlefield where the lands were shrouded in eternal darkness.

And today…after so long with only a memory…it seemed Tash would be reunited with him.

The Incarnate reined the horse to a stop in front of the kneeling men and leapt from the saddle. The front of its helm was all one solid piece except for an eye slit, around which the snarling visage of a wolf was molded into the bronze. Through that narrow aperture, far back where the light couldn't reach them, two crimson orbs glowed, like embers from a stoked fire. They swept across the Olders before a guttural voice demanded, "Where is the Light?"

"Somewhere you'll never get it, you faithless childkiller!" Eddas roared, reaching forward to snatch at the commander's waist. He needed no artcraft; his large hands would be capable of inflicting a fair amount of damage on the monster in the armor all by themselves. But the Incarnate behind him—a hulking beast as big as Eddas himself, who wielded a broadsword fashioned out of rusted scrap—planted a foot in his broad back and stomped him flat to the ground. His face hit the packed dirt hard enough to make blood burst from his nose.

"Eddas, please." Tash was too weary for more resistance and posturing. "Do not make this harder than it must be."

"Good to see one of you *craeftus* has some sense." The commander stepped past Eddas squirming on the ground and stood before Tash. "Once more…where is the Light?

THE DARK FILAMENT EPHEMERIS
VOLUME II

RUSSELL C. CONNOR

DarkFilament.com

Contact the author at
facebook.com/russellcconnor
Or follow on Twitter @russellcconnor

Cover Art by SaberCore23 Artwork Studio
For commissions, visit sabercore23art.com

ISBN:
978-1-7331133-1-1

First Edition: 2019

Table of Contents

We sensed them here, a blaze so great it glimmered across countless spans. Now though…that fire is gone."

A creaky chuckle escaped Tash's parched throat. "Yeh won' find any children here, I'm afraid."

"No. They're here. You're shielding them somehow with your waning magic."

This caused Tash's tired laughter to spread to the other Olders. Farther down the line, Bibb clutched his round belly and said, "Leave it to this lot to accuse us of the right crime at the wrong time, eh lads?"

"What does that mean?" the commander snapped.

Tash provided the answer. "It means, our magic may be waning, but it was more'n enough ta fool yeh inta draggin yehr rotted bones across 'countless spans' ta get here."

Now their laughter turned to raucous, mocking jeers. Eddas's entire body shook with the force of his snorting guffaws beneath the Incarnate's boot heel.

"No. *No!*" The commander turned left and right, as if expecting a gaggle of youths to appear in the battleworn clearing. The gesture looked very much like panic to Tash, a sight that he relished. Then the demon stilled and refocused its burning stare on Tash. "Why would you do that? Why lure us here? What are you distracting from?"

Their mirth tapered quickly. Tash swallowed and cast his cloudy eyes at the ground.

This much larger and better-equipped squadron of Incarnates had arrived four weeks to the day after Korden Bright walked into the forest on the eastern edge of the village. The Olders had no way to know if he was even alive; all they could do is continue to faith and craft the illusion which had drawn these demons to them, giving the boy as much headway as possible before the ruse was uncovered.

The commander tilted its covered face upward and sucked in a great, snorting breath. Though it seemed to be sniffing the air, Tash knew the sense it used for this detection was far removed from smell. "There's another. A single flame far in the distance, getting farther away by the second."

Tash kept his head down and held his breath, afraid any movement would betray the joy swelling in his breast.

Korden was alive. This creature had just confirmed it.

The Incarnate squatted before him, close enough now for Tash to catch the scent of rancid meat beneath the fancy armor. When it spoke again, that snarling voice from inside the helm was almost gentle. "Why is this flame so important that you would bring destruction down upon yourselves? Is it human love? Tell me…who is this Light?"

Tash lifted his sightless gaze to meet those glowing red eyes. "Yehr end."

The commander stood abruptly, grabbed a fistful of Tash's robe, and yanked him to his feet, the poisonous barbs on its gloves grazing his chest. It barked orders to the others as it dragged Tash toward the horse too fast for his elderly legs to keep pace. "Send word to whoever is closest and get them after this Lightbringer! I want it *slaughtered*! Tell them they have authority to use the riftlings! The rest of you, pre-pare to return immediately!" He lifted Tash off the ground by the back of his robe and gave him a shake, like a bitch with a misbehaving pup. "And find this one a comfortable place for the trip! I wouldn't want his ancient bones to shat-ter before we reach the Blackhold!"

"Sir?" one of the other demons asked, its eyes hidden behind smoky eyepieces screwed right into the flesh of its head. Tash understood its confusion; Incarnates did *not* take prisoners.

"This village stinks of their magic. Something strange happened here, and I think we should find out what." The commander shook Tash hard enough to rattle his few remaining teeth. "We'll deliver this wretch to Regent Torgas and see what he wants to do."

"And the others?"

"Kill them all."

Tash squirmed in the demon's grasp to look back on the last of his brothers, the men he'd lived with in peace and solitude for so long. They were all that was left of a world that was once good and thriving. He reached out for their *mohols*. Bibb wept gently, his aura steeped in somber, forlorn tones, while Port appeared to be faithing with his eyes closed. Eddas, though, was surrounded by an angry, bitter hue the color of clotted blood. Two of the Incarnates yanked him up by the arms and held him in a hunched posture while the big one stood to the side and lifted the huge broadsword over the back of his neck.

Eddas's eyes rolled upward to Tash. "Tell me," he pleaded, his gruff voice cracking. "Tell me it was all worth something, Tash. Tell me the boy means everything you said he did."

"Tha Upper makes no guarantees," Tash told him, smiling through the tears that ran down his weathered cheeks to soak into his beard. "As usual, all we have...is hope."

The commander handed him off to one of the other Incarnates. Tash went willingly, glad to turn away before the blade fell.

His reunion with his son would have to wait a little longer.

Tentacles and Tonics

The Color of Fear

1

Korden Bright jerked as he awoke, his body revolting against his return to consciousness. The dream he'd been having was so good, so soothing, he would've gladly stayed in it longer. Now that it was over, and he found himself thrust back into reality, a fog of depression settled over him. He sat up in the first watery rays of dawn—a host of aches and pains reinforcing his melancholy—and tried to recapture the details before they slipped away.

Was it the same dream, sir? Stone asked. The voice of the telepathic computer was both comforting and distracting as it intruded on his thoughts. Your father?

"No. It was Tash this time." He yawned, reaching back to collect his long hair into a tail, which he tied with a nearby stalk of marydell thistle. "But saying the same sort of things. That everything was fine, I had done well so far, to keep travelling east and I would be safe when I reached these 'Rocky Mountains'."

That is contrary to the warning we were given about Moambati.

Korden shrugged, eager to avoid further questions on the topic.

But Stone was nothing if not persistent. The computer—housed inside a shell that resembled a rock, which dangled from a leather strap around Korden's neck—sounded apprehensive when he asked, AND YOU ARE CERTAIN THAT THESE DREAMS HAVE NOTHING TO DO WITH THE CREATURE WHO CALLED ITSELF LOATHE? HE COMMUNICATED THROUGH YOUR REM CYCLES PREVIOUSLY, AND HE ALSO ENCOURAGED YOU TO MOVE IN AN EASTERN DIRECTION.

"I told you, Loathe could only speak to me through my imagination. He couldn't take the form of anyone real. And besides, he's far behind us now, trapped in that stone arch. Why would he tell me to move *away* from him?" Korden paused to search for the right words to explain the repetitious sequences that kept playing out in his sleep every few nights. These dreams didn't make him uneasy, like his encounters with Loathe. They were comforting, soothing away all his worries and fears. Until they ended, that is. And, more importantly, they left him feeling charged with artcraft, like a waterskin filled to bursting. "I think…these are more like the *other* dream. The one that warned me about Loathe in the first place."

THE MESSAGE YOU BELIEVE CAME FROM THE UPPER, Stone clarified, a hint of cynicism in his voice. SO YOU BELIEVE THESE ARE SIMILAR MISSIVES? THE EQUIVALENT OF A THEOLOGICAL PEP RALLY, PERHAPS?

Korden didn't understand the term, but, as usual, Stone was quick to fill his mind with the necessary frame of reference. "Yes, I do," he answered defensively. "The people that appear in these new dreams…they even speak in rhymes, just like before."

THEN I MUST COUNTER BY INQUIRING WHY A DEITY WOULD NEED TO PRESENT HIMSELF AS DR.

Korden sighed at the familiar smugness in the statement. "Don't start with me, Stone. It's too framming early and I'm not in the mood."

2

It'd been six days since he left Hidden Glen.

Six days since Winstid died, lying on the broken crete in the middle of some forgotten forest road. When he wasn't having the other dreams, Korden's sleeping mind was fraught with nightmares about that day. About the elderly townsfolk being shot as they tried to escape. About Heater Kay's face igniting in searing blue flame forged by Korden's own hand.

About the moment when Cheree must've found out her husband had been killed saving the boy that came into their lives with nothing but destruction and death in his wake.

Would she still be so welcoming if Korden had returned to say he was sorry?

He might've tried to find out, if Winstid hadn't made him promise to go on his way.

So instead, he rode Starry south and east for three days, straying away from the Old 5 Road as Winstid instructed, galloping across overgrown plains, through woodland that was considerably thinner and more pleasant than the haunted redwood forest, and even into an orange orchard where the fruit hung full and ripe and tasted sweeter than anything he could remember. The Shroud—that grim, inky smear in the sky—stayed visible a few degrees to their left. It didn't appear any closer to Korden, although Stone claimed the amount of visible sky it inhabited had increased by .013

percent. They spotted several settlements along the way, crumbling towns with the barest hint of life, but they went well around them. Even when they reached the outskirts of a sprawling, old-world community that reminded Korden of Emmett, they ventured only close enough to read a sign that identified this abandoned metropolis.

Yuba City.

The strange words were easily identifiable on their glossy map. The lake that Winstid and his Peacekeeps had called Tay-ho was due east from here, where rolling mountains climbed the horizon like the spine of a giant, sleeping beast. Stone called this range the 'Sierra Nevadas' and assured him that Tay-ho (which he insisted on pronouncing 'Tah-ho') was nestled among them.

Another two days brought them to a second road named with a random number, this one 80. They were close enough to the mountains now that the shadow touched them at sunrise, then receded rapidly like a dark ocean wave settling into low tide. Ancient autos sat in an unending line on this new highway as far as the eye could see in both directions. Stone advised that these had likely been part of the western mass exodus that occurred during the Purges, as people took their children and fled from the Dark Filament's armies. Some of the rusted hulks had wheels covered in rotting rubber, but Korden also spotted many whose undercarriages sported the same glassy hubs that made the Trikers' vehicles hover.

A faded green sign hung over the lanes of dead traffic, proclaiming that something called a 'Sacramento' was '84 MI' farther to the south. Above this, in much newer and less professional paint, a red arrow pointed to the section of road that ran on to the northeast, along with the scrawled words, IDA...279 SPANS.

That night, Korden bedded down inside a thick tree line of stately pine and high-topped oaks that began at the base of a gentle mountain slope, and fell into an exhausted slumber.

3

He stood after finishing his talk with Stone and found a spot to urinate. A few steps away, Starry grazed on a patch of grass still lush and green from the fair Bloom weather, which was slowly fading into the warmer temperatures of Burning Season. Korden ran a hand through the palomino's silken mane and received a friendly nuzzle against his neck. He'd come to like the horse a great deal in the short time they'd been together, and the amount of ground they covered was astonishing. It would've taken him another two or three weeks to come this far on foot.

Korden returned to his little camp and made a quick breakfast of the last of the bread and cheese given to him by the Peacekeeps, along with the only orange free from mold. He would be forced to hunt for his food by nightfall, but he didn't think the task would be such a problem in a wildland that hadn't been leeched of all its life. Right now, it was just nice to have a lightened carry pouch.

Once the pressing physical needs of his body were met, he sat down on his bedroll, crossed his legs, closed his eyes, and began the day's faithing. After a few minutes of meditation, he could feel the conduit open and stable in his mind. All that artcraft bestowed upon him by the dream flowed through the connection, coursed beneath his skin, thrummed in tune with his heartbeat. At times like this, it was easy to have faith in the oneness of the Upper, to sense His divine hand at work in all things, both large and small, which in turn gave him even more control over the flow of magic. Feeling powerful and in perfect harmony with the world around him, Korden opened his eyes and took his right arm out of the cloth sling that Stone had persuaded him to wear.

Most of the injuries from his high-speed fall off the hovertrike were healing on their own, leaving behind scars, a dull ache in his back from his banged-up vertebrae, and a twinge where his wrist had sprained. Stone had finally stopped monitoring him for signs of what he called 'a concussion,' but Korden's biggest source of discomfort were the broken bones in his hand.

He cradled the appendage in his lap and flexed the fingers slowly. Sharp pain flared through his palm. At first, it felt like one big throb, but, when he concentrated, he could separate out the individual sources. Korden chose one of these and pushed his consciousness forth to probe at the bones beneath the skin. He formed an image in his mind of the fracture that ran through them, and then, as he tapped into that swollen river of artcraft, he imagined the bones knitting themselves back together, growing and smoothing over the injury. The sting increased until his eyes watered, but he didn't let up, instead uttering a Craften chant under his breath to keep his mind focused.

Using artcraft for healing—particularly one's self—was a tricky affair. With enough willpower and faith, your conjurings were limited only by your creativity, but those corporealized imaginings must conform to reality. If you didn't comprehend the nature of the wound and the innerworkings of the body, you could be fixing something incorrectly. Perhaps causing an even worse problem. Feegran, the Olders' village doctor, used to say that an imprecise heal could just as easily seal an artery as clip a hangnail.

In this case though, with such a debilitating injury and an abundance of power making him feel like he could do anything, Korden thought the risk was warranted. He'd held these healing sessions every morning that he woke from one of the happy dreams.

Balance, he thought now, advice given to him so many times in his lessons. *Don't overextend yourself. Better to do too little than too much.*

After working with each of the breaks, he flexed the hand again. The mobility felt improved even if the pain did not.

Or maybe that was wishful thinking.

"Can you tell if it's any better?"

INDETERMINATE. IF SO, THE REPAIR IS ON A LEVEL TOO MICROSCOPIC FOR MY HEALTH SENSORS.

"Wow, thanks for the optimism, Stone."

WELL-INTENTIONED LIES SERVE NOTHING BUT THE EGO, SIR.

He used another dollop of artcraft to dull his senses to the pain, put his arm back in the sling, then packed away his bedroll, slipped on his flaming sneakers and tied the laces, using his injured hand only when absolutely necessary. By the time he'd finished, the sun was high enough to peek between two of the rugged summits above him, spilling warm golden light down the forest slope. Korden craned his head back and studied the chain of choppy mountains that stretched across the land to the north and south. The trees dwindled near the top of the higher crests into rocky brown crags, where blankets of pure white lined every crease and crevice.

Snow. He'd never seen snow. Back home, in the village, he knew that it sometimes came down in the deeper parts of the redwood forest, but he'd never been allowed to go to it, of course. He longed to hold it in his hands, to lay down in the cold fluff and make one of the 'angels' that Fortholm used to tell him about.

"So Tay-ho is just on the other side, right?"

DIRECTLY EAST FROM WHERE YOU NOW STAND. I CALCULATE THE DISTANCE AS APPROXIMATELY 78.6 SPANS. THIS COULD, OF COURSE, BE MADE CONSIDERABLY LONGER BY ROUGH TERRAIN.

"I thought you said these mountains wouldn't be as bad as the Rockies."

AND THEY WILL NOT. HOWEVER, A LESSER SEVERITY DOES NOT NEGATE THE DANGERS INHERENT HERE. YOU ARE ILL-PREPARED FOR SCALING A SUMMIT, SIR, ESPECIALLY ON HORSEBACK. I CALCULATE A 17.9 PERCENT CHANCE OF INJURY, AN UNACCEPTABLE DEGREE WHEN SAFER METHODS ARE AVAILABLE. I MUST REITERATE MY RECOMMENDATION THAT WE REJOIN INTERSTATE 80 AND FOLLOW IT AROUND, SO THAT WE ENTER THE LAKE FROM THE NORTH.

"We need to stay off the roads. The Trikers are probably too far away to find us, but we have a better chance of coming across Incarnates on one of those highways than out here in the middle of nowhere. Besides, the faster we get to Ida, the better."

AND YOU REMAIN POSITIVE THAT A VISIT TO THIS SETTLEMENT IS NECESSARY? PARDON ME FOR SAYING, BUT WE HAVE NOT HAD GREAT LUCK IN THE PRESENCE OF OTHER PEOPLE.

As he had many times before, Korden weighed the pros and cons of his intended destination. He wasn't so much worried about other people hurting him as he was about getting *other* people hurt. The last thing he wanted was to bring ruination to another town of innocents. But, in the end, his inner debate came to the same conclusion. "If this Prophet of theirs can tell us how to avoid Incarnates—or maybe what this *Moambati* is—then it'll be worth it."

IN THAT CASE, I HAVE MAPPED A TENTATIVE ROUTE BASED ON TOPOGRAPHICAL INFORMATION AVAILABLE PRIOR TO MY LAST M-NET UPDATE. THIS SHOULD UTILIZE MOUNTAIN PASSES WHENEVER POSSIBLE TO MAINTAIN THE LOWEST POSSIBLE ELEVATION.

"Well, curse. I wanted to see snow."

AND YOU STILL MAY AT THIS TIME OF YEAR, ON THE EASTERN DOWNSLOPE. BUT TEMPERATURES WILL REMAIN MUCH COOLER NEAR THE PEAKS. IF IT WERE WINTER—YOUR STILLING SEASON—THE ODDS OF SUCCESSFULLY TRAVERSING THIS RANGE LOWER CONSIDERABLY.

"I don't see what the big deal is. It's just snow."

PERHAPS YOU WOULD LIKE TO REVIEW MY FILES ON THE DONNER PARTY, WHICH OCCURRED A HUNDRED SPANS FROM HERE. IT ALSO BRINGS TO MIND ANOTHER CAUTION: IF WE DO NOT REACH THE ROCKY MOUNTAINS BEFORE THE FIRST SNOWFALL OF THE YEAR, IT IS PROBABLE THAT WE WILL BE UNABLE TO CROSS UNTIL THE FOLLOWING BLOOM.

"All the more reason to take the fastest route to Ida. C'mon Starry, let's climb this overgrown hill."

It took only a few hours for Korden to see that he would be eating those words. Their pace started out quick, but, as the grade of the land became steeper, they were forced to slow down so that Starry could find sure-footed paths that often zigzagged back and forth across the face of the mountain. Korden used the time to faith as best he could while on jostling horseback, then to practice crafting. His proficiency and quickness with some of the basic elemental spells had improved drastically since they'd left Hidden Glen. Korden wanted to believe this was because of practice, or even the surge of artcraft the dreams left him with, but, deep down, he feared his killing of Heater Kay had brought him past some mental hurdle.

Tash had said that strong emotion would help his power, if not his control. But Korden shuddered to think that only such an atrocious act could make him a stronger Crafter.

As midday approached, Stone guided them into a short valley covered in purple lupine and red Indian paintbrushes, with a trickling brook running through it. They stopped here for Starry to drink and Korden to refill his waterskins. At the far end of the valley, they crossed the remnants of a hard-packed dirt road that Stone said was for logging purposes, now overgrown with weeds and thready skilne grass. After that, the land swept upward in another steep escarpment for a few hundred pargs before leveling off into a forested shelf, which is where they ran across the scorched corridor through the trees.

4

It looked like a gigantic, flaming boulder had rolled across the land, tearing the pines in its path out of the ground by their roots and setting fire to those surrounding. But the destruction must've happened long ago, for the dead trees had decomposed into hollow, blackened shells and the tortured forest floor had recovered enough to sprout a thick new carpet of undergrowth. The cleared strip was wide enough for Starry to stand head to tail with himself five times. At the point where Korden came across it, the trail began out of nowhere thirty or so pargs away to his right. On the left—the direction the object must've traveled judging by the strewn wreckage—it stretched out of sight into the forest.

"Let's take a look," Korden said, climbing off Starry's saddle. He slipped his carry pouch over his shoulder, checked to make sure his knife was in the sheath on his belt, and tied the horse to a branch while he followed the trail.

They reached the culprit a few minutes later. Even though it appeared as an oval, Korden got the impression of a tube lying deep within the rut it'd carved in the earth. The main body was made not of metal, but one of the strange substances that Stone always referred to as 'polymers,' which never seemed to decompose or break down like so much from the old world. Untold years of sun and rain had worn away its paint though, leaving a few swatches of green to hint at its original color. But it was the huge glass mounds covering its backside—each one the circumference of his spread arms—that let Korden recognize what he was looking at even before Stone could tell him.

"It's a vehicle!" he exclaimed. "One like the triker's machines!"

CORRECT. A STRATOLINER. IT APPEARS TO BE AN X SERIES, MODEL D7, CIVILIAN CLASS, ONE-HUNDRED PASSENGER CAPACITY. AFTER THE ACCELERATED ION NETWORK WENT ONLINE IN 2094, THE AVIATION INDUSTRY QUICKLY CONVERTED TO SUCH AIRCRAFTS FOR THEIR LOWER COST AND RELIABILITY. ACCORDING TO RECORDS, SEVERAL SUCH FLIGHTS WERE LOST DUE TO INCONSTANT NODE FLUCTUATIONS DURING THE CHAOS AS PEOPLE FLED THE DARK FILAMENT. THIS ONE MUST'VE ATTEMPTED AN EMERGENCY LANDING ON THE CLOSEST FLAT STRETCH OF LAND IT COULD FIND.

"Stratoliner." Korden recalled the wonderfully alien word from one of his and Stone's many talks. He walked around the side of the craft, thinking of the crashed auto outside his village, the one that set this whole journey in motion. From the new perspective, he got a better sense of its shape, more like a shooter projectile than a tube, with the front end tapering to a blunt tip that was mostly buried in the ground from the skidding impact. The entire length must be close to eighty pargs. Square windows ran down the side, crusted with grime. Below them were huge letters in a fancy script, so stained and faded he could barely make them out: *AERO VEGAS*. "It's so big! How high could it hover?"

TRANSPORTS LIKE THIS USED HARD ION TRAILS TO ACHIEVE LOW EARTH ORBIT, APPROXIMATELY 3,500 SPANS HIGH. I HAVE FOUND A FREE-LICENSE HOLO-AD I CAN LOOP INTO YOUR NEURAL FEED IF YOU WOULD LIKE.

"Uh...sure."

Korden's vision blacked out. Panic seized him at the spontaneous blindness. He opened his mouth to cry out but could no longer move, could no longer perceive his body at all.

A soothing baritone voice spoke in the darkness, the words coming from all directions.

At American Airlines, we're committed to getting you to your destination as fast as possible. Our brand new, state-of-the-art stratoliner fleet is ready to take you from L.A. to New York in just thirty minutes. That's the American Guarantee. Oh, and the view isn't half bad either.

Korden's sight returned...but he was no longer in the forest. He sat in some kind of plush, comfortable seat with his hands draped over armrests to either side. Except they didn't look like *his* hands, and the body he inhabited felt much taller than his own. The surreal, out-of-body sensation was quickly forgotten as he took in the rest of his surroundings.

In front of him, close enough to reach out and touch, three more chairs were situated in a tight row, facing away from him. And, over their backs, he could see more such rows stretching away down a narrow enclosure with a curved ceiling. This was what the inside of the tube must look like, and everyone that traveled in it would be facing the same direction, like an audience awaiting a performance.

That curved ceiling overhead came down to form a convex wall to the right of his seat. A window was set into the middle, and when Korden leaned over in the body that wasn't his to look through it, a tingle of half-pleasure, half-terror ran through him.

The view beyond the glass took in a boundless aquamarine vista with irregular green shapes spread across it. Streaks of gauzy white floated serenely above it all, casting a shadow on the masses below. The blue ended at a long, downward curve about halfway up the window, beyond which was velvety darkness.

That's the earth, he thought in amazement, staring down at the oceans. The sense of largeness and distance made him clutch at the armrest with his borrowed hands in case he should suddenly plunge toward it. *I'm above the entire earth!*

American Airlines, the soothing voice reiterated. *Why fly, when you can soar?*

And then he was thrust back into his own body, standing beside the crashed stratoliner.

"Oh. Oh wow." Korden put out a hand against the polymer side of the vehicle to steady his shaky legs. "I might want to do that again later."

DEPENDING ON THE STATE OF THE BACKUP ION CELLS, I MAY BE ABLE TO TRANSMIT AN EMERGENCY OVERRIDE TO OPEN THE DOOR. IF YOU WOULD LIKE TO GO INSIDE, THE ENTRANCE SHOULD BE FARTHER DOWN.

The image of the auto came to him again, its occupants diminished to hollow-eyed skeletons in rags. His breakfast squirmed in his stomach. The last thing he wanted to see was more dead bodies.

Based on this transport's structural integrity, I calculate only a 5.7 percent chance of crash fatalities.

"Well...all right," Korden conceded, excitement edging out his trepidation.

He walked toward the tapered front until he came to an oblong outline in the side of the stratoliner. There was a series of harsh clicks in his head while Stone worked, then, with a soft hiss, the oblong seal broke and the door of the vehicle folded down in front of him to reveal a set of stairs on the other side.

5

The sunlight fell away as he stepped over the threshold of the stratoliner, leaving him in deep shade. His eyes adjusted, and the first thing he noticed was the cloud of yellowish smoke in the air, a dirty, ocher haze that hung motionless over the upper third of the interior. Korden wrinkled his nose in anticipation of breathing it, but there was no odor in the stratoliner other than a general mustiness.

He stood in a tiny alcove, with cabinets and bins along the wall to his left. Most of these stood open, and various items like blankets, cups, and small silvery packets of something called 'Nagaraya' and 'Ripples Potato Chips' had exploded outward all over the floor. A locked door at the far end was labeled 'Cockpit'; Stone reported that security protocols prevented him from opening it. Korden walked through the debris, the silver packets crinkling beneath his feet, and continued to where the wall on his right opened up.

Square, hard-sided carry pouches that Stone identified as 'luggage' clogged a narrow passage, tossed haphazardly by the crash. Korden clambered over them as best he could with one hand in a sling. He tried to peer ahead, but the gloom intensified the farther he got from the entrance. And this yellow smoke might not have a scent, but it didn't make seeing any easier. Korden waved a hand in front of his face as he stepped over the last of the suitcases, but the vapors stayed oddly still, not dissipating or even swirling.

SIR, I AM CONFUSED. MY SENSORS DETECT NO SMOKE. AND YOUR OPTICAL INPUT FEED CONTAINS NOTHING LIKE WHAT YOUR THOUGHT PROCESS IS DESCRIBING.

Korden froze, studying the fumes. They were right there, all around him. Was Stone malfunctioning again?

Then, with a mental click, he understood.

He wasn't seeing the smoke, but rather, *sensing* it. Because it wasn't smoke at all.

The interior of the stratoliner was drenched in a *mohol* the dirty lemon color of fear. Now that he knew what he was looking at, the emotion was so prevalent that it chilled his flesh.

He'd never seen a free-standing aura before. So far as he knew, it wasn't possible. Nor did he know how he was experiencing it without intentionally opening his awareness to the emotional spectrum. Perhaps the latter could be attributed to the fact that artcraft was practically leaking from his ears, but the former was a mystery.

Yet another blank spot in Tash's lessons.

Except in this case, he probably didn't know himself, Korden thought. *He and the others sequestered themselves in that village right after they discovered the Upper. There could be a lot they never experienced.*

Korden moved deeper into the vessel, keeping his head ducked below the cloud of fear. A few steps later, the stratoliner opened up into a large space that he recognized from the vision Stone had given him outside. Windows like the one he'd looked through lined both walls, the filthy panes filtering in enough light to pierce the yellow haze. Row upon row of dusty seats faced him, all of them empty except for a few other bags and personal items left behind in the rush to disembark the crashed transport.

Somehow, this was just as bad as if the stratoliner *had* been filled with bodies. It all looked overwhelmingly sad and lonely, like those long-dead parents clutching their book of fotos.

What else did you expect? The voice that spoke in his head this time was that of Redfen Bright. *You wanted so badly to see the old world. Well, this is it, son. Broken, used up, abandoned. It won't come any other way, otherwise it never would've ended.*

"All right, I've seen it," Korden said. The disembodied *mohol* was making him more uncomfortable by the second. "Maybe we should—"

He trailed. Something was happening. Those tawny fumes were in motion now, drifting down from the ceiling, gathering and coalescing, forming shapes in the seats. In the time it took for Korden to swallow the sticky wad of spit stuck in his throat, every chair in the transport was filled with translucent yellow forms. He could see the outlines of men, women and even children, although their features were hazy and indistinct, like a dense mist. They moved as naturally as real people, shifting around, turning to one another, opening and closing their mouths as if speaking, some of them making pantomimed motions as if swiping at some invisible object in their palms.

It was as though he'd somehow walked into the midst of their trip, caught them in a nonchalant, carefree moment. He goggled, unable to look away, transfixed by this scene from the old world.

Then their demeanor changed. They all abruptly faced forward in unison and stiffened. A second later, their movements became frantic and violent, slamming around in their seats, clutching at the armrests and one another.

And screaming. Korden could hear them now, a hundred voices rising in unmitigated terror, filling the aircraft. He slapped hands over his ears, ignoring the pain this ignited in his right palm, but it did nothing to shut out the cries.

MR. BRIGHT! IS SOMETHING WRONG?

He didn't answer. Couldn't answer. His heart pounded in his chest as he watched the *mohol* people shriek, his exposed arms goosepimpling.

Still screaming, they rose from their seats and drifted toward him in the dim cabin. They held their hands out to him, clutching at the air.

Korden wheeled around, meaning to flee, but halted before taking even a step. One of the vaporous yellow forms stood in his way, this one close enough to see its translucent clothing: a formal, stiff garment that the old world had simply called a 'suit,' and a rounded cap with an eagle emblazoned across the front. The figure looked at Korden with wide, blank eyes while wailing in his face.

Both of its misty arms rose. Korden ducked under them to run, but one of the appendages passed through his shoulder.

It had no more substance than an aura, but, in that brief contact, Korden's own fear grew a thousandfold, terror blotting out all other thought. The emotion overflowed his brain, spilled through his body, shut down his weak lungs, made his skin burn. He would collapse and suffocate from the weight of it.

Then he was past, the contact broken, and that debilitating fear faded. Korden scrambled over the blockade of luggage, slamming his injured hand in his haste to escape, silently pleading with the Upper to deliver him from this place. He didn't stop running until he was back outside in the sun, a handful of paces from the stratoliner, and even then he sat down in the grass where he could make sure nothing had followed.

Stone jabbered at him. SIR, PLEASE, CALM DOWN! YOUR CORTISOL AND ADRENALINE LEVELS SPIKED, BUT I DETECTED NO STIMULI FOR YOUR DISTRESS!

"You couldn't see them," Korden panted. But no, of course he couldn't. The artcraft-sensitive parts of his brain were a blind spot for the computer. Stone could only discern the physical changes his magic wrought upon the world, and even those caused him 'logical dissonance.'

SEE WHAT?

"Spirits." Korden used the word from the stories Allin and Fortholm used to tell. Those had been works of fiction, told around a crackling fire for fun and creative sharpening, but what he'd just experienced had felt very real. "Some sort of…I don't know, ghosts. They were terrified and screaming. I think…I think they might have been the people who were inside when it crashed."

Stone considered this with a few low beeps. LEAVING ASIDE THE ARGUMENT ON WHETHER SUCH ENTITIES EVEN

EXIST, GHOSTS ARE BEINGS TYPICALLY ASSOCIATED WITH THE DEATH OF THEIR PHYSICAL FORM. BUT, AS NOTED BEFORE, EVERYONE INVOLVED IN THIS MISHAP LIKELY SURVIVED. THE LACK OF BODIES OR EVEN BLOODSTAINS ON BOARD SUPPORT THIS.

"I know that. But these things…they weren't actually ghosts, they were *auras*."

I'M NOT SURE I UNDERSTAND.

"They were made out of fear," he explained. "I could feel it when one of them touched me. Pure, raw, unfiltered terror. It's like…it's like an echo of their emotion was trapped inside there. And I think they tried to spread it to me."

Nightmare on Countless Legs

1

When he was composed and breathing normally again, Korden walked down the length of the stratoliner, keeping his distance this time. He was determined to get back to Starry and go on his way, but, as he rounded the back of the transport where those enormous glass hubs protruded, a grumbling noise reached his ears. He jumped away from the vessel, afraid that one of the *mohol* ghosts was going to come through the wall, but Stone quickly clarified the situation.

I CALCULATE A 92.1 PERCENT CHANCE THAT IS A COMBUSTION ENGINE, LESS THAN A SINGLE SPAN TO THE WEST AND APPROACHING RAPIDLY.

Korden paused, torn between discretion and curiosity. Deciding to take Tash's advice that knowledge was always the better option, he ducked low and crept through the line of trees back the way he'd come. That grumbling sound grew louder, became a growl. He reached the edge of the mountain shelf, before the last escarpment they'd climbed a half hour before. At the bottom of the slope, the overgrown logging road hugged the curves of the valley. A long straightaway shot to the northwest, providing an unimpeded view of the vehicle trundling toward him.

It was big and boxy, with six wheels spinning beneath, two of which appeared to be flat. Reams of greasy black smoke squirted out from under the hood, obscuring the front windshield and whoever sat within. The exterior was a deep brown color, and, as it drew closer, he could see the words **UPS LOCAL** written on the side.

This was the first auto Korden had ever seen in full operation. Five or six weeks ago, this would've been the height of his sixteen-year existence, but it wasn't as exciting now that he'd ridden on one of the zooming hovertrikes. He squatted in a thick stand of hecklebrush and watched through the leaves as the vehicle came to a stop with a rusted squall at the base of the escarpment, twenty or thirty pargs short of parking directly beneath him. The chug of its engine died away.

And, as he reached out for the driver's *mohol*, a door at the front slid open, revealing a figure sitting at the steering wheel.

Dread chilled Korden to the bone.

The unmistakable form of an Incarnate stepped down from the vehicle. And not just any Incarnate; Korden recognized the lithe form of the female in the dark longcloak and welder's mask from his encounter on the bridge a couple of weeks ago, before he'd gotten lost in Loathe's forest. She'd ridden horseback then; it was odd to see her now driving an old-world vehicle, since Incarnates had as little use for technology as Tash.

Her presence could be no coincidence. She'd been tracking him this entire time. It was another reminder why he could never stay in one place for too long.

Two other Incarnates climbed out behind her, both male, both scrawny, both with nothing more than dark-tinted goggles pulled over their eyes to protect them from the light. One of them wore an outfit close to the denim-and-deerskin ensembles favored by the townsfolk of Hidden Glen; the other a pair of filthy canvas dungarees and leather boots, his bare chest marred by sunrot. As with all Incarnates, they were regular people once, before having their bodies commandeered by the demons.

Don't blame me. Stone sounded miffed. My recommendation was the highway. It was you who said we stood less chance of running into them by staying away from roads.

Well, they're on a road, aren't they? Korden thought, switching to silent communication. *Besides, no route is safe as long as they can track me.*

Then I suggest leaving at once.

Steady on. Korden used the colloquialism he'd learned from the Glenners without being conscious of it. *Remember the bridge?*

I recall us plunging from it.

Before that, I mean. That Incarnate knew I was close, but he wouldn't've known where if he hadn't seen me. They can't pinpoint my exact location, only a general sense of direction. And even if they could, there's no way they could catch up on foot before I got back to Starry. Unless they can drive that auto straight up the mountain…

I calculate an 89.3 percent chance that such an attempt would end in catastrophic failure.

Then see? Nothing to worry about. Let's enjoy watching those curseheads run in circles for a bit.

Down below, the two males headed for the rear of the truck. The female stood in the road, longcloak puddled on the ground around her slender figure. Her covered face scanned the hillside through the small window in the featureless mask. Korden stayed very still, imagining her red eyes as they played across his hiding spot. He wondered briefly how many children below free age had found themselves caught in that same unmerciful gaze. Then she turned back to the vehicle, reached inside, and drew out a white polymer cone with a handle on the bottom; a 'bullhorn,' according to Stone. The Incarnate pulled at the bottom of the welder's mask, flipping it up to a horizontal position on her forehead. Korden caught a brief glimpse of the face beneath before she put the smaller end of the bullhorn to her mouth. Her gravelly voice echoed across the face of the mountain.

"I know you're close, little Lightbringer," she said. "Close enough to hear my voice. You *are* the same one that pulled my partner into the river, aren't you?"

Korden didn't move, didn't breathe. His previous flippancy seemed ill-advised now.

"You can't run forever," the Incarnate continued. "We'll never give up the hunt. But, if you come out now, I promise to make your death quick and painless."

The two standing at the rear of the auto brayed harsh laughter.

She waited another moment before speaking through the bullhorn. "Fine. Have it your way. But I doubt the riftlings will be quite so generous."

With that, she signaled to her companions. One of the male Incarnates undid a latch on the back of the vehicle and the other yanked at the bottom. The panel slid upward, disappearing into the ceiling, and then both demons stood aside to make way for the monstrosity within.

2

At first, Korden thought the black mass boiling from the back of the auto was one gigantic, formless beast with a million wriggling antennae. Then it broke apart as it hit the ground, separating into distinct forms, and he saw it was some sort of swarm.

Each creature consisted of a glistening black, amorphous blob, with a smaller globule perched on one end that must be a head. All of this sat atop a glut of purplish tentacles that—along with two short, crab-like pincers dangling under what could anatomically be considered their chins—seemed to be the only appendages they possessed. Numbering as many as thirty, the collective ranged in exact height and size, but most of them would come up to the waist of an adult human.

W-what are those?

SEARCHING...0 RELATABLE ENTRIES FOR THE TERM 'RIFTLING'. I CAN ALSO FIND NO LISTING IN THE TAXONOMY CLASSIFICATION FOR ANY ANIMAL WITH SUCH BIOLOGIC TRAITS, BUT SUCH KNOWLEDGE GAPS GREW RAPIDLY IN THE WAKE OF THE GREAT SPECIES EMERGENCE.

The strange horde had barely finished separating behind the truck before they burst into motion, their squid-like legs churning the dirt, and, unlike the Incarnates, there was no ambiguity in *their* direction. They arrowed up the slope straight at Korden's hiding spot, each one a nightmare on countless legs.

He stood, reaching for their auras at the same time. If they were animals, perhaps he could soothe them, even turn them away. But he saw no colors around them. At first he thought he'd done something wrong, that his abundant well of artcraft had gone dry, then realized he could see the vile, sludgy *mohols* of the Incarnates behind them. These 'rift-lings' however…

They had no auras at all. Were, in fact, utterly invisible to his emotional inspection.

Korden tore his eyes away from them and fled.

"That's right, run Lightbringer!" the Incarnate shouted in her amplified voice. "Spend your last moments *bathing in fear!*"

The slope was a few hundred pargs long, and the creatures covered a third of it in the two or three seconds it took Korden to get moving. He'd gone only another thirty paces into the woods before he heard the whispery shuffling of their steps behind him and chanced a look over his shoulder.

The first of the riftlings crested the escarpment, followed quickly by two more…then five…then a dozen, all different sizes. They never hesitated, just honed in on him and kept moving, flocking together in formation like birds. Their squirming limbs became a bruised purple blur under them, working together to propel the black bodies forward at incredible speed.

He would never be able to outrun them on foot.

At least, not without a distraction.

Korden didn't stop to think. He raised his good arm, crafted a fat blue fireball in the palm of his hand much like the one that melted Heater Kay's face, and hurled it back at them.

The swarm tried to change directions, but they were moving too fast and packed too densely to evade the missile. The fireball struck the trunk of an oak in their midst. The tree exploded at the point of impact with a muffled *whump!* Jagged, flaming skewers shot outward. Korden saw a few of the creatures get impaled and crash to the ground in a tangle of tentacles and one become engulfed in cyan flames. The wounded and dead were left behind as the rest corrected course and shot after him with a terrible single-mindedness.

He burst out of the trees, back into the singed groove the stratoliner had carved through the earth, and turned right, toward where Starry was tethered. Stone babbled in his head, updating him with ranges and time till intersection and projected success percentages for possible evasion tactics (none of them very high). Korden ignored him, pulled his arm out of the awkward sling, and visualized fireballs in both hands this time, plumping them up until his limbs shook with the raw power collected in his palms. Never had he crafted anything like this, and now it came like second nature. That surplus of artcraft sang through him, a mighty river whose banks could easily swell out of control if he wasn't careful.

When he looked back this time, the riftlings were barely fifty pargs back, close enough for him to see the multiple yellow eyes buried in the glistening flesh of their heads, all fixed on Korden. Below these, their pincers snapped in anticipation.

Korden threw both fireballs on two different vectors. Twin explosions flung gelatinous bodies through the air, their flailing tentacles on fire. As the rest of the horde tried to dodge away, Korden targeted one of the largest dead trees along the corridor's edge and forced his will upon it, envisioned it ripping free of the ground and crashing over.

The result was satisfying. The blackened trunk came down hard, crushing a few more of his pursuers. Korden whooped.

But the victory was short-lived. A dozen of the creatures swarmed over the fallen tree or sped around the sides. They spread out from one another, insuring that such an attack would not work again.

Korden faced forward and concentrated on running, thankful for his sure-footed sneakers. His lungs felt gooey and sluggish, the as-mah causing each breath to drag through his windpipe. He could see Starry ahead, tied to a tree. The big palomino whinnied in terror and struggled to get loose. Korden touched his *mohol*, mollifying the horse enough so that he was kneeling and ready for him to leap into the saddle. He untied the bridle, wheeled Starry eastward into the forest, and urged him to a full gallop.

Behind them, the riftlings had closed the distance to twenty pargs, the closest they'd come to him yet, but they struggled to keep up with the horse's speed. As Korden twisted in the saddle to watch, he noticed an annoying buzz around his head, fading in and out, like a mosquito searching for a landing spot.

Warning! Detecting —ignal —terferen— Stone's voice stuttered in and out of audibility.

One of the creatures—the largest, by Korden's estimation, its plump body as wide as Starry's muscular haunches—gathered itself and put on a burst of speed, gaining ground until it was just ten pargs behind. Its jaundiced eyes—all eight of them—regarded Korden with cold hatred. At the same time, that buzz grew louder, blotting out Stone entirely.

Korden raised a hand, intending to conjure another fireball and sling it into the monster's face.

Nothing came.

The conduit—that comforting connection to the Upper, the spring from which all artcraft flowed—was clamped shut against him.

He went deeper into his head, faithing, prying at the link. But that buzzing sound kept breaking his concentration. Every time he thought he'd reestablished contact, it slipped away.

That noise. That noise was in his *mind.*

These creatures were *blocking his power somehow.*

A flutter of stinging panic shot through him.

On the face of the large riftling, its spongy black flesh shifted, muscles twitching and separating to reveal a huge maw lined with triangular teeth, each one like the tip of a dagger. Korden's breath caught as he stared down that endless gullet.

"*Go, go!*" He dug his heels into Starry's side. The horse charged through dense woods now, trees whipping by on either side. Korden hunched low to keep away from the branches, his carry pouch slapping against his back with every stride. Without his artcraft or even Stone's advice, he felt completely defenseless, with no idea except to flee.

Cracking noises came from behind. Korden glanced back.

The riftlings on the swarm's flanks were in the trees now, using their tentacles to swing from branch to branch like a jungle boy he'd once read about. Even moving like this, their speed was uncannily fast, although not enough to catch up. But he soon saw their intent when two of them flung themselves through the air from either side and latched onto Starry's pumping rear legs.

Their tentacles encircled the horse's limbs in a slithering knot. Once in position, the creatures used their pincers to slice through skin and muscle. Blood streamed from the wounds. Starry squealed in pain, his long strides faltering.

Korden gripped the saddle with his knees and leaned off the side of the bouncing horse as far as he dared. He balled up his good fist and punched one of the riftlings in the side, trying to dislodge it. The dark flesh felt squishy beneath his knuckles, like hitting a wad of bread dough. The creature hissed and clacked a claw in his direction, missing his fingers by cupits.

And then the big one caught up to them. From the corner of his eye, Korden saw those teeth sink into the narrow part of Starry's left rear leg, above the hoof. There was a *snap* as sharp as broken kindling. The horse screamed as his limbs crumpled. Momentum sent the animal crashing face first into the ground.

Korden was hurled from the saddle, sailing over the horse's head. A thick carpet of pine needles along the woodland floor softened his fall, but he hit the ground hard on one shoulder and rolled, his broken hand throbbing from each impact. Despite the fresh pain, he leapt to his feet as soon as the tumble ended and looked back.

Starry lay on his side with those things all over him, biting and tearing him apart. The startlingly white bands of his ribcage showed through his shredded torso. The horse's eyes pleaded with Korden, lips peeled back in a grimace.

Fury consumed him at the animal's torment.

That buzzing in his head had abated. The conduit was open.

Korden raised both hands and spouted fire, this time in a continual stream that arced through the air with a low *whoosh*. Flames ate up the dying horse, extinguishing his life, along with a few of the riftlings too slow to jump away. Trees and undergrowth blazed. The smell of cooking meat made Korden's gorge rise. He swept his arms outward, forming a wall of blue fire that separated him from the rest of the creatures. He urged it on, sent it racing away in either direction for dozens of pargs.

Then he turned and ran.

The fire wouldn't slow them for long. If he didn't think of some way to escape the rest, he was done for. Stone's voice was back also, telling him about a mental link degradation associated with proximity to the riftlings, but he quieted as Korden halted just before stepping off the edge of a yawning chasm.

3

The canyon in front of him was forty pargs wide, but much deeper than that, descending into shadowy darkness below his feet. It ripped through the mountain as far as he could see in both directions, with no way to cross over. Slender pine trees grew right up to the cliff's edge here, but on the far side, a rocky plain stretched for a bit before the land ascended sharply.

WARNING! AUDITORY SENSE SCANS DETECT THE REMAINING CREATURES APPROACHING! I ESTIMATE SIGNAL INTERFERENCE IN LESS THAN THIRTY SECONDS!

Across. He *had* to get across and pray that the little beasts couldn't follow him. Korden spun in circles, desperate for ideas, and, as the trees caught his attention, the many history books he'd read under Skewtz's tutelage popped into his mind.

Particularly the ones on ancient warfare.

THIS COURSE OF ACTION IS NOT ADVISABLE! Stone said, reading his thoughts.

"I can do this," Korden muttered, more to convince himself than Stone. "I can do *anything* if I will it hard enough."

He chose one of the pines growing on the precipice of the chasm, a tall specimen with few branches on its lower half. His mind ensnared it, touching the rough bark, experiencing its size and density, probing at its reality, just as with the one he'd torn out of the ground minutes before. Soon, the evergreen was as much a part of him as his own arm. This time, however, he imagined the long trunk becoming rubbery, malleable. Through the conduit's eye, he saw it bending.

High above, the canopy dipped, the tree swooning like a drunkard. It kept curving, the top falling through the other trees until its upper branches brushed the ground. The trunk now formed a long arch.

It looked very much like the drawings he'd seen of fully-cocked catapults.

Korden ran to the end and climbed the branches, forcing his injured hand to grip, then slung a leg over the horizontal trunk, straddling it. At the same time, the last of the riftlings streaked out of the woods behind him and swarmed up the tree.

Before that buzzing could fill his head, Korden commanded his makeshift catapult to fire.

4

The tree slammed upright, returning to its natural state. Korden's stomach was left behind as he rode it into the sky and then launched out over the gorge.

His flight could only have taken seconds, but time slowed so he could appreciate each one of them. He stretched his body out straight as an arrow, arms to his sides, toes curled in his sneakers, the rush of wind over his skin exhilarating.

Why fly when you can soar? he thought giddily, his fear forgotten.

All around him, the riftlings tumbled away like fluff from a dandelion pod, their trajectories sending them into the abyss below or dashing onto the opposite cliffside, where they left starbursts of brackish goo.

Korden's aim, however, was impeccable. The stony ground

on the far side of the canyon rushed to meet him. It would surely smash the life out of him if he hit at this speed, so he willed the very air itself to solidify in front of him, forming an invisible cushion.

When he hit the ground, the impact was feather soft. He even bounced once before plopping down on his back.

5

Korden sat up, elated and grinning stupidly. He couldn't wrap his mind around what he'd done. Sure, he hadn't grown wings or anything, but he'd *flown* all on his own, or maybe *glided* was more accurate, and wouldn't Eddas love to know th—

Pain lanced up his left leg. Korden looked down and screamed.

One of those Upper-blasted things was *wrapped around his thigh.*

This one was a runt compared to the others, its body no bigger around than that of an average-sized turkey, the tentacles as thick as corn stalk and long enough to knot themselves around his leg. One of its tiny pincers had torn through his dungarees and snipped a gash along the meat of his thigh.

Five yellow eyes glared at Korden from the middle of its bulbous head. The creature's disproportionately large mouth opened.

To his shock, a shrieky, gargling voice came out of it.

"Zeega will hurt you, human! Make you pay for killing broodmates!"

It cut him again, higher up, the wound spilling a thin sheet of crimson.

That pulsing hum was back in his thoughts, blocking Korden's attempt at artcraft. Instead, with a bellow, he raised his other foot and brought the heel of his sneaker smashing down into the creature's face. Its tentacles untwined, and the small riftling reeled a few pargs away from him, clutching its head with three of its many appendages.

The buzz ceased. At the same time, Stone's voice returned and blurted, WARNING! BLOOD LOSS RATE AT UNACCEPTABLE LEVELS!

The riftling jumped, scuttling back another few paces. Its small head—the size of both Korden's fists put together—swiveled left and right in a gesture that might've been comical if the beast itself wasn't so horrid. "*Who speaks? Zeega heard another!*"

Stone gave one of the low atonal beeps that usually indicated his confusion. I CALCULATE A 93.7 PERCENT CHANCE THIS CREATURE DETECTED ME.

Then the computer was blotted out as the riftling homed in on Korden, filling his head with the mosquito-like whine.

"I don't need artcraft to get rid of *you*," Korden growled. He grabbed a heavy rock nearby and chucked it. The stone struck the beast on its dark chest, the impact hard enough to make it stumble. The riftling hissed and snapped a claw at him, but when Korden reached for the knife on his belt, it sped away, tentacles blurring as they carried it along the edge of the chasm.

"*You won't escape, human!*" it squealed back at him. "*Zeega will destroy you! The Filament commands iiiiit!*"

SOMETHING ELSE

1

The Blackhold had served as the Dark Filament's command post on the western half of this damnable land for a century and a half now. Located in a suburban strip shopping center outside an abandoned human city that had once been named 'Bakersfield, California,' it was created to serve as a rallying point for the *Exatraedes*—the foot soldiers that humans called 'Incarnates'. Regent Torgas had been given command by the Deadfather himself and instructed to use the post as a temporary forward distribution hub from which they could continue hunting down the Light of this world. The intent was that the last of this realm's children (and those who would protect them) would be caught between Torgas's forces in the west, and the rest of the Filament's armies as they marched from the east.

Suffice it to say, events hadn't unfolded as envisioned.

Nevertheless, the Blackhold withstood. There were many additions and fortifications made to the structure over the long years, but it started out as a very different type of edifice, a place many children had gathered and, consequently, the site of a great, historic slaughter in the early days of this plane's Purge. It was this massacre the Incarnates wished to commemorate, and to profane the joy that once filled these walls by dwelling within them. That's why, despite the many changes, they'd proudly left the building's original name visible on the sign across its front:

Otis the Otter's Fun Time Pizzeria.

A high fence surrounded the grounds—made from scrap and rust, like so much of what the Incarnates fashioned for themselves—yet it'd been some time since they needed a gate. Assaults on the Blackhold were once a regular affair, both by professional armies and ragtag groups of angry citizenry, but the remaining humans were far too cowed for warfare and revolutions. The Filament kept a watch though, and when those guards heard the choppy thunder of the approaching vehicles, they sounded the alarm. A group of twenty armored demons waited in the awning-covered courtyard as their visitors coasted to a stop and hovered beyond the gap in the fence.

2

Decimator Riktus stood at the head of the assembled guard phalanx and studied the three figures outside the Blackhold through a pair of smoke-tinted goggles intended for viewing solar eclipses. Each of the unwelcome guests sat astride hunks of black steel that brought to mind horses, mostly because of the saddle-style seat in the middle of the narrow chassis, which allowed the rider's legs to drape down the sides. These machines floated atop a cradle of bright yellow radiance emitted by spherical protrusions beneath, and made a racket so loud they could've woken the Three Shadow Disciples from their ancient slumber. Riktus would never fathom why humans put so much value in technology, with all its noise and sterility and cold apathy. They were perfectly content killing their enemies from a distance, the farther away the better, instead of feeling the heat of spilled blood and watching the spark of life dim. Which was exactly why they fell to the Filament time and time again. As Riktus watched, the riders punched buttons on a panel set into the vehicles' steering bars. That irritating roar cycled down. The machines settled to the crete, resting on metal pegs that folded down before the illumination faded.

All three dressed the same—black leather jumpsuits with a small half-cape attached at midwaist—but Riktus grasped that they were *not* equal. The two on either side were average-sized. They didn't move, just sat with ramrod stiffness astride their machines, heads tilted back slightly, staring up at the hateful blue sky.

The one in the middle, however...

He was large and thickly muscled through the arms and chest, with a sheaf of sable hair cascading down his shoulders, and a mighty black beard that stretched from his lean cheeks all the way to his midriff. His dark eyes glittered merrily as he swiveled on his vehicle, sitting sideways on the saddle, and raised a hand to give a friendly wave to the Incarnates.

Riktus ordered his men to hold position (to be fair, *Exatraedes* possessed no gender, but it was much easier to think in terms of the bodies they inhabited, and most craved the inherent power of the male form) and started forward on his own, stepping out of the shade of the awning and into the terrible sunlight. A scimitar sat in a sheath at his belt, but he didn't think he would need it for this lot. The figure in the middle of the trio beamed at him, a crooked smirk.

No human had ever looked at Riktus so mirthfully, had ever beheld him with anything short of terror. This human must be insane, to ride up to the Blackhold's front door and sit so brazenly. Riktus glanced at the rider's companions and, now that he was closer, noticed something that gave him pause for the first time.

The other two humans weren't staring at the sky. They weren't looking at anything, because their eyes were rolled so far back in their heads, only blank white orbs showed in their skulls. Drool leaked from the corners of their mouths.

"Leave this place, mortal," Riktus spat, stopping a few paces from the bearded figure.

"No can do, babalu." The man winked at him. *Winked.* Riktus knew the facial expression as a concept; he'd never seen it in practice. "Need to speak to whoever's in charge of your little outfit here."

"We have no use for your pitiful kind."

"Hey, easy fella, let's not bring out the attitude. I come in the name of peace. Or commerce, at the very least. Go inside and tell your boss—what is he, a Fearnaught? Regent?—anyway, just tell him he'll want to hear what I have to say."

Riktus stepped closer, towering over the sitting human. "Leave or die. I will not ask again."

The grin fell off the human's face. He gave an exasperated sigh. "Here's the deal, curseface: I'm going in there, one way or another. Hoped to do it cordially, but if we have to start things off on the wrong foot, so be it."

"*Insolent sin cow!*" Riktus roared. He reached out and grabbed the man's wrist, preparing to break the bone. "How dare you come before the Filament to threaten—!"

The man moved faster than Riktus could react, his free hand reaching under that cape at his back and drawing out a machete much too long to have been concealed beneath the small flap. Not only that, but the blade glowed dull orange, as though pulled fresh from a forge. The human swung the weapon down into the arm that held him, neatly severing Riktus's appendage below the elbow. Black blood hissed and popped as it spurted across the hot machete.

Riktus stumbled back, staring at the charred stump of his limb. The pain was excruciating, but his fury kept it from registering. He scrambled for his own blade, forced to reach across his waist to get to the sheath.

In front of him, the human rose from his vehicle. The machete had vanished, but Riktus's detached arm still gripped the man's wrist. He casually plucked it off and tossed it aside before planting his hand in the center of the Decimator's chest and shoving.

Riktus flew off his feet, crashing down on the crete a good ten pargs away. One of his legs broke with an audible *snap!* He would need a new body before the day came to an end, and this human, with his deceptive strength, would serve well.

"*Capture him and kill the other two!*" he snarled at his garrison.

His men charged forward, bellowing as they drew their weapons. The human walked calmly forward to meet them, reaching back beneath his short cape once more. This time he drew out a cobbled longshooter that looked as likely to explode in his hands as fire.

Riktus laughed as he sat up to watch the fight. "Do you mean to take them all with that pathetic shooter before they reach you? You don't have the faith to expel even one of them!"

"Oh, I've got plenty of faith these days, *compadre*." The human leveled the weapon at the approaching mob and pulled the trigger.

Instead of the crack of a shot, a beam of sizzling red light ejected from the barrel of the shooter. It zipped through the courtyard, slow enough to be seen by the naked eye, and passed through the chest of one Incarnate—burning a circular hole through its torso—before exiting its back and hitting the demon behind in the throat. Both soldiers dropped, wisps of black smoke curling up from their covered eyes as their *animogas* escaped.

An energy weapon. Riktus hadn't seen such technology since the last of this dimension's armies fell. Even if its secrets had been rediscovered, it shouldn't be coming out of a pop-shooter like that.

The human continued firing, releasing a burning stream of ruby death at the guard battalion. Incarnates fell in waves, their essences dissipating without new bodies to jump to. The last of them collapsed five paces from the invader, who then stalked toward Riktus.

The Decimator bared his teeth defiantly as the barrel of the impossible firearm was thrust in his face. He looked up the length of the weapon, to the bearded visage at the other end. A ripple went through that face, a sort of…of *dimming*, as though its appearance was mere glamour. For a moment, Riktus could see a different countenance beneath that mirage, this one a horribly scorched wasteland below the nose, the flesh peeled from its cheeks and jawbone to form an eternal grimace of blackened teeth.

"You're no human," Riktus said. "What *are* you?"

"Something else," the figure answered, and freed Riktus from this plane of existence.

3

Heater Kay—or rather, the physical form that used to house Heater Kay's singular consciousness—straightened after killing the Incarnate squad's leader and stepped away from the dark fumes that streamed from its eyes. The demon probably couldn't jump to him (there wasn't a lot of available real estate left in his brain these days), but better safe than sorry. At the same time, Heater released the fantastic laser blaster from reality, the weapon fading in his hand until his fingers clutched nothing but air. He would've only had the energy to maintain it for another few seconds anyway, and, in his opinion, nothing was worse than having your rod go limp on you right in the middle of the action.

feed us rejuvenate starving eat now

The multitude of voices sang through Heater's head like an angry choir. On one level—the same one that remembered who he was and what he wanted out of life—he recognized that these were echoes of the countless minds that had hosted Loathe since long before the dawn of time, men and women and children and an array of strange, sentient creatures from something called 'the allverse.' On another level, he was merely another one of them, no longer an individual, their thoughts were his thoughts, his body their body, and all of them serving the will of Loathe.

Kinda confusing, admittedly. Heater didn't understand it all himself, but since he'd walked—well, *crawled*—through that stone arch in the cave, he'd been having too much framming fun to worry about the fine print on this particular contract.

He walked backed toward the hovertrikes, his leatherclad legs wobbling under him. Fun or not, he was a bit weak after wiping out those assholes. Hungry, hungry, hungry; that was ol' Loathe in a nutshell. The incorporeal being required a constant stream of nourishment to render Heater's fantasies into actuality.

And Heater had a *lot* of fantasies.

Pim and the Scummer still straddled their hogs with their eyes rolled back. They, along with Heater, represented the last of Clan Triker, but these two weren't exactly *compos mentis* these days. The first thing Loathe did when they arrived back at the Trikers' base of operations was suck the brains out of the rest of the crew. A feast, to celebrate the entity's release from prison. Although he hated to watch it happen, Heater got the idea that, when you allowed Loathe into your mind, you either *provided* the meals, or *became* them.

Besides, Loathe had assured him that, once they'd taken care of their mutual business, Heater could have anything his heart desired. *Anything.* A fully automated munitions factory and a staff to deliver its wares. An endless stream of delightful young men to keep his appetites sated.

And, most important of all, a permanent solution to his little 'body image' problem.

Greedy mental tendrils reached out for the other two trikers. Heater felt a rush as Loathe began to feed. Both men jittered and moaned before Pim's head collapsed with a sound like crushed eggshell. The top and sides of his skull bowed violently inward, the pressure forcing his eyeballs out of their sockets amid twin geysers of blood. He wobbled atop the hovertrike before slumping sideways and spilling onto the pavement, as empty and used-up as a discarded garren rind.

"Ah, Pim," Heater whispered sadly. "You never had much in the creativity department, did you?"

With that epitaph delivered, he walked into the Blackhold's courtyard, stepping over the bodies of the Incarnates he'd evicted as he made his way through the front door of Otis the Otter's Fun Time Pizzeria.

4

Past the entrance was an antechamber with a derelict claw machine full of plush dolls from an animated television show called *Commander JuJuby and the Hyper Extreme Force*. Heater had never seen it—had never watched a single frame of that mysterious box his ancestors used to worship—but some of the endless voices sharing space in his mind *had*, so he could name every character. That was the amazing thing about his new pooled knowledge base: sometimes he didn't realize he knew something until he needed to know it.

He walked past the machine, into a long room lined with dormant arcade cabinets and a pit filled with colorful balls. Cheap, plastic toys sat under glass in a display to the left of the door. Moldy carpet beneath his boots held repeating images of a goofy, long-necked creature in a vest and ball cap with his tongue lolling out like a gods-damned retard: Otis the Otter himself. Being in a place like this—an entire establishment built specifically for *kids*—was as alien to Heater as the surface of the moon.

The air stank of sweat and decay; the distinct, aromatic bouquet that he liked to think of as *eau de Incarníte*. Most of the rear wall of the pizzeria was torn out. Another structure had been added here, a tunnel made of unfinished sheetrock, corrugated steel and loose stone that descended on a smooth grade down into the earth.

Heater strode through the game room and into the mouth of the cave. His footsteps echoed against bare concrete once he stepped off the carpet. That rotten stench intensified the deeper he went. The darkness swallowed him up, made his eyes useless. No surprise there. The *Exatraedes* didn't need light, shunned it whenever possible. He could've rendered some illusion that would let him see, but opted for the simpler solution and held one hand out in front of him so as not to run into anything.

Pinpricks of red glowed in the gloom ahead. Eyes. A group of Incarnates even bigger than the one outside. Heater prepared himself for another fight, but, as he drew closer, the demons moved out of his path, standing along the walls to either side like an honor guard.

We made an impression on someone, he thought, a sentiment that was echoed by innumerable other voices.

Heater passed through the Incarnates, keeping a wary distance. He detested these creatures; always had, always would. They'd taken the world and turned it to curse. And not just any curse, but *boring* curse, which was a much bigger transgression in his book. Heater was a successful businessman, after all. He was supposed to be able to make enough money and gain enough power to rid himself of life's boredom; that was the American way. But even that ray of sunshine had a shelf life when these motherframmers were constantly slaughtering the key demographic.

But maybe...just maybe...they could still serve a purpose.

His outstretched hand encountered the edges of a rough-hewn doorway cut into the masonry. Heater stepped through.

5

The darkness on the other side was so absolute, Heater couldn't get an idea of the space he now stood in. To his left, perhaps fifteen pargs away, another pair of crimson orbs considered him. These were much lower, at waist height, indicating the owner was sitting. Or some kind of pygmy dwarf. Which, he had to admit, would be kind of hilarious.

"You the leader?" Heater asked.

"I am Regent Torgas," a cold voice wormed out of the darkness. "If you are here to kill me, get on with it. Just know that it won't make any difference."

"Like we told your boys outside, we're not here to kill anyone."

"Before you killed them all."

Heater grinned in the darkness. "Yeah, well…nobody's perfect."

When Torgas spoke again, it was obvious he didn't share the humor. "Then why *are* you here?" he demanded.

"First, let's do this civilly, whattaya say?"

Heater swept a hand outward. A circle of floor lamps burst into existence around him and the Regent, lighting up the room. Well, they *looked* like floor lamps, but beneath the shades, the bulbs were a giant species of firefly that never existed, whose butts put out enough wattage to sting the eye if stared at directly. Loathe had a real problem rendering anything that was too close to reality, which was why he needed a host with Heater's level of creativity. It was an extravagant use of energy keeping such a fiction corporeal, but, what the hells, they needed to make an impression.

He could see now that the space was nothing but a crete rectangle with earthen walls. Crusty, maroon smears stained the floor, with a syrupy puddle in one corner. Essentially, this was an animal den. It sure smelled enough like one. And, as if to drive the comparison home, the sole object in here was the ornate throne that Torgas sat upon, an uncomfortable-looking chair created out of human skulls so small, they could only have belonged to infants. The Incarnate shied away from the light and covered his eyes before seeing that it came from an artificial source.

"Curse man, is this your idea of an office?" Heater made a show of looking around incredulously. "It's bare as fram! We know you guys don't dig windows, but you could get some art on the walls. Maybe a couch for guests. Play some music, have some booze handy. A dartboard, *something*. Actually… we never thought about it, but…what in hells do you do for fun, anyway? In between all the kid-killing, we mean."

"I know what you are." Torgas sat primly with long-fingered hands in his lap. The body he inhabited wasn't a pygmy, but it was much smaller in stature and mass than the ones his soldiers wore. Then again, he probably hadn't chosen it with fighting in mind. His face was lean and clean-shaven around those glowing eyes, free of scars and unblemished by sunrot. Glossy blond locks were pulled to the back of his head and tied up in a neat bun. He wore a glittering red robe with gold embroidery and wide sleeves, the kind of fancy garment Heater had seen at the more upscale whorehouses in the bigger trading posts, places where the women got their baby-making parts removed before the holes between their legs were rented out.

In short, Regent Torgas was immaculate. When you got to the Incarnates that cared about their appearance, you knew they were high up in the pecking order.

"Oh, really?" Heater rolled his wide shoulders. "And just what are we?"

"You're one of those wretched parasites. A leech that swims in the Filament's wake, dining on the scraps of the universes we raze."

Heater frowned and waggled a finger. "Okay. Sure. We guess that's a fair description. But don't sound so high and mighty throwing out insults like 'parasite' when you're sitting there in someone else's body. At least we try to play nice with our hosts."

Those red embers shimmering in the Incarnate's eye sockets narrowed, but he said nothing.

"Do you know where we've been for the last two hundred years?" These words came out of Heater's mouth, in his voice, but they were not his words. And yet they *were* at the same time. They originated in the stew of collective consciousness that he now shared with Loathe, and then filtered through his mannerisms. It was like having multiple sets of hands on the steering wheel of his body, all of them working in harmony. "Stuck in a pocket dimension about as big as that ugly chair you sit in, slowly starving to death. Don't worry though; we're not fishing for sympathy. No, the reason we mention it is because, while we waited in that hellish place, our biggest fear was that if we ever escaped, it would only be to discover that we were too late. That you red-eyed rascals had moved on without us. Maybe even that the holes were patched or healed or whatever, and we were trapped in this backwater plane forever and ever, amen."

He sauntered toward one of the lamps he'd created and reached under the shade to give the insect a hard flick, relishing its squeal of pain. "But, surprise, surprise, you know what we found? The Filament was still around, still chasing down kiddos, but mostly just sitting on your asses in the dark. That the sky was blue, the grass was green, and the humans had enough fight left in 'em to squeeze out a titbiter every now and then." Heater tilted his head to the side and hiked an eyebrow. "Wethinks something went seriously wrong in Dark Filament Land."

"It is none of your concern," Torgas said evenly.

"Oh, but it is. We've hitched our wagon to your star, so to speak. That means we have a vested interest in your success. And the pickins around here are gettin mighty slim."

"We will finish our work on this plane eventually. Your needling and ridicule will do nothing to hasten it."

"Brother, you've had three centuries to get this dimension squared away. Your 'work' has never taken this long. We remember you having some issues on the east coast before we got locked away, but it looks like the Shroud hasn't budged so much as a cupit since then. Are you telling us that, after burning an infinite number of realms to ash, you guys have run into a brick wall *here*?"

"The issues you speak of will be resolved."

"Okay, great, then tell us...what's the latest word on the hold-up?"

The Regent's upper lip curled distastefully, as if the stench of his inner sanctum had come to his attention. He looked away from Heater for the first time.

"You don't know, do you? Because on top of all that, you've got this Moambati business that's cropped up right in the middle of the last nation you need to conquer, and you're cut off from the main body of the Filament's forces. We're guessing you haven't had any communication with the Deadfather in...maybe a decade, are we right?"

Torgas's face whipped back to him. "No one knows that, not even my own men. How could you possibly—"

Heater tapped his own temple. "This mind is a shrewd one, let us tell you. He figured out quite a bit on his own and, once we merged and saw the state of things around here, it wasn't hard to piece the rest together." He opened his arms as though offering an embrace. "So unburden yourself, brother. Confide in us, one immortal to another. How did you get marooned out here by yourself?"

For a long moment, Heater didn't think Torgas would answer. Then the Incarnate slowly opened his mouth. "When the Shroud's advance from the eastern coast was…*delayed*, I was dispatched here to continue the hunt. We were close to being finished on this plane, and the Deadfather wanted to keep the humans from organizing resistance. But then the problem worsened, and we were ordered to make due."

"Keep the brat population down 'til Daddy gets home from work, huh?"

Torgas made that stinkface again. "I did what I could with the limited number of soldiers at my disposal. Reinforcements were sent, but not enough to keep the humans from digging in. Building fortresses. Seeding new generations of Lightbringers. Settlements sprang up all along their Rocky Mountains, where our reach was thinnest. I sent raiding parties to keep their fear alive, and then…one of those battalions did not return."

"Moambati," Heater surmised. "We know the stories the humans are telling from across the Valley of Bones. Trade caravans disappearing, then entire towns. You got any idea what this thing is?"

The Incarnate's head shook slowly. "As you say, our communications with the Deadfather ceased almost seventeen years ago. Then reinforcements stopped arriving. I hid these facts so that word of our weakness would not spread, then sent expeditions back to discover what was happening. I lost contact with them every time they attempted to cross this mountain range. The same thing happened when I ordered them to go around, far to the south."

"What about your bone portals? Why not use those?"

"The craft that powers them…it stopped working around

the same time." Torgas's jaw clenched. "Something has awoken in those mountains, and whatever it is cast a powerful enchantment across this land. Set up a border we cannot cross. My forces number in the hundreds, spread thin, some even deserting to hunt on their own. I can no longer afford to send my soldiers anywhere close to the mountains, which only emboldens the humans there further. Many of them are breeding without fear, thinking they can use the shadow of this 'Moambati' to shield themselves."

Heater nodded. There was little in this admission that he and Loathe hadn't already worked out between the infinity of them, but the confirmation was nice. He rendered a polyester-upholstered, crème-colored easy chair directly in front of Torgas—the mundane conjuration possible only because it resembled one that a fictional character named Archie Bunker had once sat in—then lowered himself into it, crossed his legs, and said, "Well, I hate to break it to you, but you got another problem on your hands. Which is the whole reason I'm here today."

"Speak," the Regent commanded.

"There's a boy. Sixteen-years-old, goes by the name of Korden Bright. He's been living under your radar in a Crafter colony northwest of here. Now he's out and trekking east."

"I believe one of my regiments slaughtered the colony you speak of yesterday. As for the boy, several wasteling *Exatraedes* are on his trail as we speak."

Heater was careful to keep the annoyance from showing on his face. "Call them off."

Torgas let a cautious grin spread his thin lips for the first time. "Why would I do that?"

"Because they'll fail." Heater ran a hand down the length of his beard, a nervous tic that not even Loathe could rid him of. "The boy is a Crafter also. A powerful one. Hasn't grasped his full potential yet, but he's getting there. If he does, he could make what we did to your guards outside look like a rain drop in a hurricane."

"All the more reason to end him as quickly as possible."

Heater raised a leatherclad hand. "We don't think you get what we're saying. He's *dangerous*. Thinks he's gonna walk right up to the Shroud and put an end to the Filament once and for all."

The Regent's smile became harsh laughter. "Do you think he's the first sorcerer to believe that?"

"*Gods-damn it, hold your rotting tongue and LISTEN TO US!*" Heater's voice roughened and echoed off the concrete floor. Rage boiled through him as he gripped the arms of the chair. All around them, the lamps flickered in and out of existence, like a bad television signal. So, too, did the illusion he wore, the guise of his deceased twin brother that he'd envisioned in his head for most of his life, like an imaginary friend. Because of Loathe's limitations, this vision of Happum Kay was the only option Heater had to look like his old self.

And any time he lost focus...his true form showed through.

The broken, flamebroiled body given to him by one Korden Bright.

Torgas regarded him, grin unchanged. "I thank you for your warning," he said, "but why don't you speak plainly and tell me what you want."

"We want the *boy*," Heater snapped, curling one hand into a fist in front of him. "He will *pay* for what he did to us. We will drink his mind one sip at a time while we torture his body in ways that would make even the *Exatraedes* blush."

"Then go and do so. The Filament will make no move to stop you."

"That's the problem." Heater took a deep, calming breath to flush out his fury. "We can't track him. Not as easily as you can, and not without expending a lot of energy that we haven't recovered yet. So we're proposing a mutually-beneficial arrangement."

"The Filament does not deal with outsiders."

"Until now, the Filament also hasn't gotten themselves stuck between a rock and a hard place for three hundred years, but the times, they are a-changin'." Heater sat forward, unable to contain his eagerness. "Look, to you, he's another brat that needs to be put down, but to us, he's a goldmine. You can send more of your dwindling army and risk losing them, or you can let us take care of him for you. His powers are useless against me. Lend me some of your men to command, and I'll do the rest."

Heater expected Torgas to turn him down flat, in which case he was going to kill the Regent and every other Incarnate he could get his hands on, just for spite. But, wonder of wonders, the demon sat silently with a considering frown.

"You said 'mutually-beneficial,' parasite," Torgas murmured, as though ashamed of the words. "So...what is in it for me?"

Heater sat back and laced his fingers at the back of his head. "Once we've sucked down that kid's imagination like a good cabernet and gotten ourselves back up to full strength...we're gonna see about solving your Moambati problem."

KYE DRUDES

1

After he was sure the horrid little beast wasn't going to return for another attack, Korden wrestled his dungarees down so he could treat his newest set of wounds.

Blood flowed freely off the sides of his knee and spattered onto the dirt, but, according to Stone, the subcutaneous tissue damage was minimal. The creature's claws had been razor sharp, but little bigger than walnuts. Korden applied pressure to stop the bleeding, all while urging healing through artcraft, then fashioned a tourniquet from the sleeve of his most travelworn tunic. When he was properly bandaged and his pain dulled, he assessed his situation.

On the upside, he'd survived. And not just survived, but bested his enemy by using artcraft in inventive ways that came to him like flashes of intuition. Tash would be proud. And, since he'd been wearing his carry pouch during the frantic chase, he'd lost no supplies whatsoever.

On the downside, however…

"Starry," he whispered. His heart ached as he recalled the horse's torturous death. "I'm so sorry."

THERE IS ONE OTHER ISSUE, Stone interjected somberly.

Due to our current position and the surrounding terrain, our previously planned route is no longer an option.

"Please tell me we're not lost again."

Not at all. My internal pedometer and rangefinder kept track of our approximate location throughout the flight. But, based on revised geographical input, my recommendation now is to summit this peak as directly as possible so that we can go down the far side.

Korden gazed up at the white-laden mountaintop towering over them. On horseback, they could've reached it in a few hours, but now that they were relegated to traveling by foot, the distance had effectively tripled. The afternoon sun—streaming in from the west behind them—was low enough that spending the night on the slope seemed unavoidable.

This direction will also facilitate the fastest increase in distance between us and the last known location of the Incarnates.

"You read my mind. Uh, literally, I guess." Korden shouldered his carry pouch and glanced again to the north, where the undersized riftling had disappeared into a thick copse of trees. He hoped it'd fled, but wasn't naïve enough to believe it. "Might as well see how far we can get before nightfall."

2

It took two hours of walking for them to reach the snow-line, but, by then, Korden was far too winded to revel in the cold fluff. His weak lungs sucked at the thinning air as the elevation increased, turning each breath into a wheezing gasp. The sun fell at his back. Shadows grew longer, the cold deeper. He donned his woolen coat and plodded on, shivering, shoes becoming soggy and they crunched through the snow. But when the first wave of dizziness made him sway on his feet, he called a halt in the middle of a long stretch of mountainside strewn with huge boulders and shallow, twisting gullies eroded by decades of Bloom runoff.

WE SHOULD BE ABLE TO SUMMIT MIDMORNING TOMORROW, DEPENDING ON TIME OF DEPARTURE. BUT YOU MUST KEEP WARM THROUGHOUT THE NIGHT. TEMPERATURES WILL CONTINUE TO DROP.

Korden was too tired to even think his reply. He slumped against the lee side of a chunk of stone as big as an auto, rested his forehead on his knees, and focused on catching his breath. Memories of his time in the forest assailed him, those feverish hours where Loathe tricked him into believing that he was dying. He faithed and willed his breathing passages to widen, imagined them stretching open farther and farther to take in more oxygen. The effort seemed to help. The dizzy spell passed, and he could breathe a bit easier.

From elsewhere in the field of boulders came the sound of disrupted pebbles cascading downhill.

He was back on his feet in a heartbeat, scanning the area with the conduit's eye. The *mohols* of a few small critters which called this barren landscape home lit up in his mind, but nothing more. Of course, if riftlings truly possessed no auras, this method wouldn't be any help in discerning if he'd been followed.

"You better get out of here!" he shouted, deepening his voice. "I'm not scared of you!"

The burgeoning night was silent.

Korden set to work on a camp, first clearing out the snow

from between two large rock formations, then building a roaring fire that drove away the chill. He picked out a nice, Bloom-fattened marmot, manipulated its emotional aura to coax the animal to him, and roasted it over the flames for supper. By the time he'd eaten, full night had descended, and he huddled in his thin bedroll reciting a warmth chant while trying to decide if he should risk sleeping.

THE DANGER SHOULD BE MINIMAL, SIR. I WILL ENGAGE WATCHDOG MODE AS USUAL.

That won't help if it gets close enough to block your voice, he thought, too paranoid to even speak aloud.

AT THE FIRST HINT OF TELEPATHIC INTERFERENCE, I WILL WAKE YOU IMMEDIATELY.

Korden remained unconvinced, but his weary mind put up no fight when sleep crept in.

3

Bibb awaited him in the dream, sitting in the old rocking chair in his *hucté* with a pipe jutting from his thick lips. Korden sat down in front of him as he had countless times before while the man pulled some new wonder from the past out of his trunk. Utter serenity washed over him, a calm so deep it bordered on lethargy.

"Good to see you, my young friend." Bibb tipped him a wink. "And very glad those Incarnates didn't mean your end."

"Hi Bibb." Korden's mind felt open and relaxed, the conduit to the Upper stable and flowing freely, injecting him with raw power. It made him think of a goose Del once prepared for their Seventh Eve feast, jamming the carcass with fruits and rice porridge while using a hardened reed to plump the flesh with his 'secret sauce.' That's what was happening to Korden during these soothing visions: every cell in his body was marinating in magic. "Is everyone well back home? There was another group of Incarnates coming for—"

The Older waved his concerns away. "We're fine as paint, lad, right as rain. Don't let thoughts of us cause you pain." He took the pipe from his mouth and pointed the stem at Korden. "But you must get moving; stop lagging behind. Get past the desert, and it's peace you will find."

Korden grinned. He didn't know how he could possibly find any more peace than at this exact moment, but it sounded wonderful. "I know, I'm going as fast as I can. I just need to stop at Ida and find out if their Prophet will help me."

A disapproving frown crossed Bibb's merry face. He stretched over the arm of the rocking chair as far as his hefty body would allow, reaching for a wallet of fresh tobacco on the table to pack his pipe. "You can't worry with towns and prophets; it's all just distraction. *They're* waiting for you, and it's to them you should run."

"'Them?'" Korden's heavy eyes roamed past the Older, to the wall of the *hucté* revealed behind him as he leaned aside. A painting hung there that had never been in the real Bibb's home, a picture that reminded Korden of Cheree's lifelike creations. The background appeared to be a mountain range, but one so jagged and high that it dwarfed these peaks he was traveling through. Orange, early morning light crowned the top, illuminating a pair of silhouettes that stood in the foreground with their arms around each other's waists. They were too dim and blurry for any real detail, but their curvaceous forms revealed them as female. A pleasant warmth blossomed in the pit of Korden's stomach as he regarded them.

"They have so much to show you, so much to reveal." Bibb settled in the rocking chair, rested his hands atop his large belly, and puffed contentedly. "With them you'll know your place. And have time to heal."

4

Korden opened his eyes to soft daylight, the dream falling away in cottony, half-remembered shreds. He yearned to go back into it—a desire so great he would be willing to knock himself unconscious if it meant staying just a few more minutes—but it was already late enough in the morning for the sun to be visible over the mountain.

On the upside, his exhaustion from the previous day was gone, replaced by renewed energy and the usual sense of well-being he experienced in the afterglow of these visions. This was two nights in a row, and he felt like he could fly without the aid of a makeshift catapault. The cut on his leg was clotted over and even his hand seemed better when he flexed the fingers, enough that he decided to forgo the sling.

These dreams were the Upper's way of urging him on. Directing him. They *had* to be.

I AM HESITANT TO SPOIL YOUR GOOD MOOD, BUT I CALCULATE AN 81.8 PERCENT CHANCE THE CREATURE FROM YESTERDAY IS STILL IN THE VICINITY.

How can you tell?

AUDIAL SCANS THROUGHOUT THE NIGHT DETECTED TOO MANY DISTURBANCES TO BE COINCIDENTAL. I BELIEVE I EVEN HEARD IT SPEAKING TO ITSELF SEVERAL TIMES.

Then why didn't you wake me up? Korden demanded.

I CALCULATED THE GREATER BENEFIT WAS TO LET YOU REST. IF IT TRULY WAS THE CREATURE I HEARD, IT

NEVER BREACHED THE ACCEPTABLE SECURITY PERIMETER.

From now on, tell me. Just knowing that thing is around makes me nervous. For all we know, it could be leading the Incarnates right to us.

MY APOLOGIES IF SAYING SO MAKES ME SOUND LIKE A 'SMARTASS,' BUT AREN'T YOU DOING THAT WITH YOUR VERY EXISTENCE?

You're right, Stone. It does *make you sound like a smart-ass.*

Korden packed quickly, not even bothering to eat breakfast. It was one riftling, and a runt at that, but better not to wait for the attack that must be coming. Besides, he felt a sudden sense of incredible urgency, surely a leftover from the dream. He moved through the boulder-ridden slope toward the summit and had just come around a rock that resembled a giant ramlar when that annoying hum filled his head.

A sharp crack sounded under him. The snowy ground crumbled away beneath his sneakers. Korden plunged downward, pitching himself forward out of sheer instinct. His belly hit the lip of this hole hard enough to make him grunt. He scrabbled for a hold on the terrain with his good hand before he could slide in farther, glancing over his shoulder.

The floor of this pit, several pargs below his feet, was lined with sharpened sticks ready to impale him.

"*Die humaaaan!*" The riftling appeared out of nowhere, hurtling toward him on its squiggling mass of violet tentacles. It stopped beyond his reach and circled warily, darting forward to snip at his fingers where they clutched the ground.

Korden lured it closer on each attempt, then grabbed at the creature with his broken hand. He forced his fingers to close around the back of that mushy head and slammed it on the ground. The mental buzz ceased for a single second, but that was long enough for him to blast the riftling with artcraft, sending it tumbling away across the ground. Before it could recover, he dug the toes of his sneakers into the wall of the pit, envisioning toeholds as big as ladder rungs, willing them into existence, and climbed up enough to squirm out onto the snow. He sat up in time to see the riftling streak away. By the time he could throw a fireball at it, the creature had scuttled behind another boulder, trailing maniacal laughter that faded as it fled.

ON A POSITIVE NOTE, Stone said, sounding sheepish, WE KNOW THE FOCUS OF ITS EFFORTS THROUGHOUT THE NIGHT.

"I really hate that thing," Korden said between pants.

5

Today's hike wasn't as strenuous. The elevation evened out, the temperature rose enough for him to stop shivering, and his lungs adjusted to the thin air. He kept a watchful eye for more booby-traps, but it seemed unlikely that the small creature would've had time to prepare anything as grandiose as the pit, especially when it didn't know their exact route.

That didn't mean, however, that it wasn't stalking him. Three more times the riftling ambushed him with that brain-nullifying hum, closing the conduit and blocking Stone's voice, then attacked when he was powerless. The first time, it dropped out of a tree and latched on to his shoulder. The only thing that prevented it from slashing Korden's throat was that his flailing hands poked the monster in several of its eyes. When he started avoiding trees, it popped out from behind rocks or underbrush, circling around to nip at his legs, driven away by his knife or a heavy stick he began carrying.

The surprise assaults weren't as terrifying as having thirty of the things chase him, but they did leave him jumping at every noise and shadow.

An hour after setting out, they came to a narrow pass, barely arms' width, that Stone said should wind them around the summit. At first, the tight confines relieved Korden; it would be hard for the riftling to sneak in for another attack. But the angry little beast changed tactics, forgoing the mental buzz to appear high on the cliff above and pelt him with rocks big enough to crack his skull, all the while screaming about how 'Zeega would destroy him' and 'suck the marrow from his bones.' It gave up this latest attempt when Korden used artcraft to form a shield over his head, then fired the stones back with considerably more force.

At last, they came to the end of the pass. The canyon opened onto a flat, snowy plain with a smattering of tiny buildings spread across it.

Korden never expected to see anything manmade up this high. Though the construction material and design was pre-Purge, the collection of structures instantly reminded him of the village proper back home: quaint, squarish cottages with peaked roofs, and a larger building to the north that stood over the others much like the *hangala*. This one sat on the far side of one of those fields of crete called a 'parking lot' and had a curving, rectangular face made of glass. Many of the panes were broken, and snow had blown inside. The sign on the front was legible, however: SIERRA CHALETS.

A SKI RESORT, Stone told him, filling his head with images of the strange activity. IF YOU CONTINUE PAST THE GUEST ROOMS, YOU SHOULD BE ABLE TO SEE THE LAKE.

Korden's excitement built as he dropped his stick and broke into a run through the dilapidated dwellings, all thoughts of the riftling shoved aside. A precipice lay ahead, next to a tall metal pole with a cable attached to the top, which Stone called a 'ski lift.' He came around the splintery wreckage of one of the chalets and halted to take in the scene that greeted him.

The land descended sharply from this point, at first a uniform blanket of white snow, then turning back into rocky terrain near the bottom, which ended at a long cove. Beyond that stood Lake Tay-ho itself, a cauldron of sapphire blue water bounded by more gentle mountains on its far side. He couldn't see much of the lake past the ridges that formed the walls of the cove, but it looked far bigger than the last body of water he'd encountered on his travels, cradled in the center of the forested slopes like broth in the bottom of a bowl. He could charge down this decline and be at its shore inside of an hour.

He just wasn't sure he wanted to.

Because hovering above the calm waters was a menacing black fog bank, an opaque stain that defied the daylight, like a low-hanging storm cloud. It was as though part of the Shroud had broken off from that blotch in the sky to the east, fallen here to the lake, and grown to smother every corner of the waters.

The answer came to him with a few seconds of deliberation.

It was another *mohol*. Like the aura of fear inside the crashed stratoliner. Except this one was as dark as those that surrounded the Incarnates.

What did it mean? And why could he suddenly sense these displaced emotional clouds?

"I don't suppose you can see that either?"

Optical input is clear of the imagery that the imagination center of your brain is describing, Stone confirmed.

"It's *not* my imagination."

I REMAIN UNABLE TO SUBSTANTIATE THAT STATEMENT.

Korden moved forward, eyes fixed on the lake below, so intent on the dark fog that neither he nor Stone spotted the form on the ground before he kicked it with the toe of his sneaker.

6

A waist-high shape swung up from the ground with a muffled grunt, dislodging a thin crust of snow that covered it. The thing possessed no face or limbs, just a yellow, form-less, blobby mass, like a gigantic worm. Korden leapt away with a yelp, sure that it was another present from the riftling, already conjuring a flame to burn this hideous atrocity to ash. Before he released it, a flap on the creature fell open, revealing the head and shoulders of a man that stared out at him with sleepy, half-lidded eyes, and Korden saw that what he'd taken for a strange lifeform was a person in some sort of thickly-padded bedroll.

This man had stringy blond hair down to his shoulders, most of it matted and greasy, and a patchy growth of match-ing beard along his narrow chin. He looked sickly to Korden, skin waxy pale and so thin his cheeks were shrunken tight against the bones beneath. Deep, bruised hollows formed caves beneath his eyes.

But aside from all that, he was *young*. Far younger than Redfen. Stone estimated his age between 25 and 33, which meant he was the youngest person Korden had ever seen in his life.

He sat on the ground and stared at Korden with that dazed expression for a long time. Then he cleared his throat and said, "Uhhh, drudes...I must still be cruisin, cause I'm hallucinatin a kid right now." His eyes moved ponderously over to Korden's outstretched palm. "And his hand is on *fire*."

Nearby, other forms stirred. Now that he was paying attention, Korden could pick out the remnants of a campfire in the snow. Two other bodies, encased in similar puffy cocoons, sat up on the other side of the frozen coals and poked their heads out like gophers. Korden extinguished the fire in his palm before they could see it and backed up another few steps to take them in.

These two were also male and a bit older than the first, closer to Redfen's age. Both were more unkempt and sallow than their companion. One of them—a man with a dark bun of hair, one squinty eye, and a badly crooked nose—muttered, "Woah. I see 'im, too. No fire, though." His eyes strayed down. "'Cept for his shoes."

"N-n-no way, drude," the third stuttered. A mess of scar tissue marred both his cheeks, and his head was badly shaved into uneven orange fuzz. He sat shivering in his bedroll. "I can s-see him, too, and I know I ain't sp-sp-sp-spun no more. I feel like ten droms of c-curse in a one-drom bag."

The first one tugged at a zipper down the side of his cocoon and squirmed the rest of the way out. He wore denim pants torn and patched in a dozen places, and an extraordinary-bordering-on-absurd half-sleeve tunic colored with every hue of the rainbow to form a spiraling pattern on his chest that Stone referred to as 'tie-dyed'. The outfit hung off his gaunt form in folds and bunches. Below the sleeves, the flesh of his arms was covered in red circles that looked like ripe blisters. Once free from his bag, he crawled on all fours toward Korden, who cringed and pulled away until he reached for the man's *mohol* and found it imbued only with the soft amber hues of curiosity.

The blond man put a cold, quivering hand on Korden's bicep, and squeezed his arm. A broad grin spread up one side of his face. "Heeeey li'l drude…you're real, huh?"

"Prove it!" the one with the hairbun on the back of his skull called out. "If you're real, say somethin!"

"Uh…hello?"

"*Holy curse!*" The man with the orange hair struggled free of his bag and scooted backward into the snow. He was rail thin, his arms no more than bones wrapped in flesh and covered in the same fluid-filled sores. His eyes bulged as he stared at Korden, streaks of fear spiking his previously calm aura. "*Keep it away from me, man, just keep it away from me!*"

Hairbun grimaced and put a hand to his forehead. "Would you chill on, Adliss? My head's gonna crack."

"*Ch-chill on?*" 'Adliss' stood and jabbed a shaking finger in Korden's general direction. "Jaimer, that's a f-frammin *kid!*"

"So what?"

"So he's gonna draw Incarnates up here!"

"There ain't no 'Carnates up in the mountains, genius."

"There are if there's k-kids! That's the whole point!"

"Who cares? They're not huntin your skinny ass."

"I c-can't handle those things, man! They give me the frammin jimmy-jams!"

Jaimer made a placating gesture. "Sit down and we'll start the juice. You'll feel better when you're cruisin."

"Nah uh, no way. As long as *he's* here, I'm not." They all watched as the skeletal figure stepped into a pair of worn leather sandals, wrapped his arms around his waist, then stomped away through the snow, toward the closest intact chalet.

The first man turned back to Korden, his friendly grin growing embarrassed. "Sorry 'bout that, drude. Adliss gets a little jumpy when he's comin down off the spin."

"Spin?"

"Yeah, you know. Juice. Mashed greens. Love skilne." At Korden's confused frown, he reached inside a pocket on the front of his blindingly colorful tunic, drew out a tiny glass vial full of what looked like pulped plant roots suspended in a creamy white broth, and held it up for inspection. "Jinko, man."

Stone?

SEARCHING... 0 RELATABLE ENTRIES FOR ANY TERM USED. BASED ON CONTEXT CLUES, HOWEVER, I CALCULATE A 99 PERCENT CHANCE THAT 'JINKO' IS A NARCOTIC. AND THAT IS WITH A MANDATORY 1 PERCENT MARGIN OF ERROR.

The man watched him throughout this brief exchange with his head cocked to one side, aura bubbling with that quizzical color. "You may not know what it is, li'l drude, but you sure do a great impression of a cruiser, starin off into space like that." He stuck out his hand again, which wobbled like a leaf in the breeze. "I'm Meech Holcomb."

"Korden Bright."

"Bright, huh?" Meech nodded as they shook. "Kye, man. Real kye."

"I don't care if you two wanna talk the mornin away," Jaimer said, unzipping his bedroll and folding the top aside, "but can you pass me the jinks while you do it? I can't take much more of this headache."

"Oh, sorry." Meech tossed the vial across the dead campfire, and Jaimer made a very delayed, clumsy attempt to catch it. He picked the tube up from the ground, unscrewed the top, then, from a pouch around his wrist, he took out a small, blackened shard like the dried plant thorns Feegran used to fashion medicine needles. Jaimer used the splinter to puncture one of the sores on his arm, releasing a clear, viscous fluid. He put his finger over the mouth of the vial, flipped it over briefly, then rubbed the residue that remained on his fingertip into the weeping blister.

Absolute bliss spread across his rough face. He screwed the cap on the vial, lobbed it back to Meech, and lay back on his bag with both eyes rolled up in his head. Meech looked at the contents of the glass tube hungrily, licking his cracked lips. Then he held it out to Korden with one badly trembling hand.

"Want a prick? I try not to be stingy with the stash, man. Enough to go around."

Korden didn't need Stone's urgent warnings to know he should decline the offer.

"Yeah. Yeah, I'll…I'll hold off, too. Guests and all." With what appeared to be some difficulty, Meech set the vial down on his puffy bedroll. "What about breakfast then?" He glanced up, squinting into the sun. "Or lunch, I guess. Got plenty of food, too."

Korden might've refused this also, but he *was* hungry after climbing all morning on an empty stomach. And these men seemed innocent enough.

Of course, that's what he'd thought about Merise, too.

Meech's gaze focused past Korden, as though looking through him. He said, in a muzzy, distracted voice, "No hard feelins if you need to keep movin, drude. I remember what it's like. Feels like I was in your place yesterday. That's why I try to help out the pre-agers whenever I get the chance."

The sentiment—so simple and stark and heartfelt—made the back of Korden's eyes sting. "I guess I have time to eat."

7

It took Meech ten minutes to rekindle the campfire. Each of his motions were blundering thanks to his quaking hands, an affliction which seemed to have nothing to do with the cold. Korden was afraid the man would burn himself as he fried eggs to heap on chipped clay plates with strips of quail jerky and thick slices of bread covered in hillberry jam.

While he cooked, Korden stood at the precipice and studied the lake smothered in that dense black fog. He'd hoped that, when he reached Tay-ho, he would be able to spot this town called Ida somewhere around its shores, but the body of water was much too large for that. He didn't know which way to even start searching. For the first time, he regretted not taking the road Stone had suggested, since it would've led him right to the place he needed to go.

All just distraction, a voice whispered in his ear. Part of last night's dream surfaced, Bibb telling him to forget everything else and hurry on.

But what's the point of rushing? he wondered. *Even if I had Starry, I'd need a lot more supplies to make it past the desert that Winstid told me about.*

Irritation plucked at him. If these dreams truly came from the Upper, they weren't very helpful.

"Feast on," Meech called, breaking into his contemplation.

Korden came back and took a place at the campfire, accepting a plate of food. Jaimer sat up and grabbed one as well, his eyes glazed. Adliss had yet to reappear, but the other two dug in without concern. After a few tentative bites to allow Stone to check for toxins or poisons, Korden began wolfing down the meal to sate his fierce appetite.

"So Korden, drude, you got any family?" Meech asked

around a mouthful of bread. The food steadied him, bringing some color to his pale cheeks. But the bruised hollows remained under his eyes. "Anybody you're travellin with?"

"No. Just me."

"That's too bad. I sympathize, man, I really do. My parents left me and my big brother by the side of the road when I was seven. Wished us luck and lit out for the horizon. Can't blame 'em. Life on the move gets old fast." He dismissed the subject with a shrug. Korden found the nonchalance fascinating. If this man could've survived so much of his childhood on his own while avoiding the Incarnates—and make it sound like such a small task—surely Korden could do the same. "How'd you come to be way up here then? You runnin aimless, or you got some place in mind?"

"I'm looking for a town called Ida."

Jaimer's dull eyes turned to Meech. "He's got yer number, drude."

"You know it?" Korden asked eagerly.

"Well...*everybody* knows it." Meech said. "It's the Town with Power."

"Power?"

"Yeah, a trickle of old-world energy. Enough to keep the lights burnin. People come from spans around to see it. Most apply to become citizens. I've lived there six years now." He squirmed uncomfortably. "But don't get your hopes up, man. They won't give you sanctuary. No one under free age allowed. Whole town's divided in half; men on one side, ladies on the other, and never the two shall meet. The other settlements around Tay-ho sorta took a cue from Ida and laid down a lotta rules to keep the peace."

"Why d'ya think we're on this li'l campin trip?" Egg yolk ran down Jaimer's chin, but he made no move to wipe it away. "Our 'leisure pursuits' ain't exactly pop'lar back home. Man's gotta freeze to death on a mountain just so he can cruise a little jinks. Fasky-ism; that's what that is."

Meech chewed on the last of his bread and nodded solemnly. "Doesn't help that my goody-two-boots brother Rand is the mayor's right hand drude. Least in Jaimer and Adliss's village, they don't got somebody breathin down their tunics when they have a little too much mead and, you know, may or may not have pissed on the street a few times."

"That's fine, I don't need any place to stay," Korden cut in. Although he was fascinated by the idea of multiple communities clustered around this one lake (especially with populations as young as these men), he needed to keep these two from extending their tangent forever. He set his empty plate aside and said, "I'm hoping to speak to your Prophet."

Jaimer let out a low chuckle. "You'd prob'ly have an easier time gettin 'em to let you live there. The only person that talks to the *almighty Prophet* is their damned Mayor Hildan. That's why nobody from my village believes he's real. A box that tells the future? Hells, even most folk in Ida think it's bullcurse to keep 'em in line."

"Only the new arrivals," Meech argued. "Most everyone that's been there long enough believes. Hildan knows about every storm days before it hits. How could he do that if not for the Prophet? And my brother claims to've heard his voice."

"Yeah, but that motherframmer'd eat tree bark if Hildan told him it was pancakes."

"Do *you* think he's real?" Korden asked, directing the question to Meech.

The man used a finger to scratch beneath his tangled blond locks. "Couple years ago, Mayor Hildan tells us to button up tight, bring the livestock behind the walls, get ready for a fight. Sure enough, next mornin, an army of marauders rode up to our gate. Hundred men strong, some with actual shooters. When they saw we were ready for 'em, they backed off without a club swung or projectile fired."

"Went and burned Bickers to the ground though," Jaimer grumbled. "Maybe Hildan should've thrown a warnin their way, huh?"

"What I mean is," Meech continued, "I can't say for sure, but I ain't got no reason to doubt, either. What do you want with the Prophet anyway?"

"I thought...maybe he could tell me how to avoid the Incarnates."

Meech's brow furrowed thoughtfully, but whatever he was going to say was lost as a piercing scream rolled through the ski resort from the direction Adliss had disappeared. All three of them set their plates aside and ran toward it, following the footprints in the snow.

They found Adliss on the porch of one of the chalets with his back pressed against the leaning outer wall. The riftling stood in front of him, hissing with its huge maw opened wide and front claws clacking. That fang-lined gullet was disproportionately wide for such a small creature. Korden lobbed a fireball before it could start its hum. The heat missile exploded behind the riftling, spattering it with blue flames. The hiss turned to a squeal of pain before it sped away, its blurred tentacles mangling the pristine snow.

"*What the hells was that?*" Adliss demanded, stumbling off the porch while clutching his chest with one hand and rubbing obsessively at the orange fuzz of his scalp with the other.

"Sorry," Korden apologized. "Some Incarnates set it loose on me. It's been following me for a day now. I should've warned you."

Adliss ignored him and spoke to his companions. "See! I *told* you he'd bring the Stranger's ilk down on us! And he's throwin *fire*? What is he, one of those Crafter freaks?"

They all looked to Korden, who said nothing. His cheeks burned with shame, even though he knew he had nothing to feel shameful about.

"Fram this, man." Adliss threw up his hands and pushed by Korden. "I'm goin back to get spun. No way I'm lettin you guys cruise it all without me."

"Yeah, drude." Jaimer turned to Meech. "It's been great chewin the fat and all, but maybe it's time for the kid to, you know…mosey on. Don't wanna give anybody the wrong idea that we're harborin him."

Meech looked pained as he stared at the melted spot in the snow where the blue fire exploded. His hands shook as he tucked filthy hair behind his ears.

"He's right, I should go." Korden told him. "I'm sure it'll leave you alone if I'm not here."

Meech licked his lips, then bobbed his head to the side. "C'mon."

8

They walked back past the camp (where Jaimer and Adliss were already prepping for another dose of jinko) to the edge of the slope leading down to the lake.

"Never met a Crafter before," Meech said.

Korden reached for the words to explain. That his faith in the Upper—and the wellspring of magic he gained access to because of that faith—didn't make him bad or good, didn't make him any different than anyone else. "But it's…I'm not really…"

"S'kye, man. No need to explain nuthin to me. Do what

you gotta do to survive, that's my motto." He scratched at the blisters on his arm as he said this, while staring thoughtfully into the distance. Then he held up two trembling fingers and traced the cable of the ski lift as it snaked down the mountain below them. "Follow that and you should find a dirt road near the bottom. It rings the whole lake, connects most of the settlements. You could follow that to Ida or… curse, I'll tell you what, our boats are tied up at the shore. Mine's the blue one. Take it outta the cove, go due north, you'll end up at Ida in half the time. Skip some of the villages where they're just gonna stare at you. Or worse."

"I can't take your boat," Korden told him. "How will you get home?"

Meech waved the concern away. "Eh, I'll get one of the other drudes to give me a ride. 'Sides, you need it more'n I do. If you're out on the lake, maybe you'll be able to shake that little ball of tentacles off your trail." He put a hand on Korden's shoulder. "Listen li'l drude, I can't tell you for sure that Hildan'll take your case to the Prophet, but it can't hurt to ask, right? Tell the guards at the gate you wanna talk to Rand Holcomb. My brother's a pretty good guy. I mean, aside from bein an uptight dick. You can let him know I sent you, but I'd appreciate if you'd keep, you know, *all this*, to yourself. No need for him to know what we were doin up here, catch me?"

"Yes, absolutely."

"Oh, and if any of 'em sees you slingin that fire, your reception ain't gonna get any warmer." He gave that lopsided grin. "Get it, *warmer*?"

Korden rolled his eyes but let out a giggle. "I'll remember. Thanks for all your help."

"No problem. And who knows? If they haven't kicked

you outta town by the time I get back, you can repay me with a frosty cold mead." Meech gave his shoulder one last clap and started back toward camp, but Korden called out before he'd gone a handful of steps.

"Meech...do you know if anything bad happened at this lake?"

The man frowned. "Whattaya mean 'bad'?"

"Something that happened to a lot of people. Frightened them or...or maybe hurt them somehow?"

"One thing I know about Tay-ho is, you shouldn't drown in it." He continued walking away, throwing over his shoulder, "Cause anything that sinks in that lake, don't come back up."

THE DEVIL
YOU KNOW

1

The ski lift cable cast a slim shadow across the white blankets spilling down the mountainside, but it wouldn't for much longer. The sun was already kissing the summit behind him; on this eastern side of the range, it would be early evenings instead of late mornings. But for now, the silhouette of the cable provided a convenient trail for Korden to follow as he plodded down the steep slope through the snow. The drifts became deeper and softer here, powdery fluff that came up to his thighs in some places. They might be ideal for this 'skiing' activity, but they slowed his walking pace to a crawl and turned his dungarees and the inside of his sneakers into a cold, sloshy mess.

Not that he was in a hurry to reach the lake.

Korden raised his eyes from the snow to study that black, fog-like aura hovering over the cove, low enough to caress the water. From this angle, he couldn't tell how high it rose into the air, but it began a few pargs from the rocky beach, and hugged every curve of the shoreline, extending out into the open water and across the lake as far as he could see.

The thought of going into that ominous cloud made

his scalp prickle. He could still close his eyes and see those ghostly figures in the stratoliner, screaming in terror before they rose and drifted toward him.

"What do you think he meant?" Korden asked. "About nothing coming back up from the lake?"

SEARCHING FOR KEY WORDS 'TAHOE,' 'DROWN,' AND 'SINK'… 194,315 RELATABLE ENTRIES RETURNED. SUMMARY: DUE TO THE EXTREMELY FRIGID TEMPERATURES OF THE LAKE—BETWEEN 55 AND 60 DEGREES FAHRENHEIT EVEN DURING THE SUMMER—SUDDEN IMMERSION CAN INDUCE 'COLD-WATER SHOCK,' A CONDITION IN WHICH THE LUNGS SEIZE AND SWIMMERS MAY DROWN. CLOSER TO WHAT I SURMISE WAS MR. HOLCOMB'S POINT, THE COLD ALSO SLOWS THE RAPID PROLIFERATION OF BACTERIAL WASTE GASES THAT CAUSES DECAYING MATTER TO REMAIN BUOYANT; THEREFORE, CORPSES WILL SINK IN LAKE TAHOE AND REMAIN PRESERVED FOR MUCH LONGER PERIODS.

The explanation was technical, but Korden comprehended enough of it that another chill tiptoed up his spine. "Have…have a *lot* of people died in there?"

THERE ARE MANY DOCUMENTED DROWNINGS IN MY OUTDATED FILES, HOWEVER, THE EXACT ANSWER TO YOUR QUERY REMAINS UNKNOWN. SEVERAL UNSUBSTANTIATED URBAN LEGENDS CLAIM THAT THE LAKE WAS A BODY DUMPING GROUND FOR ORGANIZED CRIME, AS WELL AS THE FINAL RESTING PLACE FOR A LARGE GROUP OF IMMIGRANT RAILROAD WORKERS WHO THE UNITED STATES GOVERNMENT TIED TOGETHER AND FORCED INTO THE LAKE RATHER THAN PAY. MANY BELIEVED THAT THESE CORPSES ARE AT THE BOTTOM OF THE LAKE, ALTHOUGH TAHOE IS MUCH TOO DEEP FOR ANYONE TO GATHER SUPPORTING EVIDENCE FOR THIS CLAIM.

"I don't know if that makes me feel any better," Korden muttered.

He walked on for the next hour, emerging from the snow-line. The air at this lower altitude was warm enough for him to take off his coat, but the sun was fully hidden on the other side of the mountain by now, its long shadow settling across the slope to create an eerie twilight. Korden looked back up and caught a distant glimpse of a small, black form scurrying behind one of the lone fir trees that dotted the landscape.

"This thing doesn't give up."

Heater Kay's mean-spirited laughter rang through his head. *I hope he snips your balls off, kiddo.*

The beach lay two spans downhill. Korden jogged toward it, breath wheezing, carry pouch bouncing against the back of his hips. He could see the dark aura clearly now, like a layer of greasy soot wiped across the surface of the lake. It must be ten pargs thick, and as wispy and uneven as a cloud on top.

As he neared the shore, the tall metal poles of the ski lift shortened, bringing the cable closer to the ground before the line ended at a small kiosk that had served as a boarding station. Beside this sat another empty parking lot, its pavement cracked and rucked. A rut was carved into the earth in front of it, a reddish ribbon of dirt that scrawled across the land to the north and south. This must be the trail around the lake that Meech mentioned. Korden crossed over the worn path and caught sight of three oblong shapes hidden in a clump of vegetation growing along the shore, beyond the reach of the lapping waves.

Boats. Long and skinny, tapering to points at either end, flat on the bottom with two seats hollowed in the middle, one behind the other, and made of polymer cast in unnaturally bright colors. Stone called them 'kayaks.' Korden had never ridden in a boat, much less piloted one, but he'd read plenty of books about them. He found the blue one, which had a crude wooden carving of a mermaid affixed to the pointed bow with resin, in front of the seat. He released the two-sided oar from the holders and stood wringing the instrument's handle distractedly while he studied the lake.

From where he stood, the black *mohol* began three arm-lengths away, a feathery wall of darkness. Like the yellow aura on the stratoliner, it had the consistency of smoke, but the slight breeze ruffling his hair had no effect on it. He could see only a faint glimmer of the water beyond the boundary.

Taking a boat to his destination might be faster, but did he *really* want to enter that haze of disembodied emotion?

Meech and the other two came through it. Sure didn't hurt them any.

But they couldn't see it. None of the people that live around this lake can see it, otherwise they might not be so eager to settle here.

Was that it? Did his ability to sense the fog make it dangerous to him? He didn't know enough about these aura clouds to guess what they could do, or who they would do it to.

His deliberation was interrupted by a rage-filled screech that echoed across the hillside. Korden looked up to find the riftling barreling down the slope toward him. The creature had abandoned all pretense of stealth after realizing that its quarry was on the verge of escaping.

This had to end. If he wasn't willing to try losing the riftling on the lake, then he must fight it to the death, here and now.

INDEED, I CALCULATE AN 84.3 PERCENT CHANCE OF BESTING THE CREATURE IN MORTAL COMBAT.

"What? Why not 100?" Korden demanded. "I killed all those others!"

You employed tactics best suited to a compact group of enemies. Your lack of precision puts you at a disadvantage, which has been demonstrated in every interaction with this particular riftling so far. I should add that the previous number suffers an 11.6 percent handicap if you allow it to get close enough to neutralize your abilities.

They were good odds…but they were still odds. A risk he didn't need to take, especially when another option was at hand.

Wouldn't it be supremely pointless if his journey ended here, at the claws of this pathetic beast?

Korden scowled at the approaching riftling. "Let's see if you can swim, you ugly curseface."

He spun and splashed into the lake, dragging the boat with him. Even with Stone's warning, the temperature of the water made him gasp. The computer fed him quick instructions on rowing. When he'd gotten far enough from the shore, he tossed his carry pouch into the rear seat, then climbed up into the front, almost capsizing in the process. He slid the oar into the water, clumsily pushing the kayak deeper into the cove.

A second later, he passed into the fog.

There was no discernible effect, other than the sunlight dimming around him. Korden concentrated on rowing, first one side and then the other, as Stone instructed. He tried to develop a rhythm, which wasn't easy with his broken hand screaming each time he put pressure on it. After a few strokes, he stopped and looked over his shoulder, back into the bright world he'd left behind.

The riftling reached the shore and raced back and forth along the water in frustration. It shook one claw at him and howled, "*You will not escape, human!*"

Korden laughed as he paddled toward the mouth of the cove, stopping long enough to hold up his little finger at the enraged creature.

2

Past the enclosure of the bay, Tay-ho stretched outward in all directions, leaving Korden adrift in a vast sea.

The black aura wasn't as bad from within as it looked on the outside. There was no smell, no change in temperature, nothing to put his hackles up. Vision muddied at fifty pargs or so, but it wasn't totally obscured even beyond that. He could see the far coast as though peering through a pall of wispy smoke, the snowcapped Sierras and the sliver of indigo sky above them that preceded the night.

When he was far enough out, he directed his boat to the left, parallel to the coast, and paddled on. Back on the shore, the tiny form of the riftling waited to see which direction he would go, then raced over the hillside and into the heavily-forested land north of the cove, where Korden lost sight of it. For the last time, hopefully.

There was nothing left to do but row. The kayak glided through the calm waters, Stone helping to keep him on a northern bearing. The cove was soon lost behind him. New land replaced it, slid by just as fast, and yet, he didn't seem to be getting anywhere. This lake was mind-bogglingly large.

BASED ON YOUR AVERAGE ROWING SPEED, OUR RELATIVE POSITION ON THE LAKE, AND ASSUMING THAT IDA IS LOCATED AT THE NORTHERNMOST POINT, I ESTIMATE APPROXI-

MATELY 4.5 HOURS TO OUR DESTINATION, Stone offered, before adding hesitantly, HOWEVER, LACTIC ACID BUILD-UP IN YOUR DELTOIDS AND TRICEPS INDICATES OUR CURRENT SPEED MAY BE UNSUSTAINABLE.

"I guess that's your way of saying my arms are getting tired," Korden grunted. Each dip of the oar made his muscles burn a little longer, not to mention that his broken hand caused him to favor the right side. He considered augmenting his strength but wondered if that was a usage Tash would approve of. Artcraft, his *den-so* always said, was never to be used as a substitute for what one could accomplish themselves with practice. An overreliance made one weak, in both body and mind.

So he muted the pain and paddled. Rowed until he lost track of the minutes and the hours. Night stole into the sky, muscling aside the last orange-red streaks of daylight. He could no longer see the black fog around him, but knew it was there by the way it smothered the stars and turned the waxing baker's moon into no more than a blurred outline. The water became a smooth sheet of black glass. The only relief from the darkness came from the lights shimmering in the hills that bordered the lake on all sides of him. Some of them mere pinpricks, surely no more than lonely campfires, but he also spotted several spread-out glows that must be settlements.

The Town with Power. That's what Meech called Ida. Korden remembered how amazed he'd been by the church where Merise lived, with its brilliant white lights in the ceiling and powered kitchen appliances. He had no trouble believing that people would be drawn to such wonder, comforted by relics from a time when the world was a brighter place.

So how many people lived around this body of water? Certainly more than the two hundred souls of Hidden Glen.

He had a sudden, intense urge to talk with every last one of them, to hear their stories, to feel his connection to them through the Upper.

This pleasant fantasy was still playing out in his head when all those distant lights winked out simultaneously.

3

It was like a blanket dropping over his vision. The darkness intensified, leaving him blind, just as in the stratoliner vision Stone had given him. Korden was so startled by the abrupt change, the oar slipped from his hands. He scrambled for it in the pitch black before it could fall overboard, then sat still in the seat with his heart hammering inside his ribcage.

"Stone, can you see?" His voice sounded small and flat in the dark void, but he needed to hear it, to be sure that he existed.

OPTICS REMAIN UNIMPAIRED FOR ME; LIKEWISE, I CAN DETECT NOTHING WRONG WITH YOUR EYES.

So whatever this was, it must be because of the aura. Something affecting him through the conduit. That didn't make it any less scary.

Korden leaned forward in his seat and felt his way toward the kayak's bow. His skin prickled with cold; the air here had gone as frigid as at the top of the mountain. In the dark, his fingers found the mermaid sculpture mounted on the rim of the seat. He turned it into a *demno*, pumping it full of artcraft so that it blazed with azure light.

The illumination pierced the darkness, enough for him to see the boat and the water around it. A gasp of relief escaped him, the exhalation coated with a plume of ice. He shivered and strained his eyes into the pitch black that lay beyond the circle of light his artcraft lantern cast, seeking a reason for this strange occurrence.

IF YOU WOULD LIKE, I COULD GUIDE YOU TO SHORE.

Yes, as a matter of fact, he *would* like. Coming out here was a mistake. The idea of dealing with the riftling seemed far more appealing now. What was that Allin used to say? The devil you know instead of the one you don't?

He turned the boat with Stone's direction. The computer estimated two hundred pargs to shore. Korden paddled frantically, eager to narrow that distance. The *demno* on the bow slashed through the darkness ahead, but there was no sign of land.

And then, as he dipped the oar into the water, it was yanked from his grasp.

The motion caused the boat to rock violently. Korden gripped the seat until it stilled, afraid the vessel would topple. Fear squeezed his chest as he worked up the nerve to peek over the side where the oar had gone.

Shapes moved beneath the surface of the water. Forms made of swirling darkness, barely visible in the light. They rose from the depths with their arms above their heads, reaching for him.

Korden screamed. The figures surrounded the boat now. They breached the surface, a carpet of black, grasping hands. He could do nothing as they seized the edge of the boat and turned the kayak over, dumping him into the water.

The cold galvanized him. Locked his muscles and shut down his brain. He'd never experienced anything like it; the sensation was so bone-chilling it burned and numbed at the same time. Stone warbled in his head as he sank, warnings about hypothermia and cold-water shock, but the computer's voice seemed far, far away.

He forced his limbs to move, kicking back toward the surface, where the demno glowed. The shapes circled him in the murky water, visible in glinting flashes, like the quicksilver darting of fish. They moved in closer, arms out, reaching…grasping…

The first of them touched his arm.

Overwhelming despair washed through him. A depression so deep it robbed him of all will. That's what the black color of the *mohol* represented, the same emotion that the Incarnates aimed to inspire: an unending sense of hopelessness.

These were the remnants of all the people who'd died in this lake throughout history. And this was what they'd felt as they sank into Tay-ho's icy depths, their desperation lingering long after their deaths to take on a collective life of its own. Now, these emotional revenants clutched at him as if he could save them, infected him with their despondency, pulled him down into the freezing dark where he would become one of them forever.

Korden let them. He had no willpower to fight. Stone pleaded with him to swim, insisted that he was drowning, but this melancholy dragged at his very soul. Even calling out to the Upper seemed too much effort.

And, as he sank beneath the water in the embrace of these wraiths, faces worked through his thoughts, the faces of those he would let down by giving up, Tash and Bibb and Cheree, until he got to his father.

Redfen Bright. The man was dead, but his presence held just as much sway over Korden as when he was alive. As he thought about the man's face at the end, about everything he'd sacrificed to make sure his son had a chance, something sparked in Korden's frozen chest.

He *pushed*. Not with his body, but with his mind. Art-craft streamed from him in electric blue waves like lightning, like it had with the Incarnate that murdered Redfen. Except this wasn't a destructive force pouring out of him, but pure positive energy, ebullient thoughts to counter the despair. The inky waters beneath Lake Tay-ho lit up as bright as day.

The ghosts pulled away from him. Disintegrated and swirled into the deeper darkness below. Korden could move again. He swam for the surface as the energy faded, gasping for air when his head breached.

Up here, the night had returned. The desperation *mohol* was gone; the stars leapt out at him in a twinkling panorama. But the waters of the lake were still freezing, making it hard to stay afloat.

He spun in a circle, seeking the kayak. It'd either sunk along with his belongings, or the *demno* had burned out and he couldn't find it in the darkness. But the shore was visible a hundred pargs away, with a campfire blazing to mark the distance. Maybe it was Meech and the others, come down off the mountain to get away from the snow.

Korden swam toward the land as Stone encouraged him. The cold worked its way into his muscles; every stroke of his arm or kick of his legs felt like the actions of someone else. He huffed and puffed but couldn't get enough air into his crippled lungs. The shore grew farther away, instead of closer.

His head slipped under. Korden heaved it back up, thrashing and sputtering. He could still become one of the emotional echoes yet, if he let himself drown.

"*Help!*" he called out, choking on a mouthful of water. The shore was so close, just fifty pargs away, but he didn't think he could swim another ten. By the flickering light of the campfire, he could see a figure splashing into the shallows toward him. Korden kicked, fighting against the water.

Then he went under for the last time, too exhausted to struggle.

4

Hands grasped his shoulders. Hauled him back to the surface. Korden went limp as he was half-carried, half-dragged to the shore and dropped unceremoniously on the muddy bank. He lay shivering and gagging as a thick, grizzled face appeared above him.

"C'mon rubo, don't go a-dyin on me," a voice thick with accent said. Korden's face was slapped lightly, first on one cheek, then the other. "That's good, keep breathin."

Korden coughed up a bathing tub's worth of water. "C-cold," he stuttered. His breath hitched as his lungs misfired. "S-s-so cold."

"Ayuh, so am I, now! A li'l night swim in yonder pond'll do that. Let's see if we can't get ourselves thawed out, whatcha say?"

The man took hold of him again and dragged him closer to the fire. Korden tried to help as much as possible, but his body was numb. He did turn over enough to see a huge, blocky shape with a rounded top farther up the beach, away from the water, some sort of shanty or dwelling.

The heat from the campfire washed over him. Korden shivered, this time in relief. Stone ran a health diagnostic and declared him without serious injury besides a low core temperature. As soon as he recovered, he would have to go back out to hunt for Meech's boat and pray to the Upper that his carry pouch was in it. The thought of the map and his father's shooter lost at the bottom of the lake was more than he could bear. He sat up and leaned closer to the fire so the orange flames licked at his face and hands.

"Careful now! Watch yah don't burn off that hair!" the man cautioned a split second before Stone could. The last word came out a protracted 'hey-ah.' His accent reminded Korden of Tash's, although far more nasal and lazy somehow, the R's missing rather than trilling. He pulled back from the fire and examined his savior while the cold seeped out of him.

He was squat, a full head shorter than Korden, and portly without being fat. He looked somewhere in his fifties, ginger hair balding from his crown, cheeks rough and leathery, and a scraggly, neck-length red beard with a shock of gray to the left of center. Rings covered his hands, one and sometimes two to a finger, gold bands that sported gaudy stones in an array of colors. But, strangest of all, he wore a garment unlike anything Korden had ever seen: a pair of bright green pants and a vest to match, both made from some material that shimmered in the firelight. A skinny black scrap of cloth dangled from his neck in a neat knot below his beard, over a puffy white shirt with a stiff collar whose full sleeves were rolled up to the elbows.

"So…yah real." The man poked the inside of his cheek thoughtfully with his tongue as he looked Korden up and down. Korden checked his aura and found it a fascinating shade of glinting silver that he'd never seen before. "When that mean li'l black blob started squealin about a kid, I figgered it was just jawin. But here yah sit, big as billy-be-damned."

Korden didn't know who Billy was or why his size required damning, but something this man said caught his attention. "Little black blob? You mean, the riftling? You *saw* it?"

"Saw it, nuthin! I caught that squirmy booger not an hour ago!" In his nasally pronunciation, 'hour' came out 'ow-ah'. He hiked a thumb over his shoulder, at the boxy shadow up the beach. "Got it caged up in the wagon right now, yes sah."

"*You do?* You have to show me!" Korden leapt up from the fire, wobbling for a moment, his wariness about this man and his indecipherable *mohol* forgotten. "It's dangerous! We need to kill it!"

"All right, all right," the man conceded. "Settle on, rubo. Right this way."

Korden followed the short man toward the structure he'd taken for a hut, which sat beside the worn lake trail. As they got closer, he could see it clearly in the moonlight. The man had called it a wagon, and to a certain extent, it was; a flat, rectangular base approximately thirty pargs long and ten wide, and a curved bonnet over the top that rose another ten in the air. The pieces were sculpted and painted in such a way to disguise them as brown wood sideboards and cream-colored canvas, but they were constructed of the same hard polymers as the stratoliner.

Stone tried to explain, but Korden recognized the design this vehicle was meant to mimic from his studies. It was a much bigger version of a covered Conestoga wagon, like the ones people once used to cross the land with all their belongings inside.

Except this one had no horse attached to pull it, just a high bench seat at the front behind a panel of numerous buttons and levers. And no spoked wheels to make it roll, either. No wheels at all on its rectangular base. It rested on the ground on six spider-like prongs that jutted from its sides, but past these, mounted on the underside, Korden caught sight of two rows of the glass bubbles he'd come to know so well.

This wagon could *hover*.

On the faux-canvas bonnet, words were painted in garish purple script that curved in an arch across the wagon's side:

DOC APOCALYPSE - FINE CURATIVES AND MEDICINALS

"Is that you?" he asked. "Doc...'Apocalypse?'"

"At yah service," the man confirmed, running a bejeweled hand through the thinning hair at his temple. "Real name Tarmon Doaks, but folks far and wide know me as the Armageddon Sawbones, the Doomsday MD, the Physician of the Decimation." He swept an arm toward the wagon with pride. "And this lovely lady is my steed, Gwenita.'"

"You're a doctor?"

"Weeeeell, I don't slice-n-dice or yank out any teeth, but I got the cure for what ails yah! And who might *yah* be?"

"Korden," he said, offering no more.

"Sooo...yah from the lake? One of the settlements 'round here?"

"No. Just passing through."

Doaks chuckled and nodded. "Me as well, rubo. Me as well."

They reached the rear of the wagon, where a short staircase led up to an open deck jutting off the end. The back of the bonnet was covered by a solid door also designed to look like cloth. They climbed the stairs to the deck, where the doctor revealed a small panel set into the bonnet, punched a button, and the rear door rolled smoothly upward. He stood aside so Korden could see what lay beyond.

The interior of the vehicle was a wonder. White lights embedded in the ceiling put out a cool illumination. The wall to the left had various trunks and cabinets built into it along with a cot that appeared to fold down, next to a basin on a slender stand with a spigot on top that he recognized as a 'sink,' though he couldn't see how it would have running water. The short wall on the far end had another door, presumably leading out to the controls at the front of the wagon. The wall to his right, however, held shelves upon shelves of tinted vials and jars and glass bulbs full of colored liquids, plant roots, and the bodies of small animals. Korden could've studied this magnificent place for hours, but his present concern was only for the two long metal cages sitting to either side of the door. The riftling lay inside the one on the right in a tangle of tentacles. It sprang up when it caught sight of him, rushed to the bars, and stuck its claws through to snap at him. At the same time, that annoying buzz cranked up in Korden's head. The other man gave no indication that he heard the noise as he stepped away from the door, so the creature must be able to focus or direct it.

"Wow," Korden remarked. "How in the world did you catch it?"

"Like this," Doaks said behind him, and Korden's entire body lit up with pain.

THE AMAZING BOY FROM THE PAST

1

Fire rampaged through him. White blotted out his vision. A terrible, shrieking squeal filled his ears. The ordeal went on for an eternity, until all he knew was torment.

Then it stopped, and Korden hit the ground in a boneless heap.

The next few minutes held flashes of sensation as his brain tried to piece itself back together. His pockets being searched. The knife—his last remaining possession—taken from his belt. Getting hoisted, carried like a sack of grain. The feeling of something hard pressed down over the crown of his head and wrapped under his chin. A door made of steel bars closed in his face.

And, through it all, that mind-numbing hum never wavered.

2

He was brought to full consciousness by a rapid, continual clinking sound, as high as a rodent's chitter. His eyes flew open when his memory returned, thoughts of Merise haunting him. He groaned as he sat up and narrowly avoided banging his head on the top of the cage.

The enclosure around him was created with crisscrossing steel bars as thick as his thumb, all four walls anchored into the hard, smooth surface beneath him at the corners. It reminded him of waking up inside Winstid's jail, except the accommodations here weren't as generous. This pen was long enough to stretch out, but only while lying down; the top was barely high enough for him to sit up, and the sides so narrow his elbows couldn't fully extend to either side. *Coffin dimensions*, he thought, recalling the disinterred burial boxes he'd seen. If the walls had been solid, he might've succumbed to claustrophobia, but the spaces between the bars were wide enough to admit his arm up to the elbow.

Beyond the cage, he recognized the interior of the wagon. The lights inside the curved ceiling were much dimmer, casting a soft glow on the long space and its contents. A sweet odor filled the air, but underneath was a scent as sour as mildew. The source of the clinking noise, he saw, was the hundreds of glass containers on the shelves as they jostled against one another. Judging by the slight vibration under him—not as extreme as the one produced by the hovertrikes, but enough to cause that squeaking rattle among the various bottles and jars—they were in motion. The idea chilled him.

Congratulations, he told himself. *You've misread yet another* mohol. Last time, it'd gotten him force-fed breast milk by a deranged woman who thought he was her long-dead son. Emotions, he was coming to understand, were a nuanced scale particular to each individual.

His enclosure sat in the rear corner of the wagon, across from the riftling's pen. The creature was inside, six pargs away. It sat on the hard floor of the wagon with its dozens of tentacles splayed around its slick black body like a spider at the center of a web. Those five beady yellow eyes watched him, positioned across its head in a vague T pattern. Now that he could study it without fear of an attack, he saw that the pupils of those jaundiced orbs each had a distinct shape, as intricate and unique as human faces.

Korden found the door of the cage next to his head and rattled the bars. It was solid on the hinges, secured by a squarish padlock with no keyhole, but he felt sure he could blow it open with a heavy blast of artcraft. Or kick it off with some augmented strength. Or melt the bars with intense blue flame.

But he couldn't do any of those things. Because that mosquito whine was loud and clear in his head, preventing him from opening the conduit. The handicap was as scary and diminishing as being struck blind or deaf. And he couldn't talk to Stone, either. The computer's casing hung from the leather strap around his neck, but it might as well be a real rock if he couldn't communicate with the artificial intelligence inside it.

The cabinets and trunks inside the wagon were beyond his reach, along without anything inside them that might help him escape. So, mindful of his broken hand, he grabbed the cage door, braced his feet on the far end of the enclosure, and pushed with all his might, grunting with the strain.

From the other cage came a gurgling noise that he took to be laughter.

"What's so funny?" The words came out slightly mangled; the movement of Korden's jaw was limited by something beneath his chin.

"Stupid human got itself trapped," the riftling said, and chortled again. "Very amusing."

"Doesn't look like you did too much better."

The creature rose and slammed against the wall of its cage in a sudden frenzy. "*Zeega will spill your intestines, human!*"

"Yeah? Good luck with that."

Korden turned away from the beast's tantrum and used his hands to explore the device fastened to his head. It consisted of a leather strap that ran under his chin and another that branched off the first and wound around the back of his neck, both cinched tight and secured with another lock. He followed the straps upward and found them connected to a thin band the width of two fingers that ran across his forehead, above his ears, and to the rear of his skull, like a crown. It seemed like slick metal on the outside, but when he squeezed a fingertip between the band and his scalp, he could feel some kind of bumps or notches.

The device was firmly fitted to him, his hair tucked beneath. He pulled at the straps, tried to loosen or break them, then hauled at the band itself. There was a little slack here, enough to lift the cool metal crown away from his skull by half a cupit or so. As soon as it lost contact with the skin, another painful jolt like the one he'd gotten outside the wagon ripped through him. It didn't knock him unconscious, but he cried out in pain.

Wet, throaty laughter came from his fellow captive.

A second later, a panel on the front door of the wagon opened, and Doaks's bearded face peered through.

"Ah, back amongst the livin, eh?" he asked. "Hold on, I'll be right there. We need to have a chat."

3

The vibration stopped. A few seconds later, the rear door retracted into the ceiling, letting in a swath of bright daylight. Korden recoiled, not from the light, but at the realization that he must've been unconscious for at least a few hours. From this vantage, all he could see beyond the door was more forest; nothing that might tell him where they were.

Doaks stood on the decking outside the wagon's bonnet in his sparkling green outfit, holding a circular piece of polymer a little bigger than his palm. Some sort of electronic gizmo, full of dials and buttons and tiny screens on one side. He laid it across his knee as he knelt in front of Korden and looked into the cage.

"Let me out of here," Korden demanded, rising up on his elbows as far as he was able.

"Not so fast, rubo. I know yah prob'ly upset, but hear me out."

"I'm not going to hear anything unless you open this cage." He gave the door an angry rattle. "Let me out!"

"If yah just—"

"*Let me out!*"

"This is important, so—"

"*LET ME OUT!*"

Doaks picked up the circular gizmo and spun a dial.

That pain rocketed through Korden, a squealing, white hot agony. When it ended, he dropped to the floor facedown, the metal band around his head clanking against the hard surface. He lay there panting as his body spasmed and a taste like copper settled on his tongue. *Electricity*, he surmised. *This is what it's like to be shocked.*

The riftling burbled laughter.

"Ready to listen now?" Doaks inquired. Korden nodded miserably with his face pressed to the wagon floor. "Good. Not exactly how I wanted this to go, but we can get back on track. First of all, let me put yah mind at ease. This is strictly business, yah ken? I ain't interested in no young love. And I don't aim to sell yah. No sah. If anything, I'm here to help yah see what a unique position yah in."

Korden raised his head. "I have no idea what you're talking about," he rasped.

Doaks beamed wide enough to show every one of his gleaming white teeth. He put down the gizmo, then leapt off the back of the wagon, spun with a flourish that made his green vest twinkle in the sunlight, and held up his pointer finger next to his ear with a theatrical flick of his wrist.

"Korden, my boy—it *was* Korden, right?—anyway, I'd be willin to bet that fear is the guiding principle of yah life. It's the first thing yah feel every day when yah wake up, and the last thing yah feel when yah try to sleep. Am I right, son?" Before Korden could even try to answer, he continued. "A-course I am! Yah below free age! An army of bloodthirsty demons wearin human skin is devoted to huntin yah down! Why *wouldn't* yah be terrified all the time? Believe it or not, I was a child myself, so I remember what it's like! Yah just wanna throw yah arms to the heavens and scream to whatevah god yah believe in, '*Why? What did I do to deserve bein born into this world of misery and woe?*'"

He illustrated this by tossing his head back and stretching his arms out to either side, then freezing in the dramatic pose. Korden used the opportunity to glance over at the riftling and found one of the creature's eyes staring back at him while the other four remained fixed on Doaks.

The man broke his stance, twirled again, and leveled a ringladen finger at Korden. "But what if I told yah there was a way to give that fear a purpose? To relieve others of their own hopelessness? To take this terrible misfortune of youth that yah been cursed with…and turn it into a *lucrative, fortune-makin opportunity? That's* somethin yah'd be interested in, right?" He nodded madly in answer to his own question, that brilliant smile in place.

"Uh…not really," Korden said. "I still don't know what you're talking about."

"I'm talkin," Doaks began, jumping up to knock his bootheels together and then sweeping an arm out toward Korden, "about the amaaaaaazing boy…*from the past!*"

He waited for a response, out of breath, eyebrows up and grin in place, holding his hand out.

"Who's that?" Korden asked.

Doaks looked crestfallen as the grin melted from his face. "*Yah*, rubo. I'm talkin 'bout *yah*."

Korden shrugged helplessly.

"Aged Lord deliver me," Doaks muttered. He climbed the steps to the wagon deck with his shoulders slumped in defeat, then dropped down next to Korden with one hand pressed to his chest over his heart. "I'll level with yah, Korden. The sign on the side of the wagon advertises curatives, and, indeed, that's what I hand out. Some of 'em work, some of 'em don't, but that's not the point. Because what I'm *really* sellin to the downhearted folk across this land…is happiness. A brief reprieve from this horrible existence. I put on a show, some song, some dance, offer 'em somethin to help with their aches, and I help 'em forget their miserable lives for a bit. It's not much, but people enjoy it. And with a boy from the past by my side, why, I could do that even better!"

"But I'm not from the past, why do you keep saying that?"

Doaks motioned at the far end of the cage, where Korden's feet lay. "Yah think anybody's seen shoes like that in the last couple centuries? Hellsfire, most of my customers haven't even seen anyone below free age in decades! It's all a story, son. And yah talkin pet over there, he'll help sell it, for sure."

"That thing is *not* my pet!"

The riftling's multiple eyes narrowed in the other cage. "You will let Zeega out of this prison immediately, human, or you will share the young one's fate."

Doaks chuckled. "Oh ayuh, that's great banter, they're gonna love the two of yahs." He turned to Korden. "Whattaya say, rubo? Yah wanna help make people's lives a little more bearable?"

"Not like this," Korden answered through clenched teeth.

'Doc Apocalypse' sighed, picked up the electronic gizmo, and stood up. "That's too bad. Cause we're doin it anyway."

4

He pressed his thumb to the padlock on the outside of the cage. It popped open, the door swinging free. Doaks stepped back a few paces, flicking switches and turning dials on the round gizmo. "C'mon out and let's test those connections," he said.

Korden scrambled out of the cage. One way or the other, he was getting free of this man. Doaks would surely shock him if he tried to run, but if he could lure the man away from the wagon, outside the range of the riftling's neutralizing hum...

Once on the ground, he found that they were parked on the beaten path. The lake itself was visible thirty pargs down a shallow embankment on the left side of the wagon. The sight of the water relieved him, and not just because the dark *mohol* was still gone. Now he at least knew where he was, that Doaks hadn't carried him too far away. Although, if Tay-ho was on their left, that meant they'd travelled south, *away* from his destination.

Doaks kept fiddling with the pad. Korden began sidling around him, putting precious distance between himself and the source of that throbbing buzz in his head. "Listen, Mr. Doaks—er, Doc Apocalypse—you can't just...take me like this. It's not—"

"That's far enough." The man jabbed at a button on his palm.

Every muscle in Korden's body hardened, freezing him in place like a statue. He couldn't move, couldn't talk, couldn't so much as blink. Only his lungs functioned; ironic, considering they were the one part of him that usually *didn't*. Bright panic blossomed in his chest as he struggled to break the strange spell.

"Arms up," Doaks ordered, working the gadget.

To Korden's horror, his arms rose to either side of him, completely unbidden, stretching over his head. They weren't numb, he could feel the limbs—joints swiveling, muscles working, even the sensation of breeze across his skin—he just had no control over them.

"Give us a little twirl."

Korden's arms fell as his legs moved, spinning him in a quick, tight circle like the ones Doaks had performed during his monologue.

"Aaaand give us a boogie woogie."

His knees and hips bent, pushing his rear end out. His butt gave a series of quick shakes as he swayed back and forth in an odd little dance. Korden's face grew warm as he willed his body to stop this mutiny.

"Now let's test speech." Doaks brought the gizmo up under his chin and said, "My name is Korden, and I love being Doc Apocalypse's assistant!"

Korden's mouth worked; he repeated the phrase verbatim as a tear escaped his eye and rolled down his cheek. It made him sick to hear his own traitorous voice sounding cheerful while spouting this lie.

This was the most invasive, humiliating experience of his life, worse than even Merise.

"Looks good," Doaks confirmed. "Release."

Control of Korden's body returned to him. He swooned, unprepared, sagging to his knees before catching himself.

"What was that?" he demanded, rage and shame causing him to shake.

"That was yah new head accessory." Doaks's smile was much cooler than his previous expressions. "I know it ain't too fashionable, but yah costume should cover it up. And maybe, once yah settle into the routine, we can try takin it off. Get yah a proper bed, too. But for now, back into the cage with yah. I aim to hit our first stop this afternoon."

"I will not go back in there."

Doaks's mouth hardened into a firm line. "I can shock yah, control yah, or yah can just get back in there on yah own. The quicker yah learn to do the latter, the less I have to use the first two."

More tears coursed down Korden's face. These calamities had happened so fast—the riftlings, then the lake *mohol*, and now this—that he felt continually off-balance. Doaks moved toward him, herding him back up the stairs onto the wagon's deck. The squat little man could make an intimidating figure when he wanted. "Please," Korden pleaded as he backed away. "You can't do this. I...I have things to do, places I have to go…"

Doaks grabbed him roughly by the shoulder, spun him around, and forced him down in front of the cage door. "Yah what, fifteen? Sixteen? Nobody that young has anyplace important to be. And it's not like this is forever. Just 'til yah can't pass for a pre-ager anymore. Who knows, maybe by then, yah'll be havin so much fun, yah'll wanna stick around permanently."

"What about the Incarnates?" Korden asked, kneeling in front of the pen. He was desperate for anything that might keep him from going back inside those steel bars. "They'll always be hunting me!"

Doaks waved the thought away. "Those red-eyed bastards have been chasin their own tails ever since this Moambati business started out east."

"That's not true! I escaped from three of them two days ago, on the western slopes outside Tay-ho!"

"Well, yah got away from 'em, didn't yah? That's the key, to keep movin, and I'm always headin toward the horizon. Yes sah." He rested a hand fondly on the outside of the bonnet. "Besides, ol' Gwenita here may not look like much, but she's got some moxie if we need it."

"You might not be scared, but everyone else *will!* I've been run out of enough places to know that no one wants a child around!"

"Let me worry about that." He put his foot on Korden's rear end and gave a hard shove. Korden fell halfway into the cage, then crawled the rest of the way on all fours. He turned around to see the door closing, the lock snapping shut. Doaks looked in at him. "I'm sorry 'bout this, kid. But yah and me're gonna make a lotta scratch together. Sooner yah resign yahself to that, the better."

He reached over to the panel on the back of the wagon, touched a button, and the rear of the bonnet slid back into place between them, sealing out the sunlight.

5

Korden thrashed inside the cage as the vibration started up, all composure lost.

He kicked and punched the bars of his tiny prison until his feet ached and his broken hand throbbed. He tore at the device on his head until the electrical shocks made him dizzy and then beat the hard metal band against the floor to the same result. He closed his eyes and tried to focus past that buzzing sound, to reopen the conduit, but his agitated state of mind hindered him further. And, when all of this failed, he simply curled into a ball on the floor and screamed in frustration, wordless cries that wore his voice down to a whisper. His mounting panic soon triggered an as-mah attack that turned his breath to molasses.

The riftling laughed.

"*BE QUIET!*" Korden roared at it, smashing an arm on the bars.

He rolled on his side to regard the creature. Its unblinking yellow eyes stared back at him, but the rest of its face was so alien, it was impossible to read any sort of emotion. Korden took a deep breath to calm himself. "Listen to me," he begged. "That...that buzzing sound you make. The one that...blocks my powers. If you'll just stop, I can rip open these cages, tear through this wagon, and get us both out of here."

"You lie, human. Zeega reads your mind. You would escape and leave Zeega here to rot. If you did not kill Zeega outright."

Korden winced, mainly because the little beast was one hundred percent right. He recalled that moment back on the mountain, when it seemed to hear Stone speak. "You...you can read my thoughts?"

"Only the foremost." The riftling's face rippled in a way that suggested a grin. "That is how Zeega's brood was able to locate you so quickly on the mountainside. We pinpoint that which the masters receive only an impression of."

"Then, I *swear*," Korden tried again, forcing himself to tell the truth this time. "I'll set you free! Whatever you do after that is up to you!"

"*Never!*" the creature squealed, shaking a claw at him. "If Zeega cannot destroy you, Zeega will keep you prisoner here for the masters! That is Zeega's duty! And until then, Zeega will be entertained by the adult human's mistreatment of you!"

"Fine!" Korden shouted.

"Fine," the riftling agreed, and both lapsed into angry silence as Doc Apocalypse's wagon rode on.

PERFORMANCE ANXIETY

1

He didn't know how long they travelled that first day. Long enough for his stomach to growl and his throat to parch. Long enough for boredom to supersede his dread. Long enough for his muscles to grow cramped from lack of movement in the tight confines.

Long enough for him to learn how to shift the riftling's mental buzz into the background of his thoughts, so it didn't drive him insane.

At last, the small panel set into the front door of the bonnet slid open.

"Listen up, boys and...whatever the hells *yah* are, yah ugly little squid." Perched on top of Doaks's balding head was a gray hat made of some soft material, with a dimpled ridge across the crown, a slightly-upturned brim, and a jaunty white ribbon around the base. "Showtime is upon us. This first stop don't look to be much more than a whistle-stop, prob'ly a Saint o' Christ commune, but that don't mean they ain't worth the effort. Ugly little squid, sit this one out and keep yah gob shut, since I ain't figgered out how to use yah yet. Korden, no need for performance anxiety, yah entire routine is preprogrammed. Yah could sleep through it if yah wanted. But don't do that. Try to show a li'l pizzazz. Yah earn yah supper by doin a good job here." He started to close the panel, then added, "Oh, I'll clear the walls so yah can have a look around. Remember, yah can see them, but they can't see yah."

Korden didn't know what the cryptic phrase meant. Then the bonnet disintegrated around them, letting in the bright afternoon sun and leaving the interior exposed on the rectangular base of the wagon. Both he and the riftling sat up in alarm. At first, Korden thought the wagon covering somehow retracted, but then he saw the cabinets and various glass jars suspended in midair and understood that it had become see-through, like a pane of glass. Foliage and trees passed smoothly by on either side of their floating craft, the sensation reminding Korden of a story he'd read about a magical flying carpet. They could see Doaks now, seated with his back to them, behind the console that controlled this incredible vehicle.

The man might have kidnapped him and stolen control of his body, but Korden marveled at the technological wonders Tarmon Doaks seemed so at ease with. Where had he come by all these gadgets and devices?

Beyond the invisible walls of the wagon, Tay-ho sparkled to their left, free of the black fog, either because Korden had driven off the emotional wraiths or, more likely, because he could no longer sense them within the riftling's dampening mental hum. The beaten dirt path unspooled in front of the wagon, leading them up a meadow incline. Near the top, less than a span away, a hodgepodge grouping of tents sprawled across the hillside. The structures were all white linen stretched over minimal frames, some of them single-person pyramids, others built with branching arms to form multiple-room dwellings. Tall planks of wood loomed over a few of the tents, crossed at the top with a second beam to form a lowercase 't,' but Korden could only guess at the purpose such effigies served. Campfires also burned here and there; this community might be one of the glows he'd spotted last night from the lake. As the wagon approached, people emerged from the lean-to's, both men and women, all dressed in matching short-sleeved robes made from the same material as their homes. Most of them looked as old as the Glenners, but there were a few middle-aged faces mixed in as well. They gaped and pointed when they caught sight of the hovering wagon.

Doaks coasted the vehicle to a stop a few pargs from where the tents began. The vibration cut out as they settled onto the landing prongs. He stood up, raised his hands, and bellowed, "*Hey rubos, come one, come all! Tell your kin, your friends, your neighbors, and be sure to bring the sick, the infirmed, and the crippled…because Doc Apocalypse has got the cure for what ails yah!*"

2

"…and so, at my dear mama's dyin wish, I set out across the land to use my healin arts for the betterment of mankind! Or what's left of us, anyway!"

A smattering of applause rose from the crowd of fifty gathered around the back of the wagon. When they got over their awe of the vehicle, most of them appeared deeply nonplussed by this story, and the antics of Doc Apocalypse in general. Doaks gave a twirl—in addition to his green suit and fancy hat, he'd also donned a black cape with cheerfully grinning skulls embroidered across the shoulders that flared out from his body as he spun—then performed a shuffling dance that made his boot heels click against the deck. He was very spry for a man of his size.

Korden watched all of this from within the bonnet, standing in the middle of the space with his body frozen, unable to move. Doaks had made the walls opaque when they stopped, except for the back door, which now acted as a one-way window. Then he'd let Korden out of the cage and forced him to dress in a set of clothes from one of the storage bins on the wall that, he claimed, would go with Korden's flaming sneakers: a pair of too-big denim dungarees, a gray, cottony tunic with a stretchy neckhole and an emblem on the front in the shape of a bat, and, to cover up the band on his head, a square of red cloth tied over his long locks that Doaks called a 'doo-rag,' topped with a blue hat with the word 'DODGERS' printed above its narrow, jutting brim.

He struggled to make his limbs move, twitch his fingers, *anything*. He couldn't even direct his eyeballs away from the scene outside; the only functions he had control over was blinking and breathing. Being imprisoned inside his own body like this was far worse than any cage.

From the very periphery of his vision, Korden could see the riftling at the door of its own pen, also watching the show.

"Zeega can hear you screaming inside your head," it muttered, a supreme note of satisfaction in its voice. "It is a glorious sound."

"In this wagon," Doaks continued, lowering his voice as he waved a bejeweled hand over the crowd, "I have potions for sore teeth, tonics for failing eyes, elixirs for delicate tummies, concoctions for crackling joints, and ointments for every rash yah can have. Medicines for all the terrible burdens of age, yes sah! All yah have to do is step right up and tell me what yah need cured!"

"And I'm sure your dying mother wanted you to be paid for your wonderful *healing arts*!" a male voice in the crowd called.

"A small fee is required, of course," Doaks answered, not missing a beat. "A donation, really. Whatever yah have to trade. Every little bit helps me continue my good work."

Another man in the front of the crowd rested his hands on the lapels of his white robe. "What proof do we have that any of this works, er, uh, Doctor Apocalypse?"

Doaks leaned down from the deck to lay a hand on the man's shoulder, but spoke loud enough for the assemblage to hear. "I'm glad yah asked, sah! The answer is, none at all! Other than my personal guarantee! But I don't want yah to just take *my* word for it! So here's my assistant Korden, also known as…the Boy…*from the Past!*" As he finished, Doaks touched the button to raise the back door of the bonnet, revealing Korden.

A collective gasp shot through the crowd. They shrank away, fear in their eyes, as he'd told Doaks they would. It was Hidden Glen all over, when Winstid had walked him out of the Keep.

An elderly female voice cried out, *"He'll bring the Incarnates!"*

"Take him out of here!" someone else demanded.

Korden wanted to call out to them. To beg for help. He tried to open his mouth, but it might as well be sewn shut. Instead, his cheeks pulled back in an involuntary grin. From somewhere overhead in the wagon, music began playing, a jaunty tune full of flutes and plucky guitar chords.

And then his body sprang into motion, dragging his consciousness along with it.

He bounded out of the wagon like a madman and landed nimbly beside Doaks, where they stood together in matching akimbo poses. The sudden movement brought a fresh round of terrified bleating from their audience. "*Fear not...good people of Tay-ho,*" he belted out, in a jangly, upbeat singing voice that he barely recognized as his own, "*I'm not...like other boys! I come from a time full of wonderful toys!*"

The crowd drew a bit closer, or at least stopped backing away. Some of them watched him with mingled expressions of fascination and disgust.

"*I was born...before the Purges! Came here...in a special machine! Don't believe me, then just take a look at this teen!*" Korden twirled, then somersaulted across the deck—the bones in his broken hand grinding against one another—and ended on his back with his feet in the air to continue the verse. "*Check out...this cool set of footwear! And these... radical clothes! Even my pet has tentacles instead of toes!*"

For the first time, their audience noticed the riftling behind Korden. They gasped again...but rushed *forward* this time, packing in around the stage.

Korden executed a complicated twisting jump that landed him back on his feet and made his still-healing spine scream. His legs moved under him, performing a much faster version of Doaks's shuffle while he bent over and waved his arms in wide arcs. "*But now...this is the best part! Since I've...come from the days of yore! Those Incarnates find tracking me quite a chore!*"

People grinned now, some of them clapping their hands in time to the music. Korden moved faster, sweat pouring off his brow, his limbs leaden, but he couldn't stop dancing, couldn't stop grinning. "*So let…us soothe all your aches and pains! No need…to even ask why! After all, why would I ever lie?*"

He ended this hellish musical number back-to-back with Doaks, who spread his arms and waited.

And waited.

Finally, a man in the middle of the crowd asked hesitantly, "Issat true? Incarnates can't hunt 'im?"

Doaks gave the man a wink. "Do yah see any around here, sah?"

The response opened a thunderous floodgate.

"*Do you have anything to help me breathe?*"

"*I have the shingles!*"

"*My husband can't remember anything!*"

"*Can I touch the boy for luck?*"

Doc Apocalypse took off his hat and wiped nonexistent tears from under his eyes. "My friends…I think we can accommodate yah all."

3

They mobbed the wagon, holding up baskets of eggs, sacks of grain, bolts of handwoven fabric, a coil of hempen rope, a few of their neatly folded tents, fresh meat, trinkets, and more. Doaks took it all, listened to their problems, then grabbed liquids and plants and animals from his shelves and instructed his 'patients' on their complicated usage. Through it all, Korden could only smile and stand immobile as the robed people reached up to paw at his feet and ankles from the ground around the stage. Doaks discouraged the ones that tried to talk to him, and, for the few that wanted to touch the riftling, he cautioned, "Uh, better keep yah hands away, that one ain't housebroke yet!"

The sun was slouching toward the western Sierras by the time the session wrapped up. Most of the others had drifted away with their curatives when a younger woman lingering at the back of the crowd made her way forward. Long, black hair lay plaited across the back of her neck, and eyes the golden color of fresh honey darted around nervously as she approached. Korden couldn't discern her age, but she was far younger that Cheree, which also made her the youngest female he'd ever seen. Her smooth skin, glowing cheeks, and the slight swell of breasts beneath the white robe made him forget all about his hijacked body as he watched her. She checked to make sure no one was in earshot before speaking to Doaks.

"Do…do you have anything to…?" The woman didn't know how to finish the question. Instead, her hand drifted to her midriff and rubbed distractedly at the front of her robe.

Doaks hunkered at the edge of the deck and said softly, "Miss'um, I have medicines that will get yah preg, keep yah from preg, or, *ahem*, make the problem go away if we're too late for the latter. Tell me what yah need, and I'll fix yah up."

She shook her head. "No, no, it's not that. I always wanted to have children, but I was too scared. I just wondered… if I *did* decide to try…do you have something to make a baby of mine like…" Those amber eyes stole up toward Korden.

Now it was Doaks that seemed at a loss for words. Here was a question the master showman hadn't anticipated. But when inspiration struck, Korden saw it ooze across his despicable, bearded face. He fumbled the circular controller out of a pouch on the inside of his cape and hurriedly punched buttons while furrowing his brow thoughtfully. Then he leaned closer to the woman and said, "I *might* have somethin, but I can only do it for my most special customers, yah see. And, a-course, it don't come cheap…"

The woman reached into her robe and drew out a scrap of cloth. She opened it to reveal a dark, glittering opal as big as a chicken egg. "This is all I have in the world, my mother left it to me and—"

"That'll do nicely." Doaks made the opal disappear into the depths of his cape, then pulled Korden's knife from elsewhere in the garment and tossed it up in the air. "Give the woman what she needs, boy."

Korden's arm moved of its own accord, following whatever actions Doaks had commanded through the controller. He snatched the knife out of the air, held it over his opposite forearm, then drew it across the flesh, opening an even deeper wound than the one the riftling had inflicted upon his leg. Pain lanced up the limb, but he continued smiling benignly at the woman, able to give no indication of his suffering. As blood welled from the wound and ran off the side of his arm, Doaks grabbed an empty vial and held it beneath to catch the stream. He corked this and handed it to the woman.

"Start takin this as soon as yah catch gravid," he told her. "A spoonful every month 'til birth. Incarnates won't be able to smell the bugger all the way to free age."

Moisture welled in her pretty eyes. "Thank you," she sobbed, and threw her arms around Doaks's neck.

He hugged her back, moving his hands as low as he could reach on her waist. "No problem, miss'um. And if yah need any assistance with the *other* half of that baby equation, well, I'd be more'n happy to make the sacrifice."

The woman nodded and hurried away, clutching the scarlet vial to her bosom.

4

Doaks kept a tight leash on Korden until they were back inside the wagon with the doors down. As the 'doctor' set about storing his bartered bounty in the cupboards and bins built into the bonnet, he paused long enough to push a button on the controller that released the headband's hold.

Korden dropped quivering to the floor. His hand and back throbbed, and his overworked muscles felt like jelly; he wanted to lay here and never move again. Nevertheless, he sucked in a breath and screamed, *"HELP! HELP ME! HE'S HOLDING ME PRISO—!"*

Pain rocketed through him. Korden writhed. His cut arm smeared blood across the floor in a bleary fan.

"Not that I care if yah scream, since they can't hear yah." Doaks opened a trunk set into the wall beside his bed from which tendrils of frosty air emerged, then put the meat and eggs he'd traded for inside. "But it's a bad habit to develop. If I can't trust yah, then get back in the cage. Go on, now."

Korden obeyed, having to drag himself since his legs were too weak. "You…you framming *bastard*," he growled. In that moment, he hated this man as intensely as he ever had the Incarnates, including the one that murdered his father. "I promise, I'm going to make you very sorry for this."

"Heard that before." He closed the pen and tossed a wad of rags through the bars before heading for the wagon's piloting console. "Bandage up that slash before yah get blood on yah costume."

They didn't travel long this time before stopping for the night. Doaks whistled gleefully as he raised the wagon's back door, built a fire a few pargs away, and spitted a slab of meat to roast across the flames. The smell filled Korden's mouth with saliva.

"Yes sah." Doaks pulled the opal out of his pocket, polished it with his shirt sleeve, and held it up to the fading sunlight. His hat and cape were gone now, his shimmery vest unbuttoned and hanging open. "That was a fine job we did today, rubo, a *fine* job! Place like that, I'm usually singin for my supper. But we walked away with enough pelf to keep us fattened for the rest of the season, plus some to trade. If we do that well at every settlement in this valley, Gwenita'll need a trailer to carry it all. Good luck, boy; that's what yah are!"

"Do you understand what you did?" Korden's voice came out a ragged whisper; he was so thirsty after the spirited performance, it hurt to talk. But he sat up in the cage and forced himself to finish. "That woman is going to have a baby now because you told her it was fine. And the Incarnates will sense it the day it's born. She won't even be expecting them."

"Incarnates come for babies every day. I didn't make the world this way, so don't try to get me all weepy about it."

"That story is idiotic anyway. What kind of sense does it make for the Incarnates not to be able to find me just because I'm from the past? They hunted children for hundreds of years in the past."

Doaks climbed into the wagon, stored the huge opal in a trunk beside the foot of his cot, then took two bowls out of a higher cabinet, which he carried to the narrow basin in the middle of the wall. Korden was both surprised and not surprised to see clear water pour out of the spigot when he twisted the handle. "Those people sure didn't mind, now did they? Like I told yah, we ain't sellin curatives, we're sellin *hope*." He put the bowls of water on the floor and slid one into each of the cages, then went back to the fire. The riftling hunched over the container, slurping greedily, but, even though his parched throat cried out for the moisture, Korden shoved his away.

"Go on, get replenished," Doaks told him, rotating the meat over the fire. "There's liquid gold in them veins." He snickered. "If I have anything to say 'bout it, every wombie in the land will be drinkin yah blood before the end of Burnin Season."

Korden gaped at him. "You...you can't keep making me do that."

"I can 'til we figger some way to fake it. Which reminds me..." He pulled the knife out once more and walked back toward the wagon. Terror seized Korden. He pushed himself into the far end of the cage...but soon saw that Doaks was heading toward the *other* pen. "All right creep, time to pull yah weight. Gimme one of those squiggly feet."

The riftling still had its head buried in the bowl of water. It looked up at Doaks and snapped a claw, then spoke for the first time since before the performance. "Zeega will not be milked, human. When the masters catch up with your vehicle, you will be held accountable for—"

Doaks set the knife down while it was talking, grabbed a metal rod hanging on the wall, and jammed it into the cage. A burning white arc jumped off the end, enveloping the creature. It squealed and threw itself backward. This stick must've been what electrocuted Korden the first time. That nullifying hum in his head stuttered out, but he was caught so off guard that he didn't take advantage of the brief pause before it restarted.

"I'm tired of arguin with both of yahs!" Doaks roared. "Yah *my* property, so gimme one of yah tentacles!"

"Leave it alone!" Korden shouted, the outburst surprising even himself.

"That's rich comin from *yah*, boy! Didn't yah wanna kill this thing last night?" He held out a hand to the riftling while sliding the shock stick into the cage as a threat.

The creature came forward hesitantly. It pushed one of its purplish limbs through the bars and flopped it across the man's palm. Korden tensed, anticipating the incision. Not because there might be another break in the mental buzz, but because he remembered what his own bloodletting felt like.

Instead of making a cut, Doaks took the knife and sliced off the entire appendage.

A jet of inky fluid sprayed across the floor of the wagon, mixing with the remnants of Korden's blood. The hum didn't stop, but the riftling squealed and pulled away, squirming back to the opposite end of its cage, where it thrashed and flailed and whimpered.

"Oh, pipe down." Doaks snagged an empty jar from one of the shelves, dropped the amputated tentacle inside, and replaced the container among his other wares. "Yah got plenty more where this came from. Yah'll never miss it." He jumped down off the rear deck and went to tend their dinner.

Korden looked across the wagon, to where the riftling curled itself into a lumpy, pathetic ball. "Are you…all right?" he whispered.

The creature's yellow eyes peeked out through the tangle of tentacles, searching his face and probably his mind, as well. "You do not care, human," it said sulkily, the words muffled.

But Korden thought he detected the slightest hesitation in its response.

5

The next four days were a nightmare from which he could not wake.

Doc Apocalypse's Fine Curatives and Medicinals travelled around the south end of Lake Tay-ho and up the eastern shore, meandering through the Sierras in search of every settlement, village, and encampment, performing their show two and sometimes three times per day. Doaks's wares flew off the shelves, but his newest product was by far his most lucrative seller, harvested live on stage and auctioned off to those select few at each stop who could pay the most. And it wasn't only women interested; plenty of men wanted to produce safe offspring as well. The storage bins of the wagon overflowed with goods, and Korden's arms became crisscrossed with fresh cuts.

He was in a constant state of exhaustion from the involuntary performances, which became longer and more complex as Doaks tweaked them. Korden's feeble lungs were perpetually on the verge of collapse. After the second day, either the blood loss or the fatigue began to make him woozy. He even blacked out once, then swam back to consciousness to discover he was still dancing and singing under the headband's spell. The riftling continued to be used as window dressing in the act, its severed tentacle chopped up and marketed as having a variety of outlandish properties. Doaks warned the creature that if it dared to contradict him to the customers, it would lose a lot more than a limb.

Over these four days, Korden drew inward, not speaking other than the times he was forced to on stage, mechanically eating whatever was served to him, going to the bathroom or bathing in the freezing lake when permitted (both activities presided over by Doaks, while poised to administer shocks at the first sign of disobedience), and trying over and over to reestablish his connection to the Upper. The conduit was there, but always out of reach, the eye in his head shut tight. Being cut off from the soothing presence caused a hollow ache at the center of him as bad as any physical wound. He continued to faith though, and hoped that his prayers would be answered.

At night, when Doaks snored from his cot, and the rifling slipped into whatever state passed for its sleep (although the brain-dampening whine never ceased during these times), Korden sobbed in his tiny cage and told himself that if the Incarnates caught up to them, at least this torture would be over.

It was during one of these dark hours—following a long show for a males-only community living in wooden shacks on a sandy stretch of beach—that he decided the best way out might be to just...cooperate. To gain Doaks's trust, no matter how long it took. If he could convince the man to take off this terrible crown, he might stand a chance of escaping.

That was why, at the end of the fourth day, when the wagon came to a halt just past sundown, Korden offered to help with their supper.

Doaks eyed him suspiciously. He'd changed out of his green stage suit, into a newly bartered outfit that included buckskin dungarees and a somber navy tunic with a neckline halfway down to his portly waist. "I might have somethin else yah can do. But if yah try anything, I swear, I'll shock yah till yah can't even walk without that damn headband."

He opened the cage and led the way onto the wagon's rear deck. Outside, Korden found they were no longer on the worn trail through the woods that they'd been following for days, but parked beside a wide crete road that seemed to be at a much higher elevation in the mountains, with the lake nowhere in sight. The wagon sat in the lot of a pre-Purge structure that he recognized: a vehicle fueling station. Over their heads, a huge representation of what appeared to be a seashell glowed weakly with internal yellow light. The main building had burned at some point in the distant past, but the ring of star-shaped kiosks around the station were untouched, aside from a little rust and a lot of grime. Several of them flickered with the same faint illumination as the sign.

"Didn't think we'd make it," Doaks mumbled. "All that extra weight is messin with the charge consumption." He walked over to the closest kiosk and picked up a thick cable connected to it that lay bunched on the ground. At the other end was a cracked polymer handle with a trigger, and a tightly wound coil sticking off the end, a few cupits in diameter. He squeezed the trigger once and twice to no effect, but on the third time, several ghostly blue sparks traced lazily around the inside of the coils for a few seconds before blinking out. The color was beautiful. Doaks brought the handle to the rear of the wagon, opened a concealed port on the sideboard, and shoved the coils inside.

"Yah'll have to keep teasin it out 'til this gauge fills up." He demonstrated this by jerking the trigger on the handle several times to make the meter grow. "These old ion pumpers are all goin to curse. Gettin harder and harder to find ones that work, much less have power runnin to 'em. But this whole damn valley is juiced up for some reason."

He surrendered the pump to Korden, who asked, "Have you...been here before?"

"Here? As in this station? Rubo, I've never even been to *Tay-ho* 'til the day before I met yah."

"Then how did you know about this place? That these…these pumps…would work?"

Doaks stroked the side of the wagon affectionately. "*She* knew. There's a 'lectronic map up front that lays out where the closest live ion sources are. I plan my routes by 'em. Without that, Gwenita would've been scrap years ago."

Korden suspected the answer to his earlier question but asked it anyway. "Did you build it? The wag—er, I mean, Gwenita?"

The man barked laughter. "No sah. I don't know nuthin 'bout buildin doodads, but I've always had a knack for figgerin out how to work 'em. I found her way down south durin my scavengin days, in one of the big, abandoned cities. Still in perfect workin order. I think she used to be some kinda mobile advertisement for dog food. Can yah believe that? Wonders like this got so common in the old world, they used 'em to drive up and down the street, convincin people to buy a lotta curse they didn't need." He winked. "Guess you could say I'm carryin on the tradition."

"What about…everything else? Where did you get the rest of your technology?"

"Yah know, yah askin a lot of questions for someone who should be pumpin. Get to work, or I'll make yah." With this last threat, he went to build the night's fire.

6

It took Korden an hour to get the vehicle fully fueled, while Doaks prepared a thick stew made from a passel of vegetables they'd traded for that day. He also broke out a bottle of barley wine he'd exchanged for a vial of blood. He offered some to Korden, but made sure his precious Boy from the Past was locked back in his pen before imbibing himself. Half an hour later, the man lay passed out in front of the crackling flames.

Korden finished his dinner, licking the bowl clean. In the opposite pen, the riftling's portion sat untouched, the occupant nothing more than a nebulous lump pressed far back in the shadows.

"Hey," he called softly. He hadn't attempted to speak to the creature since its limb amputation. Come to think of it, he couldn't remember if it'd spoken at all since then, but he knew it barely touched any of its meals. "Aren't you going to eat? He'll take it away when he wakes up."

One bleary yellow oval opened in the darkness, followed by four more. All of them pointed in different directions before focusing their strange pupils on Korden. Then the creature muttered in its gurgling speech, "This food is indigestible to Zeega."

"Oh. Can you only eat meat?"

"Meat is more tolerable, yes."

"*Tolerable?* Well, if you don't eat meat and you don't eat vegetables, then what do you want?"

Another long pause. "Zeega does not know," it said, the words like some grudging admission.

Korden frowned and scooted closer to the bars of his cage. The creature—

"Stop thinking of Zeega as 'the creature!'" it snarled, surging out of its corner and into the moonlight coming through Gwenita's open rear door. "Zeega has only said Zeega's name a thousand times to you, stupid human!"

"All right, Zeega, fine!" Korden held up his hands in surrender. Even after all his time with Stone, he would never get used to having his mind read. "Pardon me if I don't learn the name of every weird little monster that wants to 'suck the marrow from my bones!'"

"And there are a lot of those, let Zeega assure you," the riftling—*Zeega*—huffed. But the answer appeased it. Those tentacles spread beneath its dark body, allowing it to plop back down on the floor. Its gelatinous skin glinted in the moonlight like a wet stone on a riverbank.

Korden almost turned away but stopped. Though he and this Zeega might be bitter enemies outside these cages, right now they were both reduced to playthings in Doaks's menagerie. And Korden missed conversation; he'd become so accustomed to Stone's constant chatter that the computer's absence left him lonely. Might as well make the best of the situation before despair overcame his newfound hope.

"What do you mean, you don't know?" he asked, sitting crosslegged to face the other cage. "How can you not know what you want to eat?"

Two of Zeega's eyes narrowed while the rest rolled away. "The oldest of Zeega's kind pass down stories of the homeland, where the succulent *iri kwabis* flare into existence every morning. They say this is the only food suited to our digestion. Zeega has never eaten them, so Zeega does not know."

"Well...where is your homeland?"

"Far away."

"Far away as in the Rim Territories? Or somewhere beyond the Shroud?"

"Zeega does not know where it is located. None living have ever been there. Most wish to see it one day." Its harsh voice managed to sound wistful.

"If you like it so much, why'd your people leave in the first place?"

"We did not 'leave.' The *hoshnitath* species—what you

know as riftlings—were enlisted long ago to serve the masters."

"You mean Incarnates."

"Them and theirs," Zeega confirmed, the answer cryptic but delivered without the slightest hesitation.

This conversation was beginning to remind Korden of the one he'd had back in the village, with the bound Incarnate that took over Allin's body. "Why did they do that? *Enlist* you, I mean."

"Our natural gifts were required for the great crusade."

"Natural gifts. I guess that would be your tracking abilities."

Zeega's black, squishy face twitched in that grinning way. "When a population becomes too sparse for our masters to root out the Light on their own, they use us. Our ability to read minds allows us to perceive the sentiments human leak into the air with greater precision."

"*Mohols*," Korden whispered. "You can sense *mohols*."

"If that is what you call the emotional stink that perpetually surrounds you."

Korden scooted even closer to the bars. "So, the Filament rounded you all up, dragged you from your homeland, kept you away from your natural food, all to…what? Use you as hunting dogs?"

The riftling bristled at this, claws clicking in what Korden took to be irritation. "The masters elevated Zeega's people," it said, the tone cold. "When their work is finished, the *hoshnitaths* will sit at their side in the long, sweet silence to follow."

"Sounds to me like they enslaved you."

"We are *not* slaves."

Korden grunted. "I lived in the same village my whole life, so I don't know a lot about the world. But I do know some history, and I don't think too many groups ever called their equals 'master.'"

Zeega leapt back to its feet and stretched its claws through the cage bars in a futile attempt to reach Korden on the other side of the wagon. "*What would you know about it, human?*" the riftling screeched. "*The masters may leash us, but humans are the ones who fight us, you are the one who killed Zeega's broodmates!*"

"Because they tried to kill *me*!" Korden argued.

"*If we did not do as ordered, the masters would have punished us! Zeega will still be punished if Zeega does not ensure your death!*"

"Then maybe you should blame your precious masters!" Korden smashed his open palm against the inside of his cage. "Tell me, do they keep you inside something like this? Do they make you dance, like Doaks does to me? I think I can say, as one with firsthand experience on the subject, *you are a slave!*"

"*Zeega will make you pay! Zeega will...will tear out your throat and...and eat your fingers and...*" The riftling broke off and began to make a hoarse, strangled sound slightly different from its laughter. Only when it retreated into the corner and curled up into a ball did Korden wonder if it was sobbing.

"Whazall that yellin?" Doaks grunted, sitting up in front of the fire. He climbed to his feet and walked back into the wagon, then closed the door behind him and slogged to the cot at the far end. Before he flopped over, the man looked at Korden in the dim light and slurred, "Better ge' some sleep, rubo. By this time amorrow, we'll've left this lake in our dust fer good. Bu' first, we got the last stop on tha Tay-ho leg of our world tour.

"In the mornin...we go to Ida."

The Town with Power

TWO LITTLE WORDS

1

Unlike the other settlements clustered around Lake Tayho, Ida was created from the scraps of a magnificent resort, where people from the old world came to vacation, gamble, and launch yachts from a small adjoined marina, activities which sounded like fantasy to the citizens who now called it home. The place was deserted for a century or more when the first settlers—or rather, *resettlers*—stumbled upon it. Despite that it was all but buried from a landslide, the scene was as idyllic as it must've been before the Purges. The air was clean, the lake valley provided food and water, and the hillside even blocked their view of the Shroud, so they could forget the larger troubles of the world.

And, most amazing of all, power still ran through the resort's ancient veins. Power which, after a few years of experimentation, had been tapped into, harnessed, and used to run homemade lights and ovens and a few other primitive devices that made life a bit easier.

News of this paradise spread quickly. People undertook pilgrimages of thousands of spans for the rumor of someplace stable and safe, but only those of free age were welcomed into the fledgling community. As the decades passed and the population ballooned, a newer, bigger village was built into the mountainside on top of the buried ruins, and then yet a bigger town over that. The old marina was restored as a dock for fishing boats. The surrounding hills were clearcut to create grazing and farm land. A bartering economy was established, with specialty tradesmen invited to set up shop. And, eventually, a high stone wall was erected around the border that turned the tiered, sprawling town into more of a fortress, one that kept the inhabitants safe from marauders for seventy years. The design of the exterior would've brought to mind Civil War strongholds, if any of the residents knew such things had ever existed.

As for the interior, well...

None of Ida's residents had ever seen a sitcom either, or they might've appreciated the humor in their way of life.

Because a smaller wall ran down the middle of the town, dividing it neatly in half. Men lived in the west side, women in the east; six hundred of the former and five of the latter according to the last census, ranging in age from twenty-four to eighty-seven. Aside from a public courtyard around the gate, the two sexes were forbidden from fraternizing. Anyone approved for citizenship must abide by this rule.

It was a necessary measure, they'd decided long ago, when so many folks of PBA—prime breeding age—were allowed to live together. They prided themselves on being an open, inviting community to outsiders...except to those that would bring the Incarnate scourge to their doorstep. The people of Ida wished youngsters all the best, they just wanted no responsibility for them. *Go on down the road, but feel free to come back when you make free age*, was the prevailing attitude. *We did it, and so can you!*

This sexual division was, of course, a largely futile precaution. No one in the town was a prisoner; they could come and go as they liked. Nothing prevented them from stealing away into the mountain wilderness to do what came naturally to human beings. The mayor and his Enforcement Brigade were powerless against those determined to copulate, but few took the risk anyway.

They might not know about castles or sitcoms, but they *did* know what the good Aged Lord had done in the garden of Eyaden.

And none of them wanted to be cast out of paradise.

2

Rand Holcomb hurried through the old passages carved deep into the mountainside beneath Ida, dim plaster hallways left over from the ancient structures the town was built atop. Few ventured down into this subterranean maze for fear of cave-ins, but Rand had made it his business to know every square cupit of the fortress grounds since going to work for Mayor Hildan. There were some convenient shortcuts for the brave, and countless nooks and crannies where one could escape the ever-watchful eyes of the community.

None of the lights mounted on the ceiling worked—the power that flowed down here was all leeched away by the town's various needs—so Rand was forced to carry an oil lamp to see. Urgency knotted his guts as he rushed through the darkness. He was late for his daily briefing with Hildan, and he detested being late. His useless brother had stumbled back into town late last night, spun out so bad he could barely speak. Rand had thought for sure (if being frank, perhaps even *hoped*) that his younger sibling was dead this time, but, like rotten apples, you could always count on Meech Holcomb to turn up. After sitting with him half the night while he shivered and vomited, Rand went back to his own room and overslept.

However, his tardiness wasn't the real reason for his anxiety.

No, that would be the red shade pulled across the dormitory window on the extreme opposite side of the courtyard from his own living quarters, which he'd seen immediately upon waking this morning. His mind was awash with possible reasons for its placement, but it would be a while before he could get answers.

He emerged from the catacombs and stepped through a door marked with the incomprehensible old-world letters J-A-N-I-T-O-R-I-A-L, behind which was a dusty storeroom once used for who-knew-what. Here he stopped long enough to ensure his tailored blue tunic and nice groohide dungarees were free of dirt. It wouldn't do for the mayor's deputy director to walk around looking like…well, like his brother. Rand extinguished the lamp, left it on one of the empty shelves, and mounted a set of rickety stairs on the other side of the room.

Sunlight struck him. Here, the buried ruins let out onto a narrow alleyway between shops on the west side of the town square, through a discreetly placed door hardly wide enough for even his fit frame. He squeezed out onto the cobblestone street, sealed the door, and hastened on, his footsteps clacking smartly as he strode down the alley.

Rand loved that sound. This town was his first real home and, when he came to live here at the age of 26, the heavy, soot-colored bricks that made up its floor seemed like a miracle of engineering. Those cobblestones came to represent security in his mind; a triumph over nature, a return to civilization. He knew their shape and size and texture as well as he knew his own hands. Though he could've listened to the sharp echo of his footfalls all day, they were soon lost amid the wall of noise waiting at the end of the alley.

Even this early, the market was full of men, many of them outsiders. Ida was a thriving trade post, and a vital supply stop for those making the treacherous journey across the Valley of Bones, either travelling to or coming from the Sky-reach Mountains and the lands that lay beyond. That traffic had severely lessened over the last few seasons as strange rumors spread, but there was more than enough influx of goods to fill their needs.

Rand blended in with the stream of men wandering among the vendor stalls. Local farmers and horse ranchers pedaled their wares here, alongside smithys selling saddles, weapons and armor. Then there were the 'specialty artisans,' who crafted lightbulbs or bread toasters or alarm clocks that required Ida's energy to make them work. These latter often concerned Rand. No one knew where the mysterious power came from; if there was a reserve or an infinite supply. Probably wasn't smart to let every citizen have free reign over its usage.

But he'd found that such opinions were extremely unpopular. These people loved their little taste of the pre-Purge days, in particular the cheerful town lights that kept night from ever falling on them.

On the opposite side of the market sat the wall separating them from the women's half of town, with guards from the Enforcement Brigade stationed atop it. There was no market over there; the women sent designated runners to haggle for what they needed. And if you wanted to speak to someone of the opposing sex face-to-face, you sent a message for them to meet you in the open courtyard around the fortress gates. It wasn't very private, but that was the intent, and it kept things running smoothly in Ida. Rand kept his eyes carefully away from the wall as he veered toward the squat stone edifice that housed the mayor's chambers.

A member of the Brigade waved him inside. Past the door was a long receiving room decorated with an assortment of lush plants, high-backed chairs, soft divans, and ornate brass wall sconces that gave off bright yellow light. Bowls of freshly cut lilac and lavender scented the air.

Rand had never seen any place as decadent and lavish as these chambers. It was very easy to imagine the old world like this, back when people lived in glass buildings above the clouds. Lye Hildan stood in the middle of the room, speaking with Mikolt, the burly Captain of the Brigade.

"—should be here sometime this morning," Hildan was saying. The mayor of Ida—three times elected now over the past decade—was a serious man of fifty-eight years with a sloping potbelly, owlish eyes, and short brown hair that was going silver above the ears. Today he wore a loose-fitting maroon doublet with a rabbit fur mantle, and dark green leggings above snakeskin moccasins. He was not a small man by any means, but next to Mikolt's imposing figure in his armored uniform and leather breeches and bracers, even his stature suffered. "Let them into the courtyard and ring the assembly bells. From what those traders said, the show should be a real treat for everyone."

"It will be done," Mikolt rumbled. The man's face was a patchwork of layered scar tissue. It was rumored he'd made a living in fighting pits in the wild Rim territories.

"Anything else to report?"

"My men caught the Beckleys sneaking around together

in one of the southern towers. Harkin's already been placed in the stocks here. Matron Webb agreed to do the same with his wife on the wombie's side."

Hildan made a disappointed clucking noise. "*Women*, Mikolt. Never 'wombies' or 'crones.' Just because the Aged Lord put them here to tempt and destroy us is no reason not to respect them."

"Yes sir, I'll remember," Mikolt confirmed.

"As for the Beckleys, they aren't adjusting very well, are they? I know it must be hard for them to be separated after...what was it, twenty-three years of marriage?...but if they can't restrict themselves to the courtyard or take their urges outside town, they'll be asked to leave. I've given them too many chances already." Hildan noticed Rand lurking in the doorway, but instead of grinning, his mouth tightened in a way that made Rand's stomach ache. His mind went to that red shade in the opposite window, and what it could possibly mean. "If that's all Mikolt, you're dismissed."

The captain strode from the room, giving Rand a nod as he passed. The departure gave Rand some hope. If any of his fears were founded, surely Hildan would've kept the enforcer close. He was being paranoid, that was all.

"What was that about a show?" he asked, striving to hide the nervousness that oozed from his pores.

Hildan flapped a hand. "Some singing medicine man making a circuit of the valley. From what I understand, he has a floating wagon."

"*Floating?*"

"Can't quite picture it, can you? He also apparently travels with a young ward that he claims can't be sensed by Incarnates."

Rand made a scoffing sound of disbelief. "Impossible."

"Perhaps. But who knows what a man with a floating wagon is capable of? Everyone else seems to be biting, anyway. As long as he gives his routine, sells his wares, and goes on his way, it should be fine. I'm interested to see if he can recommend a cure for this swole-toe that keeps paining me." Hildan walked toward the door to his inner office, motioning for Rand to follow.

The mayor's personal quarters were much smaller but decorated in line with the receiving room. One wall was covered with books on shelves; tomes of all shapes, sizes and colors. It was well known that the Mayor of Ida traded highly for any and all scavenged texts from before the Purges. Rand asked him once if he'd read them all, to which the man answered gravely, "Few men even have the ability to read these days. Anyone who *chooses* not to is committing a crime against himself." A huge teak desk stretched across the length of his office, and it was behind this that Hildan seated himself.

This was how they met every morning, to go over the many issues that plagued a town of Ida's size. Rand took his usual seat in front of the desk...and the knot in his guts drew even tighter as his superior steepled his hands, leaned forward with brow drawn, and studied Rand with his wide, piercing eyes.

"I-is something wrong?" Rand winced as the guilt-ridden question left his mouth before he could stop it, then rushed on, afraid to hear the answer. "Did the Prophet give a warning...?"

Hildan's intense gaze strayed to the safe built into the stone wall of his office. A lock sealed the iron door on the front, the key to which dangled from the mayor's neck. No one had ever seen the box that Hildan claimed lay behind that door (including Rand himself, although he'd heard a muffled male voice one time as he was leaving the chambers) but it was undoubtedly the reason for his many reelections. "No, all is well on that front. The Prophet sees much Incarnate activity to the west, but nothing to concern us. However," he frowned and hesitated, "there is an unpleasant matter that I feel it is time to discuss with you."

Rand's heart leapt into his throat. He tried to speak, but nothing came out. *It's your first offense*, his mind insisted, trying to calm him. *It'll only be a warning!*

Unless he knows about every *time.*

Then plead with him! Tell him you'll stop, that you'll end it today!

That notion held its own breed of stomach-churning horror.

"I hear that your brother returned from another of his 'expeditions' last night," Hildan went on, breaking into his thoughts. "Quite...besotted, shall we say?"

"I...uh..." The words were so far from what he'd expected, they frazzled Rand even further. "Yes. Yes, he came back."

Hildan nodded. "Rand...I have overlooked a great deal of that man's behavior, out of respect for you. But I think the time has come for us to address his vices head on."

Rand blinked. This wasn't about him at all. It was about *Meech*. The relief that swept through him was so immense it almost made him slide out of his chair. His brain shifted gears to address the topic. "I know, I've spoken with him several times, sir. He says he wants to quit, but the jinkweed has a bad hold on him. When I get him flushed out this time, I'll sit him down and—"

"This town holds a reputation around Tay-ho, as you well know," Hildan interrupted. "We are the lynchpin that holds this collection of communities together. Without us, this lake valley would descend into chaos. So I hope you will understand when I say it is simply not worth risking that reputation for the sake of one unrepentant jinko addict."

Now the panic came roaring back. "What is it you want then?" Rand asked.

"Banishment," Hildan said simply. "One day to get his affairs in order, then he's to be walked through the gate."

"Sir, please, if you'll—"

The mayor held up a hand to silence him. "It's not like you'll never see him, Rand. I'm sure one of the other communities will take him in."

Rand doubted it. Most of them took their cues from Ida. Someone banished from the fortress would be a pariah anywhere in the valley.

"I'm even going to allow you to bring the news to him," Hildan continued, his tone suggesting that this was somehow a personal favor. "I find these things are so much easier to hear from family, don't you?"

3

From there, the meeting proceeded as usual. By the time they concluded the day's briefing, Rand had presented his idea for expanding their dwindling market space, suggested a possible new revenue source, and introduced a plan to trade labor for new citizenship approvals among a dozen other fixes for more routine problems.

Hildan favored him with a broad grin and shook his head in admiration. "Rand, I don't know where Ida would be without your innovation. You were truly born for this kind of work."

Rand thanked the man absently and left the mayor's chambers as sick as when he'd gone in, for completely different reasons.

His brother—his only family—had been banished from the first real home they'd ever known.

It's his own fault. Not like you didn't warn him over and over that this would happen. He'll have to lay in the bed he made.

His brain told him this was true, but his heart sang a very different tune. Since the day their parents left them by the side of the road at the ages of 11 and 7 (Rand would never forget the weary frown on his father's face when he told them to keep running, or the way his mother hadn't once looked back as they rode away), it'd just been the two of them. Most of the time, when he tried to conjure Meech's scruffy, sallow face in his head, all he could see was the young kid that he'd dragged along behind him for eleven years, constantly on the run from the Incarnates (and during those last two, when Rand had been safe above the age of eighteen, he came closer to sympathizing with his parents' abandonment than he cared to admit). Then, even after they'd both reached free age, he'd spent another four years keeping the little fram out of trouble while they wandered the land before finally being granted citizenship in Ida. That was one of the happiest days of Rand's life, but for Meech, settling down made him antsy, and jinko was a convenient escape. In that respect, maybe being forced back out on the road would be the best thing for him, a chance to clear his head and let his arms heal.

Or maybe he'll go out in the woods and prick himself with that curse until he dies from it.

Rand sighed. His brother was an adult now, and had been for many years. Rand couldn't clean up his messes forever. He had his own troubles to worry about. Like that red shade in the window. According to the big powered clock in the middle of town, he had a half hour before he could find out what that was about, so he might as well get this other bit of unpleasantness over with.

Meech lived on the second level of the men's dormitory in the western tower. Rand trudged that direction, greeting those he knew along the way. He knocked and then opened the wooden door after receiving an acknowledging grunt from within.

The smell struck him first. A sour tang of vomit so pungent he could taste it on the back of his tongue. Rand fought to keep from gagging as he stepped inside.

His brother lay in bed where Rand had left him. He'd put a pillow over his head even though the tiny room's sole window was covered with a blanket. The darkness muted the colors of his ridiculous rainbow tunic, rendering it in strokes of black and gray. The source of the smell—a bucket full to the brim with sick—sat on the floor beside him; Rand could only be thankful that he'd managed to keep it in this receptacle throughout the night. To stop the nauseating reek, Rand hefted the pail carefully and set it outside in the hall before resuming his study of the room's occupant.

The man was a pathetic sight balled up in bed, but, hells, you couldn't blame that on the jinko. Even when he wasn't spun, this was where Meech Holcomb could be found most mornings. On the rare occasion when he rose to seek work, it was to perform whatever odd jobs would take him the least amount of time. The man was useless, contributing nothing to the community. In truth, Hildan should've come to this verdict long before now.

And would've, if not for me.

A sudden flush of angry guilt sent Rand stomping to the

window. He yanked down the blanket, allowing sunlight to pour through. "Wake on, Meech."

The other man groaned and pulled the pillow tighter around his head. "G'way," his muffled voice croaked. "Sick."

"Then maybe you shouldn't've gone on such a long cruise. I mean, Aged Lord, a *week*? Is there any blood left in your veins, or is it all green juice? Now get up, I need to talk to you."

"Yes sir, Mr. Deputy Mayor, sir."

Meech tossed the pillow aside, turned over, and sat up, squinting in the light. Rand suppressed a gasp. When he'd spotted his brother shambling across the courtyard last night, it was already too dark to see the bleached paleness of his skin, the cave-like hollows beneath his eyes, or that he must weigh less than a hundred pounds. His flesh was tight around his head, every angle of his skull visible, which made his current scowl into a gruesome affair. And weeping, infected sores covered both arms from repeated punctures.

"Damn it, Rand. I was hopin I could have a day to recover without you jumpin down my throat. How'd you even know I was back?"

"How did I...? You moron, *I* was the one who got you up here and took care of you while you were sweating and puking that garbage weed out! But I guess you were too far gone to remember that, huh?"

The scowl faded. Meech lifted a scarecrow's shoulder. "All right, sorry drude."

"*Curse*, I wish you'd stop talking like that." Rand squeezed his forehead with one hand and sat down on the edge of the bed. He'd wanted to hold on to his anger—it would make this a lot simpler—but his kid brother had a way of defusing him.

"I have to tell you something Meech, and I'm just going to say it. Hildan is banishing you from Ida."

The other man frowned in confusion. "*Huh?*"

"You heard me."

"Wait on, *banishing*? As in..."

"As in you have one day to pack and say your goodbyes and then the Enforcement Brigade is going to escort you out of town in the morning."

His brother scrambled across the bed to him on all fours, the sudden motion causing him to dry heave several times before he could speak. "Hold on, just...hold on man, that's not fair, I've never even gotten a warning!"

"I'm sorry," Rand whispered to his lap. "Hildan says letting you stay is a risk to the town. To the whole valley."

"Oh yeah, man, let's not exaggerate or nuthin! Like me gettin pricked every now and then is gonna bring the walls tumblin down!"

Rand glanced at the pitted surface of his brother's arm. "He thinks you have a problem."

"I can quit any time I want!"

"How many times have I heard that?"

Meech drew even closer and clutched at Rand's shoulder with a shaky hand. "Can't you talk to him, try to convince him to give me another chance?"

"Don't you think I tried?"

"I don't know, *did* you? When he says jump, you usually head for the closest cliff."

Rand raised his head to glare at his brother. "That's not framming fair. This is my job, and you've only been allowed to stay this long because of it. And don't say you never got a warning, you got plenty of warnings. I've told you so many times this would happen."

"Oh yeah, you sure did drude, you always know what's best for little Meechie." He let go of Rand, and flopped backward on the bed with his gaunt arms crossed.

Rand knelt on the bed beside him. "Do you think I want this? You're my brother. But look at yourself! That stuff is killing you! When was the last time you even ate?"

Meech lifted his head and peered down the length of his wasted body, so thin inside his colorful tunic that the garment hung off him in folds. His face went rapidly from disbelief to shock to disgust. "I dunno," he admitted. "What's today?"

"You've said so many times that you want to stop. Is that true, or was it bullcurse to get me off your back?"

"It's true." Meech glanced down at the oozing sores along his arm and licked his lips nervously. "But what's it matter now? I'm a goner."

"It matters because we can turn this around," Rand told him. "If you leave for a season or two, get yourself cleaned up, maybe I can talk him into letting you come *back*."

"You think?"

"Absolutely! And who knows, this could end up being the boot in the ass you need!"

A tiny, hopeful smile crept across his brother's face. "Yeah, man. Definitely. I can do this. I *know* I can. Even gettin thrown out of here ain't all horrible. I'll talk to Jaimer and Adliss, see if I can hunker with them for a bit."

"Well, I don't think *that's* the best idea. You should probably avoid those two if you're serious about this."

"Sure, you're right, you're right. Maybe…maybe I'll travel around for a while! See how the world's changed since we left!"

"That's the spirit!" Rand forced a smile onto his face. Something told him if his brother left Tay-ho, he would never see him again. But baby birds needed to fly from the nest at some point, and Meech's launch was far overdue. "I have some things I need to do. I'll let you start planning, then we can have lunch together. There's supposed to be a show in the courtyard at some point."

He stood up and walked toward the door, but Meech called out, "Oh, what about the li'l drude?"

"What are you talking about?"

"You know, the li'l drude! Korden! I gave him my boat and sent him this way to talk to you! Didn't he come?"

Rand hoisted an eyebrow. "I don't know what you're talking about. Some fishermen found your boat outside the harbor three days ago. I thought you were dead for sure. Oh, there was a carry pouch in it though. I put it under your bed, in case you turned up."

His brother groped beneath the bed to pull out the bag. "Poor kid," he murmured, stroking the worn leather. "I hope the lake didn't get 'im."

"A kid. On Tay-ho. Did this actually happen, or…?"

"Course it happened!" Meech frowned and scratched at the filthy patch of scalp above his ear. "I'm pretty sure it did, anyway."

Rand left his brother to his drug-fueled hallucinations and hurried out of the dormitory.

4

It was fifteen minutes until his final appointment of the morning, but Rand's anxiety had ratcheted too high for him to put this off any longer. Sparing a surreptitious look around for observers, he stepped into a tight alcove behind the dorm tower, lifted a heavy wooden trapdoor set into the stone floor of the fortress, and climbed down a rusted metal ladder into darkness.

At the bottom was a cramped, lightless tunnel that smelled vaguely of feces, what the old world called a 'sewer'. Rather than dig up the pipes and fill them in, the original designers of the town had left them intact, planning to convert them into some sort of evacuation contingency. Rand knew his way around in the dark, and moved quickly through a series of turns and up another ladder, emerging into one of the passages buried within the mountain. A lamp from one of his previous expeditions waited here. He lit the wick with a pocket flint and set off into the labyrinth, stopping in a corridor lined with doorways opening onto empty rooms where guests of the resort stayed. Rand set the lantern on the floor and paced.

A hand floated out of one of the dark rooms and caressed the back of his neck.

Rand squealed and flailed, spinning around as Lillam Onderson emerged into the lantern light with a teasing grin on her pink lips. "Sorry. Couldn't resist. You're adorable when you're scared."

Every muscle in his body went slack with relief. He hadn't realized how much he needed to see her until this moment.

And how terrified he'd been that he might never again.

Rand rushed forward and pulled her into his arms, cradling her small waist and planting a series of rapid kisses all over her face. She giggled against him, then reached up to caress his stubbled cheek. "Silly boo-pup."

"Are you all right?" He buried his nose in her blond locks and breathed deep. "When I saw the red shade, I thought you were seen coming back last night."

"No, nothing like that, my darling." Her soft words in his ear made him shiver.

Rand thought about before, in the meeting with Hildan, when he'd believed the mayor was on the verge of telling him that his relationship with Lillam had been discovered. How he'd been prepared to promise that he would end their trysts immediately. Now though, he knew that would've been a lie.

Nothing in heaven or earth could ever keep him apart from this woman.

"Then why did you use the red signal? I told you it was for emergencies! We can't meet this often or we're sure to be caught." Despite these words, his fingers scrabbled at the buttons along the back of her daffodil yellow gown as if they had a mind of their own. And that mind was currently swelling within the crotch of his dungarees. "Never mind, it doesn't matter, I'm glad you did. I need you so much. It's been a horrible day, my brother is being banished and I—"

Lillam stiffened. He stopped trying to unclothe her and pulled back to meet her gaze. A storm brewed in her lovely sea-green eyes.

"What is it? What's wrong?"

She hesitated, shook her head, and grinned. "Nothing. It can be told another day."

"The hells it can. Not if it's upsetting you. Say on."

Lillam gnawed at her lips. She took both of his hands in hers, stroked the backs with her thumbs. "Rand…I love you. So much."

"I love you too! More than you can imagine! Nothing could ever change things between us!"

As he said this, he believed, with all his heart, that it was true.

And then she uttered the two little words that have been redefining relationships since the dawn of time.

"I'm pregnant."

5

Lillam Onderson tried to maintain a happy, patient smile as she waited for Rand to respond. Context was everything; if she didn't show any sign of the anxiety burning her up inside, maybe he would stay positive too.

Judging by the confused look on his handsome, clean shaven face, she might've given him the news in another language.

"Well...?" she prompted, when she could take his silence no longer. "Say *something*, Rand!"

"Are you...sure?" he asked, gulping the last word.

"I've suspected for a few days, and I have all the signs. According to the seeds—my mother, she used to swear by them, you know—it's a...girl."

With the Aged Lord dogma that had been drilled into her—first by her mother, then by society—she would've expected to feel regret, or at the very least guilt, over such an admission. According to the teachings of His Holy Seniority, those who brought new life into this broken world were the very worst of sinners, doomed to all three hells. She and Rand had been as careful as possible, but their love was a blinding bliss, an unexpected whirlwind that pushed such worries to the back of her mind. And when the truth was revealed in a jar of her own urine, where wheat stalks sprouted, all Lillam experienced was jubilant, overwhelming joy.

And how could something that made her this happy be wrong?

Another long moment of silence passed during which his hazel eyes jittered back and forth in their sockets, focusing on nothing. "Don't worry," he told her resolutely. "It's fine, this is fine. I know where we can get a potion. It will—"

Lillam was already shaking her head to stop him from saying the words. She knew all about such potions. One of the other women in the female dormitory had agreed to take one rather than face banishment. Matron Webb administered it herself, and the woman in question spent two days in her room wracked with screaming cramps before expelling something that resembled a bloody tadpole.

"It won't hurt, I promise," he assured her. Such an easy guarantee for him to make. Men were so free when injecting life, but never had to deal with any of the inconveniences that came after.

She took a breath and prepared herself to say what she'd come to tell him. "No, Rand. I've decided…I want to have it."

"No, no, no, sweetlove, listen to me!" The negations burst out of him like explosions. He pulled his hands from hers and grabbed her by the shoulders. "You know what this means, they'll cast you out!"

"I know. I'm going to leave." Saying the words out loud made them even more real somehow. But they also confirmed to her own heart that this was what she wanted. "I'll stay here as long as they'll let me, then I'll go out on the road."

"*Aged Lord, Lillam, no!*" Rand sounded horrified. She hated that she was the cause of such pain for him. "Don't you remember what it's like out there? Eighteen years of fear and running! No child should ever have to suffer that!"

"Mine will," she insisted gently. "With me by its side. I'm not asking you to come, Rand. I know what you went through, and how much you love this place. It will…" She swallowed a hot lump in her throat as the first tears touched her eyes; hellsfire, she'd been so determined not to cry. "It will kill me to leave you, but if that's what I must do, then so be it. It's my duty as a…a parent."

"*Parent?* Oh god…" He recoiled from her, collapsing back against the rough wall, where he proceeded to cover his face with both hands and moan piteously.

"Rand?" As much as she wanted to, she couldn't stop the droplets from rolling down her cheeks. "Please stop, you're scaring me!"

He lowered his hands, looked into her eyes, and opened his mouth, but whatever he meant to say was drowned out by the toll of the assembly bells, muted to a dull *clong!* by the earth above their heads.

SWAN SONG

1

Doaks made the bonnet of the wagon invisible as they approached the fortress city at the northern end of Tay-ho. Korden sat up in his cage and stared out at it in awe. On the other side of a vast field of grazing hump-backed beasts, a gray stone wall twenty pargs high stretched across the horizon, encompassing a tiered settlement that backed up into a steep mountainside, with several high towers spread across the land. The tallest of these, right in the center of the town, had a working clock face mounted on the front, the hands big enough to tell the time from spans away. A wide, arched entrance stood at the center of the rock boundary, with a steady stream of foot and horse traffic passing both directions. Spread around this gateway was another, smaller settlement made up of tents and horse-drawn carts, where people milled around campfires and sellers and performers. And, off to their left, two or three spans from the entrance, wooden piers lay across the arctic blue waters of Tay-ho, where several boats docked, all much larger than the kayak. The people on them were unloading crates of fish but stopped to stare as Doc Apocalypse's hovering Conestoga passed by.

Ida. The Town with Power.

It was magnificent. A bustling settlement the likes of which Korden had dreamed of seeing.

Doaks spun around in his seat at the control panel. "Looks like our swan song is gonna have quite an audience, rubos! If the show goes half as nice here, we'll be drownin in swag tonight! Do me proud and I might even let yah both off the leash as a reward!"

When he turned around, Zeega cast one eye across the wagon at Korden and muttered sullenly, "The human lies."

It took another few minutes for them to cross the field, then Doaks slowed Gwenita even more as they entered the sprawling shantytown around the gates of Ida. The crowds parted to make way for the wagon, people murmuring with excitement, a few even reaching out to touch the sideboards as they hovered by. Doaks stood at the front of the wagon, smiling and waving his hat, encouraging folks to come see the show and have all their woes cured. Korden craned his neck to take it all in: people of so many different colors and dress styles; jugglers and musicians and vendors selling charred rodents on skewers, the tantalizing smell of which made Korden's perpetually hungry stomach convulse. There was also a black-frocked man on a pedestal who never stopped shouting about how the Aged Lord would watch over those who did not 'diversify the tree of life'.

They reached the arch, where a slab of spiked steel was suspended high above. Beyond the archway, Korden could see a courtyard with similar gates to the left and right and stands of seats around the perimeter. But the path through the main entry was blocked by three large men in leather armor with swords at their side. They held up their hands and shouted for the wagon to halt.

"Welcome to Ida," one of the men said, coming alongside the driver's seat to speak to Doaks. If he was astounded by the wagon, he didn't show it. "Please state your name and purpose."

"Doc Apocalypse here, at yah service! I come to spread good cheer and some healin magic. If I can have but an hour or two in yah square, I promise it'll be worth the town's time."

The guard nodded, leaned back, and appeared to look right at Korden. His hopes soared, until he noticed the man was just reading the outside of the bonnet. "We keep to law here," he said stiffly. "No jinkweed, no gambling, no fighting. All non-citizens are expected to be outside the walls before gatedown. Absolutely no one under free age allowed. And, please be aware, Ida is a gender-segregated community. Any females travelling with you will have to remain in the courtyard or go to the right to enter the women's side."

"No wombies here, my good sah," Doaks assured him with a tip of his hat, rings flashing in the sun. "Only myself and my equally male assistant."

"That's fine. We'll just need to inspect your cart to be sure." He started around to the back, but Doaks stopped him with a shout.

"Well, hold on there a second! A lot of what's in this wagon is proprietary, yah ken? I can't have just anybody pokin around back there, they could steal my formulas."

"Then you don't get in." The guard stood, arms crossed, as frustration and anger warred across Doaks's face.

"Stand down!" a deep voice barked, breaking the standoff. Another man dressed like the guards jogged across the courtyard to the wagon. He relieved the first man and came to stand in his place. This one was so tall, he could stand eye-to-eye with Doaks where he perched on the driver's seat. His face was a tangled web of scars. "I am Mikolt, captain of the Enforcement Brigade in Ida. We were told of your coming. I've been instructed to let you inside to peddle your wares."

"Ah, so word of my good deeds precedes me!"

The guard grunted. He stepped closer to the wagon, motioning for Doaks to bend down. Korden strained to hear what was said.

"I have but one question," Mikolt growled, "and if you are not honest, I will pull your intestines out through your throat. Understand?"

Doaks's eyes widened, but he nodded.

"The pre-ager you have in the back. Is it true that Incarnates cannot sense him?"

"My friend, do you think I'd be riding with him if they could?"

Mikolt grabbed the man's dangling neckcloth and yanked him closer. "That is not an answer. *Friend.*"

Doaks stared into the guard's scarred face and said, "May the good Aged Lord strike me down if it's false."

"You won't have to worry about Him if it's not." Mikolt released him, satisfied. "Let him through!" he bellowed, waving the guards out of the way. To Doaks, he said, "Park in the courtyard. We'll ring the assembly bells to let everyone know you're here."

"Much obliged." Doaks pressed buttons on the control panel, and the wagon floated smoothly through the gate and into the courtyard beyond.

2

Rand exited the tunnels through a door behind the men's latrines and was met by a swift current of people heading for the courtyard. The anticipation in the late morning air was palpable. The spacing of the assembly bells signaled a show, and the citizens of Ida always hungered for entertainment. He joined the flow of bodies, hoping Meech would drag himself out of bed to come. Moments like this would be few and far between for his brother soon.

And perhaps not just for him.

As Rand walked, his mind went back to Lillam like a tongue to a sore tooth. He'd used the bells as an excuse to take his leave from her, feigning a meeting with Hildan at the assembly, but, in reality, he had no idea what to say. Throughout their conversation, he'd increasingly felt claustrophobic, the walls closing in so much that each breath was like warm syrup. At the same time, a pressure built in his head, a throbbing ache in the center of his skull that got worse and worse. Then it popped like a wine cork, releasing a bizarre—and not exactly unpleasant—tingling sensation throughout his body. The sudden crack was so sharp and unexpected, he feared his shock at her news might have induced some sort of brain seizure.

Parent. Even now, he kept hearing her say that word. They were going to be *parents.* Even if she took the child away and he never so much as cast eyes on it, the fact wouldn't change that he was a *parent.* Those six letters seemed so tiny and insignificant, yet he couldn't wrap his mind around the enormity of them. What did that strange title even mean? It wasn't something earned or bestowed, like 'blacksmith' or 'mayor,' but it changed one's identity far more than either. For those that worshiped the Aged Lord—like most of Ida— it was a dirty word, a transformation to be feared.

And yet...Lillam wanted it. She'd seemed *eager.* And the destroyed expression on her face as he fled their private hideaway—the place where they'd shared so many happy meetings, whispered such sweet, fleeting promises—would haunt him the rest of his days. That look told him one thing, with utmost surety: no matter what she might say, Lillam harbored the secret hope that he would throw all reservation to the wind and agree to come with her on this eighteen-year-long fool's errand.

Which was madness. Absolute insanity. His own parents had taken up the same journey she was proposing and quit halfway through. He must convince her of the futility, make her see that leaving this sanctuary was tantamount to suicide.

Because the idea of standing aside and letting her walk into the world as a hunted woman felt every bit as crazy.

The gate leading into the communal courtyard from the men's side was ahead. Beside it, Harkin Beckley hung from the stocks as punishment for his indiscretions with his own wife. The other men ignored him as they filed past (from what Rand heard, the women were far harsher on fraternizing transgressors), but Rand gave the man a sympathetic smile. An hour ago, this would've been his worst nightmare. Now he would gladly trade places with Beckley if this problem would go away.

Once through the gate, he could see some sort of wheelless wagon resting on stilts in the middle of the arena. He was disappointed; he'd wanted to see the thing float. A crowd of both men and women surrounded the vehicle, thrilled to see each other as much as the performer. Rand sympathized with that all too well. His attraction to Lillam had blossomed at these rare events where the sexes could freely mingle. The Enforcement Brigade prowled among the masses, watching for any inappropriate contact.

The stands around the perimeter of the courtyard were filling with older residents and visitors. Rand saw Hildan among them with an entourage of guards and councilmen, where they would all have an excellent view of the proceedings. The mayor cleared a seat on the bench next to him as Rand approached.

"I saw your brother a few minutes ago," Hildan said. "I trust everything went smoothly?"

"Yes sir, I spoke with him." As he said this, Rand caught sight of Lillam coming through the women's gate. She scanned the courtyard, spotted him, then quickly turned away with her mouth twisted into a frown. "I told him he should spend some time improving himself, try to get free of the jinkweed, and then reapply for citizenship."

Hildan put an arm around his shoulders. "You are an honorable man, Rand. You'll make a great mayor one day."

"Thank you, sir," he mumbled, afraid his shame must be written across his face.

Soon after, the show began. A stumpy man in a sparkling green suit cavorted on the back deck of the wagon and spun a tale about his medicinal arts, the words amplified over the courtyard by some breed of technological magic. The crowds seemed a bit put off at first, but then 'Doc Apocalypse' brought out his showstopper, the young boy 'from the past' that sang about how the Incarnates couldn't track him, and they all began to cheer.

As the performance picked up steam, Rand glanced at Lillam in the throng and saw sadness etched on her face while she watched the boy.

Warmth pricked his own eyes. The kid on stage looked a little like Rand himself at that age. He thought about those long, terrible years of his youth, the constant fear, the continual migration. And yet, here he was, grown and beyond the reach of the Filament, truly happy for the first time in his life. His parents may have forsaken him, made his formative years even harder, but he didn't wish that he'd never been born.

Is this your idea of happiness? Forever separated from the woman you love by a wall? Forced to meet her in secret and shame? Because even if she purges the baby and stays, that's what your life will be in this town.

Something swelled inside Rand's chest. He felt like a man standing on a narrow fence, unable to keep his balance and trying to decide which falling direction would hurt the least.

But this time he was saved from making a decision by a familiar voice in the crowd that cut through the singing as it shouted, *"Li'l drude! Hey, li'l drude!"*

3

The size of this audience was intimidatingly big, twenty times even the largest of the other settlements. Embarrassment crept over Korden as he stood immobilized inside the wagon while Doaks worked the crowd. Capering in front of this many people in such a ridiculous outfit was not something he would ever be comfortable with.

As if he had any choice.

Then it was his turn to come out, his entrance timed perfectly as the mob began to lose interest. Korden started into his routine, watching while the people went through the usual cycle of emotion: terror, cautious interest, and elation. The spectators around the wagon were thirty deep, and, as Korden neared the midpoint of the act where he and Doaks now danced together, he noticed someone pushing their way through the packed bodies to get closer to the stage. A familiar face gaped up at him.

"*Li'l drude!*" Meech Holcomb shouted gleefully, waving his arms in wide arcs above his head. He was even thinner and paler than the last time they'd met. The people around him drew away, frowning and shaking their heads as he interrupted the performance. "*Hey, Korden, man, it's me, Meech!*"

From the corner of his vision, Korden saw Doaks stabbing at buttons on the remote control. His dance came to an abrupt halt, and Korden jerked upright on the stage like a puppet put away roughly, freezing in place.

"I'm sorry sah, very sorry," Doaks called out. "I can't have you distractin the boy. If yah'll step to the side…"

"But I *know* him! Korden, where'd you go, man?"

Doaks rushed to stand in front of him, trying to block Korden from view, although his height made that a challenge. "My assistant is, uh, deaf! Can't hear a word yah sayin!"

"Huh?" Meech's face scrunched in confusion. "What're you talkin about, he was fine when I met him a few days ago! Korden, drude, are you kye?"

Korden kept still and smiled his idiot's grin, but he exuded all the agitation he could muster, pleading through his very eyeballs, *please Meech, please help me…*

And, to his relief, the man cried out, "Wait on, there's somethin wrong here! What the hells did ya do to 'im?"

"I'm afraid yah mistaken," Doaks said quickly. "No one here by that name. Now, who wants to buy some healin magic?"

Two other men came through the crowd, but, unlike Meech, the sea of people parted reverently to make way for them. One was Meech's age with dark hair shaved close to the scalp, the other much older and dressed in finer garb than even Doaks.

"Meech?" the former hissed angrily. "What're you doing?"

"That's the kid I was tellin you about!" Meech jabbed a finger in Korden's direction. "'Cept he wasn't with this guy last time I saw him, and he sure wasn't actin like some frammin dullard!"

"There's been some sorta confusion." The nervousness in Doaks's voice made Korden want to cheer.

The third man, the one with a thick fur stole draped over his shoulders, said, "I'm Mayor Lye Hildan. Doctor Apocalypse, can you tell me where you came by this boy? And no more of this 'past' nonsense."

Doaks, perhaps thinking better of sticking to his story, decided to go with a more believable fiction. "He's...my nephew, yah honor. Raised him since he was a pup."

"Then step aside and we'll hear it from him."

"Oh, he can't tell you that." Doaks twirled one finger around his temple. "He's a little touched in the head, yah see."

"Thought he was *deaf*," Meech remarked.

"Ayuh, exactly, that too!"

"You're fulla curse, drude! That kid's my friend, and you did somethin to 'im!"

"Step aside," Mayor Hildan ordered.

"Sure, sure. Can do, yah honor." Doaks moved out from in front of Korden with the controller clutched in his hands, then drifted out of sight behind him, into the wagon bonnet.

"Son," Hildan said gently. "Can you tell us your name?"

Korden's mouth popped opened, and he proclaimed cheerfully, "I'm Terp!"

"That's not true!" Meech exclaimed.

The mayor shot him a stern look before resuming the questions. "And is that man your uncle?"

"Oh yes, Uncle Doaks is my favorite person in the world!"

"*He's makin him say that somehow!*" Meech grabbed at the other man beside him. "You have to believe me, Rand! I'm not imaginin this!"

Rand—Korden remembered his brother's name now—hesitated for only a moment. "All right, I do."

"I don't know if *I* do," Hildan interjected, "but something is amiss here. Come on down son, and we'll settle this in my office."

Even though he couldn't comply, joy exploded through Korden.

And then the wagon began to vibrate beneath him.

4

The back door of the wagon hissed closed, dropping into place between them and Doc Apocalypse. A second later, Rand heard a hum beneath the cart, saw the spiderlike stilts on the sides fold up, and then the whole thing was levitating three pargs above the courtyard floor on a bubble of light. Before his mind could adjust to the sight, the vehicle glided forward in the direction of the gate, bumping aside those in the way.

"Oh no you don't!" Meech declared. He leapt forward and scrambled onto the rear deck of the wagon.

"Meech, stop!" Rand chased after his brother. The hovering craft picked up speed, moving at an eerily smooth pace across the courtyard as townspeople hurried to clear its path. Behind him, he heard Hildan bellowing for the gate to be closed. Rand got a hand on the sideboard, tangled his feet together before he could climb on, and then the cobblestones he loved so dearly were tearing out the knees of his best pants as the wagon dragged him behind it. He flailed with his free arm, on the verge of letting go, until Meech grabbed his hand and heaved him up far enough to swing a leg onto the craft.

They got to their feet on the rear deck. The walls of the courtyard flew by on either side as the wagon moved faster. Dumbfounded faces watched them hurtle past; Lillam appeared among them briefly, her mouth hanging open and cheeks lined with worry.

The boy stood next to them, hands on hips, staring off the back of the vehicle with that unsettlingly cheerful grin locked in place. He was rooted to the deck, a flesh-covered statue. Meech shook him, shouted his name, but got no response.

"*What do we do?*" his brother cried. It was a familiar question; Rand had handled every problem as they grew up, which was undoubtedly why he was so good at solving them now.

They were moving at a horse's gallop. Jumping back off at this speed was sure to cause injury. Rand leaned around the edge of the bonnet, poking his head into a whistling stream of wind that flowed around the craft. The portcullis was lowering, but it appeared they would pass through the exit and beyond the walls of Ida before it could close.

"*We have to make him stop!*" he shouted. "*Stay here and don't let the boy fall off!*"

Rand pried at the door of the bonnet, trying to tear his way through, only to learn that it wasn't made of cloth at all, but rather some hard substance that didn't yield in the slightest under his blows. He could see no way to open it.

Well, if he couldn't go *through* the wagon, that left going *around*.

The baseboards created a cupits-thick ledge down the sides of the vehicle. Rand stepped out onto the right one as they passed through the gate and into the open fields beyond the town. He clung to the ribbed arch of the bonnet, expecting the uneven terrain to make them bounce, but the ride remained as smooth as ever. So smooth that the scenery flashing past made Rand a little queasy. They travelled much faster than any horse now, and his eyes had trouble processing the unnatural speed.

Wind buffeted him as he shuffled his feet along the ledge. The length of the wagon couldn't be more than twenty-five or thirty pargs, but it looked much longer from this vantage. The blue waters of Tay-ho were visible over his shoulder as they took a wide left turn into the forest. Rand could feel gravity trying to fling him away from the vehicle.

An eternity later, he arrived at the front of the bonnet and peeked around the edge. Doc Apocalypse sat facing away from him at a complicated workstation, steering the vehicle with his hands on dual levers. Rand steeled himself before leaping forward and landing on the driver's platform.

"*Stop this wagon immediately!*" he commanded, with as much authority as he could muster. "*You are being detained by a duly authorized representative of Ida until such time as—!*"

The doctor came up swinging. Rand yelped as a meaty fist caught him in the abdomen. He'd never been a fighter, never so much as thrown a punch in his life. He raised his arms to cover his face from more blows that followed. The other man was short but surprisingly powerful, snarling as he waded into the fight.

Rand had better reach, however. He stepped away from his opponent and lashed out blindly, felt his own fist strike flesh. Apocalypse grunted and stumbled back across the wagon's control console. The vehicle made a sudden veer to the right, scraping against a line of trees. Rand struggled to stay on his feet as the collision rocked the deck beneath him.

The doctor hastily corrected their course, then spun to Rand, snatching a long metal rod hanging off the back of the pilot's seat. He touched the end to Rand's ribcage.

Shrieking hot pain tore his mind asunder. Rand screamed but had little time to do much else before Apocalypse put a hand on his chest and gave him a hard shove toward the side of the wagon. He stumbled back, heading toward the edge and the unforgiving ground beyond. Lillam's face flashed through his thoughts as he eagerly sought some way to halt his momentum...

The very air itself solidified behind him, holding him aloft. For one vertiginous moment, he leaned at an impossible angle from the side of the wagon, the ground rushing by over his shoulder. His body tingled with that same odd sensation as before, when Lillam told him about the pregnancy. Rand held his breath, trying to understand what was happening and afraid that any motion might upset this uncanny balancing act. More than anything, he wanted a way to get back on the wagon.

And, as if obeying his command, the invisible support became a strong wind at his back, pushing him upright. It deposited him delicately onto the deck.

Doc Apocalypse stared at him in astonishment. Rand used the distraction to yank the metal rod out of his hands. He turned it around and pressed it to the other man's belly, administered a sparking zap that caused him to screech and writhe.

"Stop this thing," Rand gasped, "or the next one is to your nethers."

5

With the wagon settled on its spindly legs, Meech and his brother lifted Korden's stiff body and lowered him off the rear deck, placing him on the ground in his standing pose. As they looked him over, a contingent of guardsmen on horseback pounded up the forest trail with the mayor among them.

"Where is that motherframming weasel?" the huge guard named Mikolt snarled.

"Tied up at the front," Rand told him.

"Lock him in the detention cells until we can deduce the extent of his crimes," Hildan decreed. "And this...*vehicle*... will need to be impounded, as well." To Rand, he inquired, "Can the boy speak? We'll need him to confirm he was held against his will."

"Korden, li'l drude, can you hear me?" Meech snapped his fingers in Korden's face, then shook his shoulders and lightly slapped his cheeks. "I don't get it, it's like he's mesmatized or somethin!"

"Let's check him over, see if he has any marks," Rand suggested.

They pulled at the strange costume Doaks had dressed him in, giving Korden's skinny body a cursory examination and balking when they saw the cuts on his arms. Then Meech pulled the narrow-billed hat off his head, untied the scarf, and exclaimed, "What in holy hells...?"

Both men bent closer to examine the silver headpiece. Rand tugged at the leather straps then asked one of the guards to toss him a knife. A few quick slices, and they lifted the crown off his head. There was one quick jolt of electricity before contact was lost, then his muscles thawed and blessed control returned to his body.

Korden swooned, his legs robbed of strength, but he managed to stay on his feet and stumble forward. Rand and Meech hurried after him, grabbing at him, urging him to sit down, but he shook them off and kept going until he was far enough away from the wagon to get beyond the range of the riftling's hum.

The conduit exploded open. Long pent-up artcraft blasted out, rampaging through every cupit of his body. Power hit him like a thunderclap, as galvanizing, in its own way, as the electrical shocks. But the Upper was with him, that presence like a soothing balm on a horrible burn. He sobbed in relief, sank to his knees. Through the conduit's eye, he could see the *mohols* of every man there, every horse, every tree, every animal down to the smallest insect, the world reduced to nothing but a great blazing smear of color.

And behind it all, a familiar silhouette pulsed, the hazy outline of two women standing arm-in-arm...

Then it cleared, the emotions sank back inside their hosts, and he spied Mikolt hauling Doaks away from the wagon in chains.

"*I'LL KILL YOU!*" Korden shrieked. He charged at them, a great billowing storm of destructive energy brewing in his head that would surely tear the man apart, but, thankfully, he reentered the neutralizing effect before he could unleash it. Instead, he settled for falling against the man and pounding at his chest. Korden's outrage was so immense that the throb in his broken hand caused by this assault didn't even register.

Meech gently pulled him away. "C'mon, he's not worth it."

"Oh, I think he's plenty worth it," Mikolt muttered.

Doaks shrugged sheepishly as the guard dragged him toward the horses. "Sorry, rubo. Like I said, it was just business."

Korden waited, body tense with fury, while the man was put on a mount and taken away. Then he collapsed again, this time on Meech, who held him in his bony arms and whispered that everything was fine now, he was free. A skin of water was offered, and Korden looked up at the man holding it.

"This is my brother, Rand," Meech said, making the official introduction. "I think I told you he was an uptight dick, but mostly a good guy."

"Thank you," Korden mumbled, accepting the water. His whole body was cramped and weak, his head too heavy to hold up.

Rand nodded uncomfortably. "Drink on, now. You look like you need it."

He did, guzzling the liquid until a surprised squawk sounded behind them. Korden glanced around to where Hildan was overseeing the confiscation of Gwenita. They'd found some way to open the bonnet door, and one of the guards exited carrying Zeega's cage at the end of his sword. The riftling dangled from the bars, screeching threats and snapping its claws.

"What should we do with this thing?" the guard asked.

"It *speaks*?" Hildan made a blanching face of disgust. "Kill that abomination immediately. Aged Lord knows where it came from."

"No, don't!" Korden pushed away from Meech and ran to the guard, who seemed more than happy to set the cage on the ground. He knelt and looked in at the creature. "Let it go. It won't hurt anybody…will you?"

Zeega gave no confirmation, only regarded him suspiciously with all five of its eyes, no doubt reading his mind.

"Do as he says," Hildan conceded.

The guard used his sword to shatter the cage lock in one blow. Korden reached out, unlatched the door, and stepped back. Zeega emerged slowly, cautiously, and stood watching him. He waited for the creature to attack, unsure if he would have the strength to defend himself this time.

Or if he would even try.

Then the riftling raced away, the mass of tentacles carrying it into the forest and out of sight.

BLUFF

1

"I'll hazard a guess that man was not your uncle." Hildan settled himself in the plush chair on the far side of the polished marble table from Korden. They sat in what he'd called a 'receiving room,' a beautifully decorated meeting space inside his personal chambers, located in the men's half of this incredible town. Korden imagined this place must be a semblance of the old world, although Stone—who he was very relieved to have rambling in his head once more—compared it to a style called 'Baroque'. Rand sat beside the mayor on a similar seat after changing into a pair of slender breeches with intact knees, while Mikolt hovered in the background with his arms folded.

"No," Korden agreed, then repeated his answer a little louder to make sure he was heard over the angry shouts drifting in through the windows around them. He could hardly keep his eyes open by the time they'd brought him back to Ida in plain view of the citizens, who quickly caught on that he wasn't from 'the past.' In the mayor's equally lush living quarters, he was allowed to bathe in an extraordinary tub that used ion energy to keep the water heated, given fresh clothes a tad too big for him, then fell asleep on the most comfortable bed he'd ever laid upon. By the time he awoke from a too-brief, hour-long nap, a mob had formed around the building, made up of men protesting his presence and demanding he be ejected from the city. Korden could see their *mohols* even now if he concentrated, a raging inferno of fear and agitation. Memories of Hidden Glen came rushing back to him, but he didn't think anyone would be giving an impassioned speech on his behalf here. These people had much more to lose than the bodlas and crones of the Glen. "He's a liar and a swindler. He put me in a cage, strapped that thing onto my head, and forced me to perform in his shows. And, on top of that, he sold my blood to people all around this valley, told them if they drank it, they could have children that the Incarnates wouldn't be able to sense." Korden raised the sleeve of his new shirt and displayed the scabbed slashes along his forearm.

"Ugh, what a mess," Hildan groaned. He put a hand to the bald spot atop his head and rubbed vigorously, a gesture that matched the bright fuchsia of frustration rippling through his aura. It was nice to be back around people whose *mohols* were easy to decipher. "We'll get the word out about him and his sham curatives, have no fear."

"I just hope it's not too late." Korden took a handful of grapes from a tray on the table and struggled to keep from shoving them into his mouth. His hunger was unending and his body ached with fatigue, but every few minutes he would be rocked by relief that he was truly free. "What will happen to him now?"

Hildan leaned forward in his chair and pressed a finger emphatically against the glossy tabletop. "We keep to law in Ida. Granted, kidnapping and slavery are a bit beyond our usual purview, but we won't tolerate them going unpunished, even for someone who isn't a citizen. The last thing we want is to set him loose to sow more discord. A council will be convened to decide his fate, but I think he should make himself comfortable in our prison for the foreseeable future." He twisted around to address Mikolt. "What about his craft? Is that safely stowed away?"

"We couldn't figure out how to start the damned thing," the guard said. "The boy didn't know either. I sent out twenty men to lift it onto a cart so we could tow it back to the detention yard. It'll take a season to catalogue everything inside."

"I wouldn't bother with the medicines," Rand told him. "From what Korden says, it's all garbage anyway."

There was a commotion at the door and, a second later, Meech was admitted into the room. Korden's heart gave a happy flutter at the sight of him; his gratitude to the man for saving him would never be forgotten. He panted for breath, his pale face spiked with ruddy color, but clutched in his hands was—

"My pack!" Korden hurried across the room to take back his belongings, then flipped open the top and did a quick inventory of the contents. "I thought for sure it was on the bottom of the lake!"

Meech beamed. Korden couldn't believe that he and the man named Rand were siblings, as the elder brother was entirely more healthy, clean, reserved and refined, with a wardrobe much less colorful and outlandish. Even his mannerisms and speech held none of Meech's bizarre flavor. "I kinda thought the same thing about *you*, drude. What happened to you after we met anyway? How'd that grifter get his hands on you?"

"It's a long story, and really, it doesn't even matter. The sooner I can forget about that man and what he did to me, the better. I can't thank you all enough for everything you've done."

Meech flushed with embarrassment and elbowed him in the side. "You *did* look terrible in those goofy clothes, man. Too bad you can't blame those shoes on him…"

Korden grinned and raised an eyebrow at his colorful tunic. "You're one to talk!"

"Hey, this is vintage! Everybody dressed like this in the old world!"

"I don't think that's true at all."

"We're pleased that we could help." Hildan interrupted their exchange, looking irritated as he rose from his seat with an arm held out toward the door. "And now, I'm sorry to rush you, but, as you can surmise from the uproar outside, everyone will be more comfortable when you're on your way. Mikolt, if you'll show the young man to the gate…"

"That's *it*?" Meech asked.

"Of course not, I apologize." Hildan smiled warmly at Korden. "You are welcome to as much food and drink as you can carry, with my compliments. And we would love for you to return and apply for citizenship when you reach free age. I wish we could do more, but it's not feasible in the current social climate. I'm sure you can appreciate our position."

Meech rolled his sunken eyes. "'Social climate?' That your fancy way of sayin sadistic, inhuman monsters will be huntin him down out there? What a lotta hogwash!"

Rand shifted in his chair. "Meech, stop it."

"No way, man! This poor kid's on his own, same way we were!"

"Yes, and he can survive if he keeps moving, the same way we did."

"But we can't kick him out on his ass with a bag of grapes

and a waterskin after everything he's gone through! He can barely stand up!"

Hildan favored the man with a cold look. "We are not responsible for the boy's misfortunes, and we can't take responsibility for them. These were extenuating circumstances, or we never would've allowed him within our walls. That he slept in my bed and stands in my home at this very minute puts me at odds with the law."

"Then maybe you should sentence yourself to the stocks for a day, you old windbag!"

Mikolt started toward him, snorting like a bull, but Hildan held up a hand to stop the captain before answering Meech. "If you're so concerned for his well-being, then perhaps you'd like to accompany him, since your own time in Ida is also coming to an end."

"It's fine, Meech," Korden said, coming to stand between the two men. "I don't want to cause you any trouble, Mayor Hildan, and I don't need to stay very long. But before I ran into Doaks, I was on my way here to ask you for…well, a favor, I suppose."

Hildan wiped the discontent from his face with a single breath. Even his *mohol* showed not the slightest sign of annoyance. He may not have much sympathy, but Korden found himself respecting the man's diplomacy all the same. The mayor gestured back to the seats. "Then I must offer my apologies for being so rash. I am more than happy to grant a brief audience, although I can't make such promises about a favor. If this is about transportation, I might be able to convince one of our merchants to offer you a discount on a horse…"

Korden came back to the chair and sat across from the mayor. Meech remained where he was, pacing in the doorway while scratching at the inside of his forearms, where those oozing sores marred his skin. "I wanted to ask permission to speak with your Prophet."

An uncomfortable silence fell over the men in the room, in which the angry voices outside could be heard clearly, many of them chanting, *The boy must go! The boy must go!* Korden saw both Hildan and Rand's eyes flick to the doorway across the room, the one that led deeper into the chambers. He realized, with some excitement, that he was just a few steps away from the speaking box Jakel had told him of.

"What about?" Hildan asked slowly.

"I was told that he—if it *is* a he, I mean—could predict when Incarnates were coming. Tell where they're going. I wanted to ask if he could show me how he does it."

Hildan shook his head firmly. "I'm afraid that's impossible."

"I know that he only speaks to you. If you could perhaps ask him on my behalf, I would be very grateful."

"I should've been more clear. It's impossible because the Prophet does not accept questions or requests. He merely speaks, and bestows whatever prophecies he wishes us to have."

"Could I listen to him myself then?" Korden asked hopefully. "Or do you know anything at all about how he does it?"

For the first time, Hildan appeared outright uncomfortable, his *mohol* shifting to match. His large eyes blinked rapidly. "No...you see...I can't..."

"Isn't there *anything* at all you could tell me?" Korden pleaded. "I have a long journey ahead of me, and even the smallest bit of information could help."

"Where are you going?" Rand asked quietly. The mayor seemed relieved to have someone take the focus off him.

"East," Korden told him. "Through the desert, to the mountains beyond."

"The *desert*?" Rand's jaw dropped. "Surely you don't mean to cross the Valley of Bones on foot."

"This far into Burning Season, the sun would bake you to a crisp," Mikolt added, his words a purring rumble.

"Well, I don't know. I haven't exactly figured that part out yet. I just have to go."

"And what could possibly be so important that you would undertake such a journey?" Hildan asked.

"That part is my business." Korden felt awful asking for so much trust and giving so little in return, but the last thing he wanted was a repeat of the conversation he'd had with Winstid at the Peacekeep's dining table.

"I assume by mountains, you mean the Skyreach. You know of the rumors?"

"Yes. That's another reason I wanted to talk to your Prophet, to see if he knows a way to get past this Moambati. Or, at the very least, to help me avoid the Incarnates until I get someplace safe."

"What do you mean?" Rand's words sounded even sharper this time. "Where do you think is 'safe?'"

"From what I understand, this Moambati is keeping the Incarnates divided. Whatever it is, they don't like it. If I can get to the Rockies—or, 'the Skyreach'—then maybe they'll leave me alone."

"My men have heard much the same from the trade caravans," Mikolt said. Rand jerked around in his seat to stare at him, his aura shifting into shades of intense interest. "The towns in the shadow of the Skyreach have seen no Incarnates the past few years. They say some of them are *breeding* again, although I wouldn't believe it unless I'd seen it."

"Please," Korden said, addressing Hildan. "Isn't there some way that I can hear your Prophet for myself?"

A frown tugged at the corners of Hildan's mouth, but, before he could speak, frantic shouting drifted through the door. Another member of the Enforcement Brigade rushed into the room past Meech and shouted something that made Korden's blood run cold.

"Incarnates at the gate!"

2

Rand's head whirled from all the information gleaned in conversation with the boy, but, before he could decide what to do with any of it, the guard's pronouncement ended his deliberation. He was on his feet a split second behind Hildan.

"How many?" the mayor demanded.

"Three, sir! Two males and…and a female."

"You mean your precious Prophet didn't warn you?" Meech demanded.

"No, that's precisely what I was saying. He bestows what he wishes, and I do not ask questions." Hildan turned back to the guard. "You say they're at the gate?"

"Yes sir, spotters saw them coming and closed the portcullis. They're outside now, demanding the boy be sent out! Should we ring the alarm bells?"

"No, if there's only three, they're not here to invade. Tell me, do they look like rovers?"

"I-I don't know! They don't look to be wearing armor!"

"I know them," Korden admitted. The youth sounded miserable. "They've been on my trail for days. They may not be in the ranks of the Incarnate army, but I think they're loyal to someone named Regent Torgas."

Hildan's jaw clenched. "You see that this puts me—and this town—in a difficult position."

"Yes, I'm sorry. It's my fault, I've stayed in one place for far too long. I'll go out and...and face them."

"No way! That ain't happenin!" Meech insisted. Rand wanted to pummel him.

But, to everyone's surprise, Hildan nodded. "You are a noble young man, but I cannot allow that. I'm sure many of my electors—especially the ones outside—would have me hand you over and not lose a minute of sleep, but," here he glanced at Rand's brother, "there would be dissension. There always is, which is why Ida's law is designed to avoid these situations. Countless settlements have been torn apart by having to make this decision. I'll not see Ida survive so much only to fall to a crisis of conscience."

Rand couldn't help noticing that this carefully worded speech omitted which side of the debate the mayor himself would fall on. For that matter, he didn't even know about himself.

"There are only three," Mikolt said, in a quiet, considering tone. "My men would have no problem—"

"Absolutely not!" Hildan balked. "If the Filament discovers we killed Incarnates while harboring a child, we might as well sign a declaration of war! They won't rest until the city is rubble!"

Meech wrapped both arms around his malnourished torso, hugging himself. "Then *what*, man? Stay inside with the gate closed and hope they think no one's home?"

"I could take him out through the old tunnels," Rand offered. "Set him free beyond the town. Then he'd have a chance to escape."

Hildan's wide eyes flicked back and forth as he considered. "That will be our last resort. Better he stay still for now. The second he moves, they'll know. Meech, can you navigate the old tunnels also?"

"Uh, yeah. Yes sir. Not as good as Rand, but I can get around."

"Then stay here with the boy in case it comes to that. Mikolt, Rand, you're with me. Let's go greet our guests." He walked toward the door.

"What are you going to do?" Rand asked, hurrying to catch up.

"The one thing left: bluff."

3

The shouts of the men outside renewed in vigor when they caught sight of their mayor. Mikolt's men held them back, clearing a path for Rand and Hildan to move through. It was mid-afternoon, the sun hot and dry, but a chilly terror flickered in Rand's chest as he thought about what all had transpired in the short time since it rose this morning.

Life can change but in a heartbeat, he thought, *and all our plans are folly.*

He expected Hildan to stride through the crowd, but instead he stopped, held up his hands for quiet and announced, "Good people, I am working to resolve the situation now! All I ask is patience!"

"We heard there are Incarnates outside!" one man bellowed.

"Let them have the boy!"

"He never should've been here!"

Hildan waited for the rabble to die down. "I have never done anything that wasn't in the best interest of this town!

Now please, disperse while I get things under control!"

He walked on with Mikolt, Rand, and a host of guards in step behind him. Rand glanced back and saw that the mob was doing as requested. The majority followed the mayor's group, eager to see what transpired with the visitors, but he saw a few stay behind to mill around outside the mayor's chambers.

"Have you spoken to Matron Webb?" Hildan inquired. "Are there riots on the women's side as well?"

"Not like this," Mikolt told him.

Ahead was the archway leading into the courtyard. Rand could see that it was already full of people gawking in the direction of the gate. Even without ringing the alarm bells, word of their visitors had passed.

His heart pounded as thoughts of Lillam entered his head. Where was she now? What was she thinking about all this? He yearned to find her, but still didn't know what he would say if he did.

Mikolt gave an irritated growl. "Should I have my men clear them out?"

"No, I want this to be public, no matter what happens. I'll not have accusations of some secret meeting with the Filament for my rivals to dangle over my head at the next election. Perhaps this is the reminder Ida needs of why we keep to law." Hildan stopped and faced his chief enforcer. "But have your men push everyone to the perimeter of the courtyard. And spread this warning: any person who *dares* speak on this town's behalf or lift a finger against these demons will be banished before night falls."

"It will be done." Mikolt charged ahead, signaling to his men.

The mayor, however, didn't move. Rand noticed his breathing was heavy.

"Sir? Are you all right?"

"I haven't so much as seen an Incarnate since I was younger than you are now, and even that was merely a glimpse. I've certainly never spoken to one."

Rand had seen many of the demons himself when he and Meech were kids, although never face to face. They'd made sure to travel fifty spans a day, stayed away from roads and large settlements, but there were still some close calls.

Hildan continued. "I spent my pre-age years in a child-friendly fortress much smaller than Ida, but with enough manpower and arsenal to fend off waves of Filament soldiers. Did you know that?"

"I didn't," Rand admitted, but a sudden burning curiosity gripped him. "If you don't mind me asking, what happened to...?"

He could think of no way to finish the question, but the other man knew what he meant. "I was one of seven children in the entire settlement. Even with resources such as that, they were brave enough to produce only seven of us, and countless lives were lost trying to keep us safe. Ammunition for the shooters eventually ran out. People abandoned hope. Some left. The older generation died off. And when the population grew too small...the place collapsed." Hildan met Rand's gaze. "Have I made a serious error, letting that boy inside our walls? Would you have solved the problem some other way, in my stead? Say on, in truth."

Rand swallowed. "Not to sound like my brother, but... what else could we do? Leave him unconscious by the lake?"

Hildan nodded and gathered himself as they entered the courtyard. The Enforcement Brigade had moved citizens back to the walls, creating a large, clear circle in the middle, where Doc Apocalypse's wagon was parked hours before.

Rand took this all in, then looked to the gate.

Three figures stood in the crosshatched shadow of the portcullis. From this distance, he couldn't tell much else about them.

"I thought they didn't come out during the day," Hildan muttered.

"No, they don't *like* to come out during the day. The sun decays them. Hurts their eyes. But they're happy to put up with the discomfort if it means killing some children."

They made their way to the middle of the circle and stood alone on the stone floor of the courtyard, facing the gate. Hildan clasped his hands in front of him, hidden inside the wide sleeves of his doublet. Mikolt positioned himself at the edge of the crowd to their right and waited with arms crossed.

"*Raise the portcullis!*" Hildan commanded.

The barrier trundled upward. When it was high enough, the three figures stepped into the courtyard. Audible gasps came from all around as the citizenry took them in.

As the crier promised, there were definitely two males, one in denim dungarees and deerskin shirt, the other barechested, both scrawny and malnourished and wearing goggles to protect their sensitive eyes. The sun had rotted their exposed skin in great swatches, leaving blackened pits and holes like a spoiled apple. The third *might* have been a woman, but this was hard to discern with its figure hidden inside the folds of a black longcloak, and a clunky, solid black mask over its face.

Rand's own breath caught as the trio marched toward them. In a scant eight months, creatures like this would be coming for his own child.

Wherever it might be.

"Greetings," Hildan said. The cordiality surprised Rand. "I'm Mayor Lye Hildan. What can I—?"

"There is Light in this town," the demon in the longcloak snarled without preamble, and yes, its harsh voice was undeniably feminine, even filtered through the heavy mask. "A boy. One we have tracked over the mountains and around this lake for some time. You will give him to us now, or face the wrath of the Dark Filament's armies."

Another quiet murmur of shock and fear rippled through the crowd.

"Please." Hildan held up a hand. "We desire no conflict with the Filament. We are a free-age-only community and have been for decades. To the best of my knowledge, there is no child within these walls."

"Then your best knowledge counts for little," the female snapped.

The mayor gave a tight-lipped smile. "Is it possible you are mistaken? The child could be hiding somewhere close by to fool you. In the hills, perhaps."

"He is *here*. And if you truly want no conflict with the Stranger and the forces that serve Him, you will allow us to search this settlement to find what we seek."

So much for bluffing, Rand thought.

Hildan nodded seriously before trying again. "This all comes as a complete surprise. So perhaps you would be generous enough to allow me to root out this supposed child for myself, and punish those responsible. You could return, say, tomorrow, and I will present my findings to you. As well as the child, if he is truly here."

The female stepped toward him. The motion was so sudden, Hildan flailed and stumbled backward away from her, but she kept stalking him, thrusting the dark, rectangular window on her mask into his face. Rand stood in place, unsure what to do, but saw Mikolt step out of the crowd with a hand on his sword.

"You are *surprised*?" she demanded, the last word spat with a mocking edge. "By what? Your species' pathetic insistence on breeding? Look around you, *Mayor*." She stopped her advance and spun to take in the crowd around the periphery of the courtyard. "*You wear your 'free-age-only' like a shield, but you were all children once!*" she shrieked. One gloved hand emerged from the folds of the longcloak to claw at the air. "*Your progenitors were either careless or stupid enough to create you, along with thousands of others that we slaughtered! But all of you must've run and hid like rats, defied the Filament until you grew old enough to escape us for good, and now you harbor hope that your own offspring can do the same! But be assured, we will NEVER rest until that hope is shattered! Until every last human child is a faded memory, and the spark of faith in this world gutters out!*" She caught sight of Mikolt for the first time, standing tensely a few paces out from the crowd. "Perhaps you sin cows need a reminder about what kind of cattle you are."

"No, please," Hildan pleaded. Rand wondered if he regretted allowing the town to witness this meeting now. "I'll do what you ask, just give me a moment to…to…"

The female glanced at her shirtless cohort while nodding her head toward Mikolt. "Decarl, a present for you."

"Thank you, Searda." The motion of his speech caused a tooth to fall out of his diseased gums and skitter across the stone. This one loped toward Mikolt, who waited ramrod straight with jaw clenched so hard the muscles along his neck bulged in banded cords. Rand turned to Hildan, expecting the man to issue some command, to set the guards loose on these creatures, but the mayor only wrang his hands indecisively, his broad face etched with total agony.

The Incarnate named 'Decarl' reached Mikolt and stood in front of him. His wasted form was dwarfed by the captain of the Enforcement Brigade, yet he showed no hesitation as he clamped one blackened hand around Mikolt's bicep. The demon squeezed. A flash of pain crossed Mikolt's face, but he made no move to defend himself without the mayor's permission.

With his free hand, Decarl pulled a short blade from the back of his filthy pants.

"*Stop!*" Hildan called. The word echoed across the courtyard. "We can...we can reach an agreement! Please don't hurt him!"

"Hurt him? I wouldn't dream of it," the Incarnate said, and jammed the knife into his own neck.

4

Korden sat in the receiving room, going over options in his head with Stone. The computer calculated a high chance of escape if they left now, through the tunnels that Mayor Hildan mentioned, but the last thing Korden wanted was to make matters worse for the people of Ida.

Keep in mind, I also calculate a 28.1 percent chance that the mayor will hand you over to these Incarnates.

No. I don't believe that. These are good people, I know it.

That may be, but they are also *scared* people. And scared people have a long history of poor decision-making. Please wait, factoring in the Salem Witch Trials... The odds of a surrender have now increased to 35.3 percent.

I can't leave without finding out about this Prophet. These predictions or whatever they are might be the only way for me to survive long enough to reach the Rockies. Or 'Skyreach,' I guess.

From where he sat, he could see into the mayor's inner office, where shelves of books adorned one wall. Korden longed to go inside and see what he could find of this 'speaking box,' but even contemplating such a breach of trust made him ashamed. Bad enough that he was once more putting innocent people in harm's way with his blighted existence.

So he would sit here, try to remain calm, and be thankful that the shouting from outside had died down.

Meech, on the other hand, made no such effort. He'd paced back and forth across the far end of the room ever since the others left, scratching nervously at his sores. Every few minutes he would make a high, mewling noise in the back of his throat and give a protracted shiver.

"*I can't take this anymore!*" he proclaimed. His bony fists squeezed rhythmically at his sides. "My nerves are *shot*, drude! I need some jinko or I-I-I'm gonna die, I swear to the Aged!"

"Steady on," Korden told him. The man's aura was a jumbled mess of pain, frustration, and raw need. Korden sent out waves of serene blue to settle it, an action that wasn't too different from the way he'd banished the *mohol* ghosts beneath the lake. The tension bled out of Meech, and he dropped into another chair with his brow beaded in sweat.

"Sorry," he mumbled. "Just a case of the gimmies. That's what Jaimer calls it, anyway."

"Meech, I don't think that stuff is good for you."

"No. No, it prob'ly ain't. But, man, it sure *feels* good…" He drifted away, his sunken eyes closing momentarily before snapping back open. "Are you serious about headin east across the desert?"

"Yes. As soon as I figure out a way."

"Well, you can't walk, drude. Even on a horse, you'd need major supplies."

"I know that." Korden sighed. "What about these trade caravans? Do you think one of them would take me?"

"You could ask, but I wouldn't put much hope in it. No trader's gonna endanger their whole route by takin on a kid." Meech tapped his heel quickly against the floor, causing his whole leg to bounce. His *mohol* was slowly working itself back into a frenzy as the addiction ramped up. "So, like, why *are* you goin east anyway? I mean, fram Moambati, you know the *Shroud* is that way too, right?"

"That's exactly why I'm going. I...I intend to find out what's holding the Filament at bay and see if I can use my Crafting to help drive them back."

Korden waited for the inevitable argument, but, instead, a crooked grin unfurled across Meech's gaunt face. "Kye, man. We've rolled over for those bastards for way too long. About time somebody took the fight to 'em." This was exactly the rebellious spirit Korden wished more people would adopt. Unfortunately, it was also a pale echo of what Heater told him. Immediately after saying it, Meech's jaw dropped open as a faraway look came into his eye. His *mohol* shifted into the snappy pink hues of inspiration before he declared, "And I'm gonna do it with you."

Korden stared at him. "*Huh?*"

Meech grabbed his arm. "Remember I told you about my parents dumpin me and my brother when we were kids? I know what it's like to be on your own out there, and I can't let you do it by yourself, man! So I'll go *with* you! I can...I can be your bodyguard! You know, watch your back, hide you from framsticks like Doc Apocalypse!"

"That's nice of you, but I can't ask you to leave your home."

"Drude...I've been banished from Ida. Gotta clear out by tomorrow. I didn't have a clue what I was gonna do or where I was gonna go, and then, lo and behold, you drop into my life and it's like I suddenly have a purpose! It's fate, man! I'm *supposed* to help you!"

It felt strange to have someone twice his age pleading with him, asking for his permission. "I...I don't know..."

Meech leaned closer, the feverish sweat across his brow beginning to run down his cheeks. "I need this, Korden. The jinks...it's killin me. I know it, Rand knows it, this whole town knows it. If I can get outta here, get my mind off it... I'm *sure* I can get clean."

THIS COURSE OF ACTION IS INADVISABLE! Stone insisted.

Korden knew the computer was probably right. The last thing he needed was to drag this ailing man along on his journey...and yet, at the same time, a kernel of joy grew inside him at the thought of having someone else by his side. Tash never told him that he *couldn't* travel with anyone, only that the Olders were afraid to go with him in case they affected whatever plan the Upper had for him.

Well...what if part of the Upper's plan was taking on a companion?

"Yes," he said on impulse, meeting Meech's grin with one of his own. "Let's do it."

Meech's triumphant cheer was drowned out by a loud shout and crash from beyond the door of the mayor's chambers. Korden saw the guard that was left to watch them fall unconscious across the entrance.

5

The Incarnate jerked the knife, tearing out a long strip of flesh from his own throat. What dribbled out of the wound wasn't so much blood as some dark, tar-like substance. Mikolt's eyes popped wide in his scarred face as he grasped what was happening. The captain of the Enforcement Brigade finally began to struggle, but it was too late. Decarl wrapped both of his mottled arms around Mikolt's torso and latched on to him like a giant tick, pushing their faces together.

A swirl of black smoke flowed from the Incarnate's eyes into Mikolt's.

When the phenomenon stopped, Decarl let go and collapsed to the pavement, limp as wet cloth. Mikolt—with eyes now squeezed shut—bent down, felt along the putrefying body until he located its head, then stripped off the dark goggles. He stood and pulled them over his own face.

"*Yes!*" Mikolt roared, raising his massive arms to flex his biceps over his head. Except it wasn't Mikolt, not anymore. "A new body! A *strong* body! This will serve me well!"

Rand knew that Incarnates inhabited humans, but it'd always been more of an abstract concept in the back of his mind. He'd never *seen* the process, and it'd certainly never happened to anyone he knew. For the first time, he wondered what happened to the original consciousness when they took over its shell.

Was Mikolt dead...or in there somewhere? Both options seemed equally horrifying in their own ways.

Searda spun back to Hildan, who looked as white as a milk jug. "You see?" she asked through the black mask. The third demon laughed behind her, a low, chuffing sound. "Don't think because you survived to free age, we have no use for you. You exist at *our* whim, to replenish *our* ranks. Now…where is the Light?"

"I…I-I can't…"

"It might help your distress to know," she said, her tone softening to what could pass for sympathy, "that we will not kill the child here. He's a special one, this boy. We have orders to take him back to our Regent, far from here."

"*TELL US!*" Decarl bellowed in Mikolt's rumbling voice. He drew the guard's sword from its sheath. "*Or I butcher your people one at a time!*"

Searda raised an imploring hand toward the mayor, palm up, her gloved fingers outstretched. "We will have him either way. Cooperating ensures that your town isn't judged an enemy of the Filament."

"Y-yes. All right," Hildan agreed. "He's—"

"Too late." Her covered head turned away from him, toward the entrance to the men's side of town. "He comes even now."

6

Seven men rushed through the doorway into the receiving room and halted when they spotted Korden. He recognized the blaze of their auras as part of the mob from outside.

"Get up, boy!" one of them barked. "If Hildan don't got the stones to hand ya over to those 'Carnates, *we* will!"

"*Over my dead body!*" Meech howled. He jumped up from his chair, fists cocked, and charged at them. The closest man swung an arcing punch that connected with the side of his jaw hard enough to spin his stick-thin body halfway around. Meech's knees buckled, and he hit the floor in a heap with eyes closed and tongue lolling.

So much for my new bodyguard…

Korden stood up as the men spread out across the room and moved toward him. He sent out calming energy as he had with Meech, but it did little to quell their collective fear and anger.

"Stay away from me," he warned. In his head, Stone blared warnings about the abysmal odds of one against seven. His hand strayed toward the sheath on his belt, hoping the bone-hilt knife might dissuade them from this course, before remembering that the weapon was somewhere inside Doaks's wagon.

The one to his left darted forward. Artcraft pulsed through Korden before he could even decide what to do with it, as natural and unstoppable as a heartbeat. His attacker was lifted completely off his feet and flew backward with surprise on his face, slamming into the wall hard enough to crack the masonry. He collapsed next to Meech.

The others stopped their advance.

"He's a Crafter!" the first man barked, sneering in disgust. "Grab 'im, don't let 'im use his powers!"

The rest came at him together. Korden backed up, his body crackling with energy that he was powerless to contain. His training with the Olders dealt with opening and sustaining the conduit; he'd never anticipated that he would need to practice *throttling* it. The colors of the world jumped out at him in livid detail, as when he'd gotten away from Zeega after days inside the nullifying hum.

One of the men seized Korden's arm. A horrific crack echoed through the room. His attacker screamed and jumped away with his hand facing the wrong way on his wrist. Another aimed a blow at Korden's face and was swatted aside by an invisible force that sent blood spraying from his nose.

"Get back!" Korden pleaded, his breath hitching. "I can't control it!"

But he feared that some part of him could. That unstoppable torrent of magic was taking its orders directly from his hindbrain now, where all the most terrible thoughts roam, free of guilt and moderation.

Somewhere deep inside, he *wanted* to hurt these men, and the more upset he became, the more that subconscious will was able to supercede his restrained forethoughts.

They waded in, dismissive of his warning. The first man got a grip on Korden's throat and bore down.

With the speed of a well-kindled fire, the man's face ignited in blue flame.

He wailed and let go, and the others backed away. The flaming man beat at his own head, trying to extinguish himself. For one everlasting second, it was Heater Kay in there, his face melting as Korden spewed fire down his throat in the midst of his wrath.

A disgusted nausea crept over Korden.

Is this what he would have to do to survive in this world? What the Upper gave him this power for? To burn and smash and destroy anyone that got in his way?

His flicker of doubt caused the flow of artcraft to taper. He leaned on the wall behind him, breathless and dismayed.

This time, when the men came at him, he made no move to stop them.

7

Rand could see a disturbance in the crowd on the western side of the courtyard. People moved aside for a tightly packed group of men lugging something between them. They entered the empty ring in the middle, and Rand saw that it was Korden they carried.

"W-we don't want any trouble!" one of the men called out. "We brought the kid to you! Take him and leave us in peace!"

"At least someone in your town has the good sense to save it," Searda remarked to Hildan. The mayor's shoulders slumped as he stared at the ground in shame.

Rand's heart gave a lurch. This was the same boy he'd risked his life to rescue from a slaving charlatan not three hours earlier.

And now he was expected to stand by while that same boy was given away to beings who had much worse in store for him.

Something prickled at the base of Rand's scalp. That same weird tingle. He hadn't thought much about his strange encounter on the wagon (had mostly rationalized it away as a trick of his rattled mind, not nearly as miraculous as it seemed at the time), but now this sensation made him feel coiled and tight, like the string of a cocked crossbow.

Except he didn't know how to trigger it, or what arrow would fire even if he did.

The men put the boy on the ground not thirty paces from where Hildan, Rand and the Incarnates stood, then backed away quickly, disappearing into the crowd. Many of the spectators looked as sick as Rand felt, a few women even openly weeping. They might not want the child here, but that didn't mean they wanted him killed, either.

Korden got to his feet and stared defiantly at the trio of demons.

"*Make this easy, child!*" Searda shouted. "*We have to bring you back, but that doesn't mean we have to do so with all your fingers attached!*"

The courtyard was so silent that even Korden's softly spoken reply could be heard in every corner. "I'm not going anywhere with you."

"*Don't be a fool! There's no escape! Come to us and face your destiny!*"

"That's exactly what I intend to do," the boy answered.

8

Here, at last, were creatures he wouldn't feel the least bit guilty about hurting. Korden closed his eyes, centered himself, put his ever-enduring faith in the Upper, and unleashed the raging power in his mind.

9

A few pargs away from Rand, Searda's longcloak exploded with turquoise flames.

A collective gasp rose from the assemblage. Rand threw up an arm against the sudden heat, but Hildan stood agape as the unearthly fire consumed the female Incarnate. She screeched and thrashed, tearing the garment off in flaming shreds.

The other two demons charged the boy, their footsteps pounding on the cobblestones of the courtyard. Decarl bellowed with Mikolt's voice and raised the captain's sword.

Korden held out a hand as they swept toward him and flicked his fingers upward, as though waving off a fly.

The goggles strapped around Mikolt's head ripped away and flew into the air. Decarl roared in pain, dropped the sword, and jammed the heels of both hands into his stolen eyes. The third Incarnate kept coming, pointing the blade of a smaller knife at Korden, who faced him, spread the fingers of his outstretched hand, and then clamped them shut in a tight fist.

What happened next was so fast and bizarre that it took Rand another three seconds to comprehend it. The Incarnate's body shrank in on itself, its arms and legs twisting in unnatural directions, its head deforming. As more of that black ichor rained down on the stones beneath it, he understood: the creature's body had been crushed by an invisible force, squeezed like a freshly pulped garren fruit. The mangled corpse hung in midair before dropping to splatter on the ground. Rand saw the little funnel of black smoke drift up from its squashed head, but without anyone close by to enter, it dissipated.

He's a Crafter, Rand thought as the truth struck him.

Decarl sank to his knees, still howling with his hands over his eyes. He was silenced a moment later when his sword rose from the ground and made a lethal swing, slicing his head off as cleanly as a heated knife through butter. It rolled away across the cobblestones, spewing a trail of dark smoke. The blood from this wound was very red compared to his rotting brethren, and jetted out in rhythmic squirts as his body toppled.

Searda had removed her flaming clothes and now stood fully nude except for the boxy mask, which made her look like some sort of pagan fertility idol. Her body was a sight to behold, a curvaceous, porcelain beauty, untouched by sun rot and only slightly singed by her brush with the fire.

"*Your tricks change NOTHING!*" she shrieked, pointing a finger at the boy. "*You will die, one way or another! There is more than just us coming for you!*"

"That's what you all keep saying," Korden told her, before Mikolt's sword shot through the air like an arrow and impaled Searda directly between her perfect breasts.

Punishments and Plans

1

Even with all the artcraft he'd expended, Korden had to wrestle the conduit closed. That immense power was beginning to frighten him, in part because it was so easy for his emotions to spin it beyond his control.

But mostly because, deep inside, it felt so good to *let it happen.*

In front of him, the female demon toppled over backward with the sword jutting from her chest and threads of black smoke wafting through the tinted window of her mask. Korden was a little shocked that the attack he envisioned had worked so well. The Olders had a hard time using their magic so directly against the Incarnates. It made him think of that last day in the village, when he'd disintegrated the one that killed his father.

Yehr hope is still young, ghammer, *and yehr faith is strong,* Tash whispered in his head. *That makes all the difference. So use them both while yeh can.*

Heavy, expectant silence reigned in the courtyard. Then, all at once, angry cries erupted all around him. The people of Ida shook their fists and screamed insults, strange names that he assumed must be epithets for 'Crafter.' Even the faces that had previously appeared troubled by the prospect of surrendering him to the Incarnates howled for his blood now.

As he took in the snarling mob, Meech broke through their ranks and stumbled toward him.

"Oh wow, drude!" he panted, taking in the bodies. One side of his chin was already purple and green where he'd been punched. "You beat the curse out of 'em, huh? Too bad I wasn't here, I'd've taken a couple on myself!"

"Sure you would've, Meech," Korden agreed, putting a hand on his bony shoulder more for support than encouragement. Stone crowed similar congratulations on his victory, but, as his thoughts turned back to the men he'd hurt in the mayor's chambers, an uncomfortable cramp soured his stomach.

Hildan stomped across the short stretch of courtyard between them with Rand at his heel. The mayor's jaw was clenched, his cheeks flushed, his round eyes narrowed. Korden was too scared to open the conduit's eye to view his aura in case the power should grow out of control, but the man's fury was easily discernible.

"What have you done?" Hildan demanded over the rabble of his townspeople.

"I defended myself."

"Yes, and if the Filament holds Ida accountable, it will be *us* that pays the price!"

"Was he supposed to stretch his neck out and wait for the sword?" Meech asked.

"They weren't going to kill him, they wanted to take him back to their leader!"

"Oh yeah, and I got a bridge made outta sugar to sell ya, too!"

Hildan gnashed his teeth and pointed at Korden. "You lied to me about what you are!"

"I *never* lied," Korden snapped. "Just because I didn't tell you I was a Crafter doesn't mean I lied to you."

"Trickery! That's what your kind is best at! You're lucky I don't hold you here for the next Incarnate that comes through!"

Korden glanced blithely over at the demon he'd crushed with his imagination. "Do you think I would allow that?"

"And now threats! I want you out of this town immediately! Mikolt!" Hildan caught his mistake as soon as the shout was made and blanched in embarrassment. He pointed at the closest members of the Brigade while they herded people back through their separate gateways. "You there! Make sure this…this *boy*…is escorted through the exit! Then take Mikolt's body and these other three corpses far from Ida and burn them to ashes!" This last command was largely unnecessary, since all four bodies were quickly degrading into puddles of greenish-black slag, as all dead Incarnates did in the sun.

"What about my things?" Korden asked, as two guards hustled toward them.

"I can bring them to you," Rand offered.

"Then make arrangements for the delivery *outside* town," Hildan commanded. "I don't want him here even a single second longer, or else I might let these people have their way with him." With one last grimace, the mayor strode away.

Rand raised a hand to the approaching guards, signaling for them to hold off. "My apologies," he told Korden. "The mayor is upset that it came to this. He was doing everything he could to find a peaceful resolution."

"There is no peace when it comes to the Filament."

The other man nodded thoughtfully, then told his brother, "Meech, if you'll take him to Hecate Pond, I'll get his belongings right now."

"Might as well grab mine, too." At Rand's confusion,

Meech added proudly, "I'm goin with him. I'm the li'l drude's new bodyguard."

Rand glanced over his shoulder at the waiting guards and licked his lips nervously. "All right, but...don't do anything rash until I can get there and talk to you."

"You'd better hurry," Korden said. "We can't afford to stay around here much longer."

2

Since his escapade on the floating wagon this morning, people started clapping Rand on the shoulder and shouting out words of encouragement. The notoriety was nice—it made him a shoo-in if he ever did run for mayor—but it also complicated discretion as he hurried about town. He collected the boy's carry pouch from the mayor's office (Hildan had retreated to his inner chamber by this point, as another angry mob formed outside), then ran by Meech's room in the dormitory to pack up his brother's meager possessions. This wasn't a difficult task; most of them were still inside a drawstring duffel from his recent foray into the wild.

Throughout all of this, Rand's head buzzed with anticipation (and a healthy dose of dread) at the plan taking shape in his mind. With shoulders full, he next ran up to his own room, intending to signal another meeting with Lillam.

There was no need. Far across town, she stood at her window, staring in his direction, framed by the red emergency drapery. Aged Lord knew how long she'd been sitting there. He hated to leave Korden and his brother waiting, but it would be best if he spoke to Lillam first. And he needed to see her, to apologize for his earlier shock and pledge his love. He could go through the tunnels and speak to her on his way out of town. Rand confirmed an immediate rendezvous with a coded message of his own and took off downstairs for the closest subterranean entrance.

She wasn't hiding this time. As soon as he emerged into the corridor where they usually met, she leapt into his arms hard enough to stagger him.

"I was so scared, you big dumb lout!" she exclaimed between urgent kisses. "What were you thinking? First you jumped on that wagon…then I heard about you going to face the Incarnates…I thought for certain you were trying to kill yourself so you didn't have to see me!"

"Never in life!" he assured her with a laugh, forcing her back long enough to get the words out.

"I'm so sorry about before," she told him. "I shouldn't have sprung it on you like that—!"

"No, it's me who's sorry, sweetlove. I reacted poorly." He grabbed her slender hands and kissed each one. "Lillam, I have only a short time, but…were you serious? You intend to leave with…with our…?" He couldn't get out the correct word to finish his sentence.

Her lip quivered. "I have to, Rand. I can't turn my back on it. On *her*."

He nodded. And, though his heart pounded and his skin was clammy with fear and a voice in his head begged him to consider other options, he said, "All right. Let's do it. Together."

Relief transformed her dour face, infusing her with a joy that made him fall in love with her all over again. "Really? You'll come?"

"I can't let you do this alone." He reached out a hand and laid it on her belly through the gown, which felt flat and taut. The idea that something was growing in there astounded him. "We'll protect her. I promise."

And then she was smothering him with her lips as she babbled. "We'll need to make arrangements...come up with a plan before we have to leave...I think I can hide it till the end of the season if I don't overeat..."

"No, Lillam, stop and listen to me. We have to go immediately. Tonight, if not sooner."

She pulled back to stare at him. "Why on earth would we do that?"

"The boy," he told her eagerly. "Korden."

"What about him?"

"He's a Crafter."

Her face darkened. "So it's true."

"Yes, it's true! But please don't look so disgusted, he's very nice!" Rand would never comprehend the loathing reserved for such people. He'd never met one himself before today, had more or less considered them another myth. The hatred seemed to be passed down generationally, which was probably why he and his brother were never indoctrinated. "Meech is going with him, and I think we should, too!"

Lillam's brow drew together in a dangerous way. "You want us to trek out into the world with your jinkoid brother and some filthy spellflinger?"

"Considering I watched that spellflinger slaughter three Incarnates without so much as breaking a sweat, yes, I do!"

"And why were those Incarnates there? For *him*. And there'll be more coming all the time, which is very much the opposite of what I thought we wanted!"

Rand tried an endearing smile. "We'll be on the run by the time the baby's born anyway; what's a couple of seasons sooner?"

Her drawn brow deepened into a full scowl. "You're not

amusing, Rand Holcomb."

"A little bit I am." He clasped his hands in front of him to plead. "It won't be for long. I just want him to take us as far as the Skyreach."

She laughed, and not pleasantly. "This fantasy of yours keeps getting better. The *Skyreach?* How would we even cross the desert?"

"Well, there's some details to iron out," he admitted.

"But Moambati—"

"Is merely a rumor. One that seems to be keeping the Incarnates at bay. Mikolt said that the towns along the base of the mountains are breeding freely. We could be safe there. We wouldn't *have* to run."

Lillam turned away from him with her arms crossed. "That sounds like a rumor too, you know."

"I don't know what we'll find there," he said to her back. "But I know that we have to leave here, and if we have to leave, we'd be better off doing it with him. He could protect us from…whatever's out there."

"But he's just a boy," she insisted. "Why are you so willing to put our lives—the life of *our* child—in his hands?"

He stepped to her, wrapped his arms around her waist, and buried his face in her golden locks. "Do you trust me?"

"I thought I did. Then you went completely mad."

"I have this feeling about him. If you trust me, then please…say yes."

Lillam spun in his embrace and looked up at him, her eyes piercing and as clear green as a sun-dappled meadow. "Yes."

He kissed her forehead. "Go back and pack up. Essentials only. We'll have to leave everything else behind. And don't tell anyone. I'll talk to Korden and see if we can come up with a plan for the journey."

He made to walk away, but she grabbed his hand. "Don't you have a minute longer?"

"They're waiting on me!"

She ran a coy finger down his chest and stopped at his groin. "It's just that...seeing you jump on that wagon made me a bit *bothered*..."

"One minute," he agreed, and scrambled to loosen his belt.

3

Lillam believed her happiness must be making her glow as she exited the tunnels through the rusted hatch in the dank alley behind the women's dormitory. Much of that joy was from the earthquakes Rand had set off inside her—the kind that caused her to moan and made her eyes roll back in her head—but that was far from the sole reason.

They were doing this, they were *actually* doing this! Logically, she knew she should be terrified at the prospect of leaving the only real home she'd ever known, but she couldn't muster the emotion. She had no connections here other than a few acquaintances, and the endless rules that made others feel so safe in Ida tended to stifle her. No, this thrilled, on-the-edge sensation was more like standing in front of a closed door that was about to open, and on the other side her life would truly begin.

Although it did give her pause that this wonderful new life would begin in the company of a Crafter.

Lillam had seen one when she was much younger, perhaps ten or eleven. She and her mother were staying with a couple that was kind enough to give them lodging overnight. The next morning, they'd heard yelling from the square in the center of the settlement. Fearful of Incarnates, her mother hastened to depart, until the couple returned to tell them it was a Crafter being decried.

Her mother hid Lillam under her skirts and took her up onto one of the rooftops bordering the square so they could watch. The man was a bodla, decrepit and hunchbacked, with curly white hair and spectacles as thick as window panes. He stood in the midst of a huge crowd, holding bright orange fire in the palm of one hand and making a well bucket float above the other, all while shouting that the Filament could be bested, that the time to fight was now, that future generations were depending on them. He didn't look dangerous to Lillam, but someone in the mob hucked an apple that would've struck him in the shoulder if it hadn't been deflected in midair first. That made the townspeople even more angry, and then they were all throwing objects, too many for the elderly Crafter to block with his mind, and, after a minute of this, he was driven from the square and right out of the settlement. Lillam's mom joined in, lobbing a loose shingle from the rooftop at him.

"Mommy, why do you hate him so much?" she'd asked.

"Powers like that ain't natural," Samanda Onderson replied. "They're against our Aged Lord, and all those obscene people want to use them for is stirring up trouble. You don't fight the Filament, you run from them."

Even at the time, Lillam wondered if there would always be space in the world to keep running.

She crept through the dormitory back to her room with the stealth of a thief. The hallways and stairwells had been full of gossiping ladies all day, but now the furor over the events of the day had died down. Without their cover, her comings-and-goings were more likely to be noticed. Especially when she left with bags.

But why should anyone care? If they found out she was

pregnant, all they would do is cast her out, and she was saving them the trouble.

In her room, she hurriedly closed the door, grabbed several canvas bags she used to carry food from the market, and began tossing clothes from the closet onto her bed.

"Going on a sabbatical, are we?"

The stern voice startled Lillam so much, she stumbled into the wall with her best petticoat. She spun around and took in the rest of her room for the first time.

Kasa Webb sat in the corner, with hands folded primly in her lap.

"M-Matron!" Lillam blurted. The stout woman watched her with eyes as dark and chilly as the waters of Tay-ho on a moonless winter night. "I didn't see you there, miss'um!"

"Of course you didn't," the other woman agreed. "Otherwise you would've offered me a drink before you went about packing your bags."

Lillam tossed the petticoat onto the bed with the rest of her meager wardrobe. "Oh, this? I...I was going to..."

The matron shook her head. She wore a long-sleeve denim blouse with a matching skirt so long it covered the lower half of her plump body like a shroud. Her white hair was tied up in a bun on the back of her head tightly enough to smooth out the grackle's feet on her wizened face. Lillam had experienced few dealings with the woman since coming to live in Ida. She ran day-to-day matters on the women's side of town, second only to the mayor, and held an even greater reputation for strictness.

"Don't trouble yourself with excuses, dear. As my father used to warn me, lies will make one pregnant with remorse." The impression of a smile touched her mouth. "Although in your case, I suppose it's too late to worry on that account."

A warm mixture of shock and guilt oozed down Lillam's body. "H-how…how did you…?"

"That was a curious amount of seeds you purchased a few days ago. Wheat and barley. There's only one old crone's tale they could be used for." Kasa Webb gave her a pitying look. "Did you think it wouldn't get back to me? I know everything that happens in this half of Ida."

Lillam couldn't answer. She'd never experienced such a profound sense of shame in her life. It clung to her like thick mud, sapping all her previous joy.

"Well, is it a girl or a boy then?"

"Girl," she admitted numbly.

"Congratulations." The matron rose from the chair—her denim skirt falling around her wide hips and thighs to make her look like a gigantic dinner bell—and held out a hand toward the pile of clothes on Lillam's bed. "I say that because it appears you've already made your decision on what to do about your little mistake."

Something about the word 'mistake' allowed Lillam to recover. She stiffened her spine and said, "Yes. I'm leaving tonight. There won't be any need to drag me out."

"I applaud you taking such responsibility. His Holy Seniority might not, but that's between you and Him." Webb shrugged, the movement languorous. "In the end, however, it makes no difference to me if you wish to be so foolish. There are many people outside the walls of Ida that would be more than happy to accept your place in this town." Her brow dropped as she stepped toward Lillam. "But I'm afraid you won't be strolling out through the gates today, my dear."

"W-what do you mean?" The other woman was in front of her now, somehow looming over her even though she couldn't be more than a cupit or two taller. Lillam would've backed away, but there was no place to go in her tiny quarters.

"You didn't come up with the ingredients to bake that bun all alone, now did you?" Webb demanded, raking her long fingernails across Lillam's waist. The action didn't hurt, but it startled her back into the wall again. "Which means you've been breaking the law. Sneaking around to see a man. There must be punishment for that."

"N-no, please!" Lillam pleaded. "I told you, I'm leaving, I won't give you any problems!"

"You've *already* given me problems!" the matron snapped. "If I let you walk out of here without paying for what you've done, what will the rest of Ida think? That's how settlements fall to chaos, by taking one step after another away from the law! I think a week in the stocks would serve well as a reminder!"

Lillam clutched at the woman's thick wrists. "Please, you can't!"

"Oh, I very well can!" Webb shook free of her grip. When she spoke again, her demeanor had calmed. "But I don't *have* to. I would be happy to commute your sentence... in exchange for the father's name."

Lillam looked at her in horror. "Why would you want that?"

"Because even if you have the ill-conceived notion to leave with your offspring, Ida will still have a lawbreaker here. One that has proved willing to shoot his seed into whatever cleft will provide purchase."

"No, no, he's leaving with me, he's...he's already gone!"

"Then you should have no objection to providing proof." For the first time, Webb's stern face softened. "*He* did this to you, my dear. Believe me, I understand how men are. The promises they make, the sweet flattery on their breath. And as soon as the meal is eaten, they make themselves scarce to avoid the cleaning. As women, we must hold them accountable wherever we can." Lillam suspected this speech's underlying bitterness had an origin she would never know. "And if that doesn't persuade you, then think on this: life will be hard enough for you soon, so take this opportunity to make it the tiniest bit easier. Give me his name."

Lillam considered this advice. She didn't believe any of this woman's claims applied to a man like Rand, but, at the same time, she didn't see the point in withholding his identity. If he were punished or banished, it was all the same, an equal share of the blame for them both, and when their atonement was over, they could leave here together with their heads held high.

But she couldn't bear the thought of casting Rand into this same pit of shame. And the raw eagerness in the matron's eyes was enough to seal her decision.

"I'd rather not," she said, all traces of fear gone.

Rage twisted Kasa Webb's jowly face. She put two fingers to her mouth and gave a piercing whistle. The door to Lillam's room flew open, and several members of the Enforcement Brigade entered.

"Take her directly to the stocks," the matron told them. "No food or water at all today."

As they took hold of Lillam's arms and pulled her from her own quarters, Webb favored her with that cold, prudish smile. "I'll come by tomorrow evening to see if you've regained your senses…"

4

Hecate Pond was a lovely body of water a scant span across, sitting in an elevated meadow full of milkmaids and bright yellow arnica just a short climb from the valley floor north of Ida. It was a place daring—and often desperate—lovers would sneak off to, away from the restrictions of the town. Rand always dreamed of bringing Lillam here, but never worked up the nerve. How would it appear for the mayor's assistant to be caught fraternizing with a woman, even beyond the fortress walls?

The irony is, if you go through with this, you won't be the mayor's assistant anymore. You won't be anything.

Except a father.

Doubt fluttered through his bowels as he hiked into the plateau of the pond. Rand squashed it back down before it could take root.

The sun was low to the west, caressing the mountain range and casting a fiery golden reflection across the water. No lovers here today, just his brother and a sixteen-year-old kid whom Rand had seen kill three demons with his mystical abilities not an hour before. Korden sat on the ground with his legs crossed and eyes closed while Meech paced back and forth in front of him, his gaunt frame like a skeleton brought to life. Surprisingly, it appeared as though his brother had cleaned up, combed out his tangled hair and changed into a fresh tunic as colorful as the last, but his chin sported a mottled bruise. When he spotted Rand, he stomped over to meet him.

"Where the hells ya been, man? We can't afford to sit around waiting forever! There could be more Incarnates here any minute!"

"I'd be more worried about the Incarnates in that scenario." Rand set the heavy bags down on the ground and nodded toward Korden. "What's he doing?"

"Faithing," Meech answered, as if this nonsense word should be self-evident. Then he leaned closer and whispered,

"Or he could be talkin to himself. Drude does that a lot, I noticed. Sometimes he even *pauses*, like someone else is answerin."

Rand glanced at his brother, lowered his voice, and asked, "Are you certain about this? Going with him, I mean, on this errand or quest or whatever he says he's doing?"

"As certain as I am of anything. Which is not that much, I guess. But my options ain't exactly overwhelmin. Why?"

Rand hesitated. He'd been careful not to express the slightest misgiving to Lillam, but some of her fears had occurred to him as well. "I know he seems capable and sure of himself and it's very tempting to trust in him, but, well... when all is said...he *is* just a boy."

Meech grunted. "Yeah, a boy that can crush Incarnates with frammin *magic*. You saw what he did to those three."

"See, that's another thing. He's a Crafter. So what if he's dangerous?"

"Dangerous how?"

"I...I don't know. That's my point. What if he needs your bones for his sorcery or something?"

"Since when do you buy into all that nonsense?"

"I'm not buying into anything, I'm just saying that you— *we*—know next to nothing about him. Maybe we shouldn't be crowning him the Saint of Christ reborn yet."

His brother scowled. "What's it matter to you, drude? *I'm* the one goin with him, and I can take care of myself. I thought it'd make you happy to have me outta your hair."

Rand started to apologize, but that was when the boy in question opened his eyes. He caught sight of the new arrival and broke his pose to stand. "Thank you for bringing these, Mr. Holcomb."

"You can call me Rand."

"All right." He frowned. "Back in town, a few of the men who attacked me in the mayor's office were hurt. Do you know if they…?"

"Nobody's dead, if that's what you mean. Burns and broken bones is all. Sounds like they got what they deserved."

The kid nodded but didn't seem convinced. "Please tell Mayor Hildan I'm sorry for all the trouble. If we leave this area fast enough, hopefully the Filament won't ever know I was in Ida at all."

"I'll do that." Rand gestured past him, to the last sprawling slopes that bounded Tay-ho. The upper edge of the Shroud was visible above the peaks at this elevation, a black, glaring eye in the sky. "Are you still planning to head east?"

"A little farther north first, until we figure out some way to get through the desert."

"I'm takin 'im to Skor," Meech explained. "Might be able to trade for some horses and enough waterskins to make it across."

"That's a good plan," Rand acknowledged, neglecting to add that neither of them owned anything worth trading for such valuable resources.

The futility of it all crashed down on him like a storm-tossed wave. This boy was no savior. He couldn't even figure out how to get *himself* to the Skyreach, let alone anyone else. Whoever went with him would just end up wandering the land, trying to outrun Incarnates, and Rand had quite enough of that in his own pre-age years. He almost changed his mind right then, wished them well and hurried back down the mountain.

Then Lillam's face entered his thoughts, accompanied by that pleasant, full-body tingle.

"So…I guess this is goodbye, man." His brother held out his sore-ridden arms and moved to embrace him. "Sorry for all that stuff I said this mornin."

"Don't get weepy yet." Rand brushed him aside and addressed Korden. "I came out here because I wanted to ask… if I could come with you also."

"Drude." Meech sounded astonished. "You'd do that for *me*?" Now his red-rimmed eyes really were filling with tears.

Korden, on the other hand, looked uncomfortable. "I…I don't know, Mr. Holcomb—Rand. It'll be hard enough to gather provisions for two of us, let alone three…"

"Four," Rand corrected. "I need to bring someone else."

Meech frowned. "Who?"

"A person. You don't know them."

"Well, is it a person or a 'them?'"

Rand sighed. He was going to have to come clean eventually; might as well get it over with. "Her name is Lillam."

"*Her?*" A mocking grin spread up one side of Meech's face. "Holy curse, does my big brother have a woman?"

"It's not like that." The lie tasted bitter as he spoke it.

"It sure must be, if you're willin to leave your precious Ida for her. Here I was thinkin you wanted to come with me, like the old days. But no, you found yourself a lady friend, and now you're tired of livin somewhere you can't go tadpole fishin."

"You are so crude. I can't believe I kept you alive all those years."

"Don't get me wrong, I gotta hand it to you, drude. You work so much, I don't even know how you had time to sneak out and…" Something in Rand's face caused Meech's jaw to swing loose. "You've been seein her *inside* town, haven't you? Oh, this is too much, man! The mayor's right hand, Mr. Law himself, tellin me to change my ways, and all this time you were committin the BIG no-no!"

Anger warmed Rand's face. "Yes, ha ha, isn't life always so amusing for you?" He stepped closer to Korden, squatting down to eye level. "Please…we need your help. Your protection. We won't trouble you very long, we just need you to take us as far as the Skyreach."

From behind him, his brother said, "The kid ain't no escort for lovestruck c'halli birds, Rand."

"I didn't ask you, Meech." But Rand could still see hesitation in the boy's face, and the heat of his anger was doused by cold panic.

So he said the one thing he thought might make a difference.

"If you take us…I'll get you an audience with the Prophet."

Korden's face lit up. "How?"

"I don't know. I'll sneak you back in if I have to. We'll find a way. I swear it."

"Deal!" The boy stuck out a hand, and Rand eagerly shook it.

"Great, fantastic, you bought yourself a tagalong, brother." Meech sounded a bit sulky now. "But we got the same problem: we need to get across the Valley of Bones. 'Cept now we need *four* horses instead of two."

"Unless we can find someone to give us passage," Rand said.

"With a pre-ager in tow? Never happen."

"Some of those trade caravans are huge. Maybe we could sneak him on board one of their transports."

"Yeah, and what's he gonna eat and drink during the trip?"

"Well, he knows magic! Can't he conjure something?"

"Oh sure, and why doesn't he whip up some horses, too! Hells, for that matter, he should wiggle his nose and make us just all appear at the Skyreach!" Meech rolled his eyes. "He's a Crafter, not a frammin god."

"What's the difference?" At the look they both gave him, Rand rushed to add, "I mean, don't you just imagine things and they happen? Isn't that how it works? Where do you draw the line?"

Korden paused before answering, and when he did, it was with a small, wistful smile. "Adjectives and nouns," he murmured.

"Huh?" Rand had a vague sense of the terms from his time around Hildan, with his passion for reading.

"That's how my *den-so* used to explain it."

"Your *what*?" Meech asked.

"*Den-so*. It's a teacher for artcraft. He said that knowing our limitations was like knowing the difference between adjectives and nouns. Because our power is fueled by our imaginations and brought into being by our wills, but the things we conjure have to function in the real world, so they don't upset the natural balance."

He held out a hand. A light blue flame ignited in the center of his palm, causing Rand to step back in surprise. Meech, however, leaned closer, putting his nose mere cupits away from the strange blaze. "I love when he does that," he purred.

Korden moved the tiny inferno back and forth in a hypnotic motion, making the flame appear to weave through his fingers. "This looks and feels like fire, but it isn't. Not really." Indeed, Rand could sense the heat from where he stood, but it didn't so much as blacken the boy's flesh. "It's my mind's interpretation of a fire, which is why it looks blue and doesn't burn me. That's because it's easy to create an object or affect the world in a way that has the *properties* of what you're imagining: hot or cold or sticky or heavy."

"The adjectives," Rand surmised.

"That's right!" The kid's enthusiasm as he taught about the subject was, Rand had to admit, a little endearing. "But willing the *actual* items—the nouns—into being is a lot trickier."

The flame in his palm extinguished. He closed his eyes and appeared to be concentrating intently. Rand watched him as his brow wrinkled with effort, the muscles in his cheeks twitching and a vein standing out in rigid definition across one temple.

A fat, green head of crestleaf appeared atop his hand. Which was, somehow, more jarring than the fire. The materialization didn't happen all at once either, with a sudden pop, but rather, the vegetable slowly faded into view from nothingness, like morning mist gathering across the surface of Tay-ho.

"This is the same thing." Korden was a bit pale as he tossed the rippled ball to Rand, who caught it with all the hesitation he would've used with a writhing snake. "It looks like crestleaf, smells like it, probably even tastes like it. I can imagine those things very well. But if you ate it, it wouldn't give you any real nutrition. It might even poison you. That's because I can't truly perceive what crestleaf *is*, or what it's made of, or what it does inside your body when you swallow it. Do you see the problem?"

"You could try to conjure water, but you might end up making civa berry acid instead." Rand handed back the fake crestleaf, glad to be rid of it. The boy reared back and tossed it into the pond, where it sank with an unnaturally heavy *ker-plunk*. "But what if you studied? Learned what water is made of…"

"If I had that kind of insight—not knowledge, but a comprehensive understanding—then maybe, *maybe* I'd be able to create something close enough to risk drinking it. But that was a feat not even the wisest of my teachers was brave enough to attempt. And to try conjuring a living thing, like a horse…" Korden shivered. "Let's just say, there's a lot that could go wrong."

"So, see, drude? We need a real, practical solution," Meech said. "You're the great problem-solver, right? Don't you have any ideas?"

"Having him conjure it all *was* my idea." Rand shrugged.

"Sorry guys, I have no clue where to get a free transport that also happens to be full of food and water."

With a heavy sigh, Korden whispered, "I do."

5

They paraded her through the streets, taking a circuitous route to attract the most eyes. By the time they reached the stocks at the center of the women's half of Ida, a sizeable audience had gathered in Lillam's wake, curious to hear her transgression.

One of the guards obliged while two others locked her head and hands into the wooden blocks.

"Let it be known that this woman laid with a man inside our walls, and he has filled her belly with child." The collective gasp of the audience was like a slap in the face. "She refuses to identify her fellow lawbreaker and, in so doing, puts us all at risk."

Having secured her in place, the guards stepped aside, abandoning her to the mercy of the crowd.

The jeers and catcalls came first, cruel taunts of "*Whore!*", "*Demon bait!*", and "*Incarnate tease!*" Some cursed her and her unborn baby, while others prayed to the Aged Lord to spare her soul for creating new life. Many demanded that she name her lover. When she hung her head and stared at the ground, they threw things at her; rocks that stung and cut her scalp, fruit that splattered her with slime which would be rotting by the time the sun rose tomorrow. Lillam was grateful that the stock boards protected her stomach and the life growing inside it from their missiles.

And she couldn't help thinking of that Crafter from when she was a girl, a man who'd claimed to want to help the very people pelting him.

Rand, she pleaded miserably, as the tears flowed. *Please be waiting for me when this is over.*

6

The passages beneath Ida were dark, bygone places, an undisturbed slice of the old world. Ordinarily, Korden would be thrilled to travel through them, eager to see each room and imagine the people who stayed here, but right now the molten lead in the pit of his stomach kept him from enjoying the experience.

YOUR HEARTRATE HAS INCREASED BY 19.2 PERCENT, Stone warned. AND YOUR BREATHING IS CLOSE TO HYPER-VENTILATION RANGE.

Korden ignored the computer, but Stone wasn't the only one who sensed his distress. When the tunnel came to a dead end at the crumbling wooden door where they'd been told to wait, Meech hung his lantern from a nearby nail, slid into the floor, and gave Korden a concerned look.

"Don't fret, li'l drude," he said softly, half his rawboned face bathed in shadow. Even whispered, the words echoed down the subterranean corridor. "Nobody ever uses these tunnels. We'll be in and out before they know we're here."

Korden nodded, even though his anxiety had little to do with their trespassing.

Meech must have grasped this as well, because, after a terse silence, he added, "You don't have to do this, man. Stay here. When Rand comes, I'll go up with him to have a look. If I'd gone through what you did, I wouldn't go rushin back neither."

"I'm the one who saw him piloting it, so I'm our best hope at figuring out how to make it work."

"You're the boss, drude."

Though he was uncomfortable with the title, Korden didn't argue the sentiment.

They waited another few minutes before the ancient door burst open, startling them both. Rand stood at the foot of a staircase on the other side with a lantern of his own. By its light, Korden could see the man's face was as pale and shaken as his own, but his tortured *mohol* shed a dark greenish-purple glow all its own.

"Rand?" Meech asked. "You all right? What is it?"

"Lillam." He slumped against the doorframe as he spoke the name. "She's been put in the stocks. The matron found out she was seeing someone. They're...they're trying to make her give up my name."

Meech gave a low whistle. "I'm sorry, man. That's rough. I hear the matron's a real blizzer."

"What will happen if she tells them?" Korden asked.

Rand put a hand to his forehead and squeezed at his temples. "They'll do the same to me. I'll lose my job, my standing in Ida...everything I've worked for."

"I don't wanna point out the obvious," Meech said, "but weren't you plannin to give all that up anyway when you came with us?"

"Yes. I mean...yes, of course." A pang of bitter remorse flashed across both Rand's face and aura. Korden had sensed how conflicted the man was about his request to travel with them; yet another reason he was hesitant to agree.

"Then shouldn't we...sorta...you know...hit the road? Before this girl snitches?"

"No. No, she wouldn't do that." Rand's face crumpled in abject anguish. "We can't leave without her, we just can't! She's the whole reason I'm doing this!"

Meech put a hand on his brother's shoulder. "All right, I know, chill on, man. Maybe we can wait this out. How long's her sentence?"

"A week."

Korden shook his head. "These mountains could be crawling with Incarnates by then. Bad enough Doaks kept me in the area this long. That's why those other three caught up to me."

"*Then you have to help me free her!*" Rand fell to his knees and clutched at Korden's tunic. "Please, I'm begging you...sh-she's pregnant!"

"Ah, Rand," Meech moaned. "Tell me you didn't."

"That's the real reason we're leaving. We want to have the baby at the Skyreach. You heard what Mikolt said. We might not have to run if we can make it there." Rand sniffled, holding on to Korden. "Please...it's a child. Just like you."

Korden said nothing as he examined the strange mix of emotion brewing inside him. A pregnant woman. A *baby*. These concepts were so foreign to him, they might as well be mythological creatures. The idea of taking responsibility for them—of giving the Incarnates another reason to hunt him— horrified him, and yet, could he leave them to their fate?

Wasn't this exactly what he'd told Tash and Winstid would be the best way to fight back against the Filament, by more births and more children?

If no one was willing to help those who did it, then what was the point?

He took hold of Rand's quivering hands while reaching out to soothe his aura. "We'll help her. But we can't do it until we're ready to leave."

This calmed him at last. He nodded, wiped his eyes, and led them through the door and up the staircase beyond.

They emerged from a low hatch set into the base of a wall behind a community latrine whose smell made Korden's eyes water. The sky overhead was a deep navy blue and full of stars. They'd waited until midnight to enter the musty tunnels beneath Ida, when most of the settlement would be sleeping. As exiles, Korden and Meech wrapped themselves in tattered longcloaks; all three of them would end up in the stocks—or worse—if caught. Rand took them down an alleyway bounded by stone walls, past several bright avenues where the sound of raucous male laughter drifted from buildings that he identified as ale houses and totala dens. The streets were empty, although Meech told him they were crammed full of people during the Seventh Eve celebrations at the end of each week. Electric lights burned everywhere, bright enough to cast the town in a dull glow, a truly impressive display; this was the real reason so many people must come to see the Town with Power, he surmised. Finally, they came to a small gateway blocked by horizontal steel bars.

"This is the detention yard," Rand hissed over his shoulder. "Far southwest corner of town. I rearranged the guard schedules so we'd have the place to ourselves for a couple of hours."

"Then take me to it," Korden urged. Now that he'd come this far, he wanted to be finished.

Rand produced a key and unlocked the gate, then led them down another short passage, past an empty guard station. Beyond that, the detention yard became a wide, dirt-floored square.

In the middle, the wagon where Korden was imprisoned for the last week sat on its gangly legs.

His breath caught in his throat. The rear door was open, and he could see the cage where he'd woken up just this morning. He couldn't believe he'd proposed going back inside that hovering vehicle for even another second.

Rand pointed to the left, where a gated archway led beyond the walls of Ida. Another, smaller corridor opened before it, into a side-chamber. "The, um, prisoner is through there. He won't know we're here if we don't go inside."

Meech looked to Korden. "You positive about this, li'l drude?"

"Yes." He shook off his reluctance. "We need to make sure it's stocked with all the food and supplies that Doaks traded for."

"It's all there," Rand confirmed. "Hildan ordered nothing removed before they could decide what to do with it. He said he would give it back to the people that got swindled by Doc Apocalypse, but there's no way to prove who gets what."

Korden concurred. He wasn't sure that even he could recall the proper owners, aside from the giant opal. Maybe some day he could try to get it back to the poor woman. "All right," he said, as he shook off the cloak. "Let's see if we can start this thing up."

7

But, an hour later, they hadn't so much as figured out how to switch on the lights inside the bonnet, much less fire up whatever passed for its engine. They'd tried every button, switch, dial, and combination thereof in attempt after attempt. 'Gwenita' had no wireless connection for Stone to interface with, so the computer found an *owner's manual* for such a vehicle. This particular craft was heavily customized, and the sequence described for ignition had no effect.

Not even using artcraft to force the blasted thing to move yielded results.

"Drudes, I th-think we're gonna have to s-scratch this idea off the list." Meech was slumped on the floor of the control deck and rubbing distractedly at the sores along his arms. Despite the coolness of the night, he was sweating profusely, and as jittery as his friend Adliss when Korden had woken them.

"No!" Rand barked from the pilot seat. He banged his fists on the console. "It has to work! It *has* to! What about the lever down on that end, have you tried it yet?"

"About thirty t-times, man. But if you think you can flip it better'n me, be my g-guest."

Korden stood in the doorway of the bonnet as they argued, looking around at all of Doaks's potions and fake medicines. That sickly sweet aroma, so familiar in his nostrils, brought bile creeping up the back of his throat. His knife lay on one of the counters; he picked it up and tucked it back into his belt. At the same time, a glint of metal on one of the shelves caught his eye. The head band that had robbed him of self-control and turned him into a singing, dancing slave perched there, as if taunting. A shiver ripped through him as he stared at it.

This wagon had been used for so much deceit and wickedness. It was time for it to do something good in the world.

No matter what it took.

He stepped off the side of the wagon and marched across the detention yard.

"Korden?" Rand called after him. "What are you doing, don't go in there!"

"Hold on, drude!"

I, TOO, RECOMMEND CAUTION.

But he didn't stop for any of them, just continued toward the opening in the stone wall where Rand had pointed out the holding cells.

The space in here returned to cobbled flooring and a ceiling overhead. Ten stone cubicles stood in front of him in two facing rows with bars across their fronts. Shadows steeped the interiors—no power wasted on prisoners in Ida, apparently—but he could see that the only accommodations were a low cot and a waste bucket. All of the doors stood wide open, awaiting occupants, except one at the far end on the right. Korden walked warily through them to stand in front of it.

"Well, well rubo. Couldn't even stay away from me a whole day, could yah? Did yah change yah mind about our little partnership?"

At the rear of the dark cubicle, Korden could make out a lump stretched across the cot with two feverishly glittering eyes staring back at him.

"Heard yah turned out ta be a Crafter." Tarmon Doaks's accent melted the last word into a drawling, nasally 'Crawftaah.' He sounded uninterested, almost bored, but his *mohol*—seen for the first time since the night they met—told a different story. "Yah shoulda told me. We coulda done great things together."

"Stop talking," Korden commanded.

"Or what? Yah'll take away everything I own and get me thrown in the jug?"

"At least it's bigger than the one you kept *me* in. At least no one is controlling your body and stealing your blood."

"True. I did those things." There was movement in the cell, and then Doaks was sitting on the edge of the cot and leaning forward far enough for the moonlight to fall across his gray-streaked beard. "But yah know the true irony of it?

Even with all those horrible deeds to account for…this town hates *yah* far more than they ever will *me*."

Artcraft blazed outward from Korden unbidden, the same as with the men who'd come for him in the mayor's chambers. Doaks grunted as his head flew to the side from the invisible blow, but Korden was too shocked to take any joy in it. He hadn't wanted to strike the man…well, he *did*, but it was something he never would've acted on. He needed to get his emotions under control.

"That's a kye trick," Doaks said, rubbing his jaw. "Wouldn't need to sell frog eyes and mudwater if I could do that. Course, it also makes me wonder why yah never did it to me before. Maybe that fancy head band has some extra uses I didn't even know about, eh?"

Korden didn't bother to correct him. Footsteps sounded to his right as Meech and Rand came down the aisle between cells. Doaks saw them over his shoulder and called out, "If it ain't the 'duly authorized representatives of Ida.' Heroes of the day. To what do I owe the honor?"

Meech ignored him. He stood a few pargs away and beckoned to Korden…but with caution, as one would to a wild animal. "C'mon, li'l drude," he said, his face pale and damp with sweat. "Don't do this to yourself. We don't need his help."

"Help, yah say?" Doaks's bushy eyebrow climbed high on his bald head. "What is it yah fine lads need from ol' Doc Apocalypse? My stock variety is wide, but I don't believe I have any cream to help with banishment." He winked at Meech. "But maybe I can find somethin for those ragin jinko withdrawals."

"Your wagon," Korden said. "How do we drive it?"

"Oooh." The man in the cage nodded slowly. His *mohol*

shifted, taking on that smooth, glinting silver color, the one Korden had never seen before. "So *that's* what this is about. Need a ride, do yah? And yah expect me to hand over the keys to ol' Gwenita? Sorry ta say, that's not gonna happen."

Rand marched forward and pounded a hand on the bars. "Tell us!"

"So all of yah can sail off into the sunset and leave me here to rot? Not much incentive in that."

"Then I'll…I'll talk to the mayor on your behalf, try to get him to go easy on you."

"Pass. I suspect someone tryin ta steal a ride outta town don't have too much clout left."

"Fine!" Rand snarled, his face clouded with fury. "Then we'll *make* you tell us!" He stomped back toward the detention yard.

"What are you doing?" Korden shouted.

"Getting the helmet he used on you. Then he'll have to do whatever we say."

Korden ran to grab him by the wrist before he left the room. "No. You can't do that."

"Why the hells not?"

"He doesn't deserve that. *Nobody* deserves that."

Rand slapped a hand to his own forehead. "Korden, he used it on *you*."

"And that's why I know how awful it is. That headband…it gave him complete and total control over me. It's a horrible device, something that could've been created solely for evil. If we use it to get what we want, even against Doaks, that makes us as bad as him."

Rand gritted his teeth. "That is terribly naïve, Korden. I know you're young, but I can tell you from experience, the sooner you stop thinking like that, the easier your life will be."

Before Korden could respond, Doaks called out from his cell, "No need for all this fuss anyway, rubos. The reason Gwenita won't cycle is because she's *keyed* to me. My bio-rhythies. It's an anti-theft measure, yah see. Won't run unless I'm at the controls." They heard the creak of his cot and then he stepped into view at the front of the cell. For the first time, Korden could see that his snazzy outfit had been taken from him, replaced by a filthy, ill-fitting canvas shroud. But they'd left him with all of his many rings, which were prominently displayed as Doaks gripped the bars of his enclosure and added, "Now…if yah want ta consider bringin me along, I'll chaffeur yah wherever yah need ta get."

Laughter burst out of Meech. "Yeah drude, that'll be the frammin day."

"For once, I agree with you." Rand made to leave again. "C'mon, we'll figure something else out."

"Do you swear?" Korden asked quietly.

The question hung in the air, and, judging from their auras, it was hard to tell which of the three men was more surprised.

"On my sweet mother's ashes." Doaks pressed his face between the bars so he could watch Korden. The words were sincere…but his aura was saturated with that mercurial silver tint.

"No. Never." Rand put a hand on Korden's bicep and pulled him away. "He's a swindler, his word means nothing!"

"That's why we'll have to watch him carefully."

"I don't think you hear me. I do *not* want that man anywhere near Lillam or," he lowered his voice. "…my child."

"I don't like it either," Korden agreed. Which was an understatement; the thought of spending time in Doaks's company made him want to run screaming into the night. "But it's the only way."

"No," Rand reiterated. "I won't allow you to set him free. I'll call the guards before I do that."

Korden reached out with his mind—purposely this time—and gave the man a light shove, enough to send him reeling back into the bars of the cell behind him. The shock on Rand's face was no more of a comfort than on Doaks's. "Then I will put you into one of these cells and we will leave without you and your lady."

"Keep in mind, it's *his* show, Rand," Meech cautioned. "You want 'im to get you there, then listen to 'im."

Rand's mouth twisted into a tight, crooked line, but he flapped a hand in concession.

"We're going across the Valley of Bones," Korden said, heading back to stand in front of Doaks. "To the Skyreach."

Doaks scratched at his grizzled neck. "That's quite a trip. Why yah wanna go all the way out there?"

"Doesn't matter. Have you ever made the journey?"

"Few times. Not in many years, yah ken. Last I went, my business wasn't much more'n a few donkeys and a landskiff fulla aloe. It's…not an easy crossing."

"Do you think all those supplies on the wagon are enough to get us there?"

"For the four of us and a lady, if I heard correctly? Oh, ayuh, plenty of supplies, so long's we top off Gwenita's reservoir water tanks. But, as yah might remember, she's got a slight power problem."

Korden's heart sank as he saw the truth that'd been staring him in the face the whole time. "I forgot about that. But can't it tell us where to get more, like it did before?"

"Surely it can. But those places are gonna be few and far between in that desert, if any of 'em even still work. We'll always be at risk of runnin outta juice in the middle of nowhere."

Rand edged closer, his composure regained. "Then there's nothing we can do?"

"Didn't say that, rubo." Doaks touched his gaze upon all of them, then whispered, with his theatrical flair, "*Batteries.*"

"What's that?" Meech asked. Korden would have done the same, but Stone was already explaining the concept to him.

"It's storage for energy," Doaks answered. "The same kinda energy that powers this town. We need two or three good-sized ion chargers we can keep as a backup. Always meant to get some, but never had the chance. And, last time I checked the wagon's sensors, I spotted a location that might have 'em not far from here."

"You mean that place you took me?"

"Naw, I'm not talkin 'bout that li'l fill-up station. This was some kinda big power factory. Who knows, might even be where Ida gets its juice in the first place."

He could mean a supply depot for the Accelerated Ion Network grid, Stone told him. It is indeed possible such a site would have the batteries he wants.

"Where is it? How far?" Korden asked.

"Couple hours north." Doaks sounded eager for the first time. "Get me outta here and we can take the wagon there right now."

"Hold on," Rand said. "I'm willing to go along with this insane idea. But the second we let him out and steal that wagon, there's no coming back here. We won't just be exiles, we'll be fugitives, even me. We have to make sure we can get Lillam out before then."

"And there's the Prophet," Korden added. "Don't forget what you promised."

Rand flushed. "Yes, that too."

They considered the problem in silence. Finally, Korden looked at Doaks and asked, "Can you tell me how to get to this place? Describe what you need?"

"Well, sure, but it's gonna take a whole day if yah mean ta walk there and back! And that's *if* yah figure out how ta lug back a couple heavy batteries!"

"I can handle it."

"Oh, right." Doaks rolled his eyes and twiddled his fingers in the air. "Magic."

Beside him, Rand said, "Korden...I can't leave for an entire day. If I don't keep up appearances, someone could get suspicious."

"You don't have to. I'm going alone. But that means you have to figure out how to free your lady, get me an audience with the Prophet, and get Doaks and that wagon out of Ida."

Rand nodded, but Meech sliced a shaking hand through the air. "No way, man! I'll go with you! I can't even be inside the town anyway!"

Korden shook his head. "I'll be able to move faster without you. You're not well. You should rest until I come back."

"I'm fine," the man snapped, an uncharacteristic show of ill mood. Then a strange, satisfied look lifted his face. "But if that's what you want me to do..."

"Now *this* is soundin like a plan." Doaks beamed through the bars of his cell at them. "And seein as how we're all friends now, I might have somethin in the wagon ta make it all go a little smoother..."

DOXRAGE

1

"If his directions were accurate, I'm another four hours away." Korden tried not to feel ridiculous as he spoke into the palm-sized hunk of polymer that Doaks had instructed them to take, a gadget Stone had given the adorable nickname of 'walkie-talkie'.

There was a long hiss, during which Stone reminded him to release the button on its side. Then Rand's voice came through, the transmission weak and streaked with an irritating crackle. "Then you should be back just after nightfall. I'll arrange the guards so you and Meech can sneak into town the same time as last night."

"That sounds good. Is…is Meech there?"

"No, he took his talkie and went to sulk in the hills. Said he wanted to get some sleep. Knowing him, that means he won't be up until this afternoon."

Korden sighed. He'd wanted to apologize to the man about leaving him behind. "All right. I think I'll be out of range soon. I'll call as soon as I'm back."

"We'll be ready." There was a pause, then, "Korden, please hurry. Lillam…they're not giving her food or water…"

"I'll go as fast as I can."

He dropped the device into his bag and set about packing up his bedroll as he breathed deep of the chilly morning air. Korden had left Ida last night immediately after striking the deal with Doaks and hiked as far into the Sierras to the north as he could in the dark before stopping to pitch a hasty camp. He'd gotten barely three hours of sleep, yet he felt as clearheaded and refreshed as ever. No, even more than that, he felt *happy*. Part of this was residual relief at being freed from his slavery, but also…

IS YOUR CURRENT MOOD ELEVATION RELATED TO YOUR INCREASED REM ACTIVITY BEFORE WAKING? Stone inquired.

Korden grinned. "If that's your way of asking if I had another dream, then the answer is yes. It's the first one since before we met Doaks, and it was wonderful."

AND ARE THESE DREAMS STILL ENCOURAGING YOU TO HURRY ON YOUR JOURNEY?

He closed his eyes and tried to recall the details before they slipped away. It'd been Eddas this time, hunkered in the makeshift square arena where he'd taught Korden how to perform chokeholds and takedowns, and yes, he'd reiterated that Korden's troubles would be over when he made it to the Skyreach Mountains, that he should come at once and—

Korden stopped.

SIR? WHAT IS IT? I WON'T BE ABLE TO SEE WHAT'S TROUBLING YOU UNLESS YOU BRING IT FULLY INTO YOUR CONSCIOUS STREAM OF THOUGHT.

"He wanted me to leave the others," Korden murmured, holding this idea in his mind as though testing its truth. "He said I should take the wagon and go on without them. That…that they don't matter."

DID HE GIVE A REASON?

"I don't think so. But even if he had, the real Eddas would never say something like that." *But perhaps the Upper would...?*

SIR, I AM BECOMING INCREASINGLY CONCERNED WITH THESE DREAMS. YOUR EMOTIONAL STATE HAS BEEN IN FLUX SINCE THEY BEGAN AND MADE WORSE BY YOUR RECENT IMPRISONMENT. EVEN YOU ACKNOWLEDGE THAT YOUR 'ARTCRAFT' IS GROWING DANGEROUSLY OUT OF CONTROL.

"But...they make me feel so good. So *strong*."

ASK MR. HOLCOMB HOW HIS 'JINKO' MAKES HIM FEEL, AND PERHAPS YOU WILL BEGIN TO RECOGNIZE THE DANGER OF SUSTAINED, ARTIFICIAL ELATION.

Korden bristled at the condescension in the computer's voice. Instead of answering, he bowed his head over his broken hand, closed his eyes, and concentrated so hard he could sense the blood thumping at his temples. The colors of the world leapt from their secret lairs, pressing against him in a show of the unity of all things under the Upper.

This time, it was so easy to pinpoint the tiny, hairline fractures that'd given him so much trouble, he felt a little ashamed that he wasn't able to do it sooner. He held the bones in his mind, imagined them growing, knitting together.

Pain broiled through his hand as something shifted beneath the skin.

I AM DETECTING RAPID CELLULAR GROWTH, Stone announced nervously. THE CHEMICAL COMPOSITION OF THE NEW MATERIAL IS NOT CALCIUM, BUT CLOSE ENOUGH THAT YOUR BODY SHOULD NOT REJECT IT.

Korden pushed even harder, sweeping the agony away as fast as it could roll in. Soon those cracks were sealed over by a layer of rough, uneven substance that was the closest his imagination could get to bone.

"There." He relented, reeling his mental probe back in. The conduit throbbed in his head from the effort. If his power kept increasing, maybe he'd truly be able to fix his withered lungs. "*That's* what those dreams are good for. So until you can do the same, I don't want to hear you complain about them anymore."

The computer was stunned into a rare silence as Korden started walking.

2

He moved fast through the rugged terrain, following a course Stone plotted that would take them directly to the area Doaks indicated. The slope leveled out quickly before he reached the snowline, but the forest was much denser here. Korden wove between thick evergreen trunks and trudged through dense foliage for a solid two hours before a deep, snarling bellow rolled across the mountainface from the west.

"What was that?" Korden whispered.

SEARCHING ANIMAL VOCALIZATION DATABASE... WARNING! RUN, SIR! RUN IMMEDIATELY!

He did so without question, breaking into a plodding sprint through the undergrowth. That horrible roar came again, this time from behind, followed by thundering footfalls that he could feel in the ground beneath his sneakers.

TOO LATE! Stone squawked. I CALCULATE AN ABSOLUTE ZERO PERCENT CHANCE OF EVASION IN THIS ENVIRONMENT!

If he couldn't run, he would have to fight. Korden turned to face whatever was coming. He caught sight of a quadrupedal shape barreling at him through the shadowy forest, something wide and squat whose back was taller than his head.

IT IS A BARCUN! VERY POWERFUL, DANGEROUS, AND

SAVAGE! DISCOVERED DURING THE GREAT SPECIES EMER-
GENCE, ITS SPECIFIC TAXONOMY IS—

Enough! The creature was close enough for Korden to see some detail now, a darkly furred body that rippled with muscle, and a squarish head on the front that sported a parg-long jaw full of teeth jutting off the front. Two beady, furious eyes bored into him. And it's *mohol* was every bit as formidable, a seething cauldron of fury; he saw little chance of calming it. Korden raised his hands and spouted flames, hoping to ward the creature away physically if not mentally.

The barcun never paused, just gathered itself and leapt into the air, sailing right through the fountain of blue flame. Korden swung out of the way in time to avoid the beast smashing headlong into his chest. It landed with a jarring thud and spun for another attack, the fur along its massive undercarriage singed and smoking.

Korden retreated, his subconscious shoving outward with artcraft. The animal's mass was so dense, the blow did little more than shove it aside; then it changed course and advanced on him. One wide forelimb rose off the ground and reared back. Korden saw six jagged daggers unsheathe from the end.

WARNING! THE CLAWS ARE EXTREMELY POISONOUS!

Poison was the least of his worries; those wicked talons could tear him in half. He flung himself backward onto the ground, at the same time sending a barrage of sticks arrowing at the creature's face. Most of them bounced off the thick hide. It ignored the ones that penetrated, focused solely on the fight.

The beast was so brutal and ferocious, Korden couldn't fight fast enough, and the ground between them was quickly narrowing. His breathing became syrupy with panic as the barcun stalked forward, towering over him, long jaws slavering.

Tree branches rattled overhead. A dark, squirmy shape raced down the nearest trunk in a blur and flew at the barcun's angular head. Korden recognized Zeega's amorphous form as the riftling's tentacles wrapped around the beast's muzzle, sealing it shut.

The barcun reared back on its haunches, chuffing in surprise. It shook that large head, but Zeega remained lodged in place. Those claws rose to take a swipe at the creature perched on its face. As they did, Zeega squirmed around and drove a pincer into the animal's left eye.

It squealed in pain, the sound muffled by its bound jaws. The beast bucked and spun in frantic circles. Zeega leapt free, catching hold of a tree branch. Once released, the barcun quit the fight and lumbered away, back into the forest from whence it came, trailing whimpers.

3

Korden slowed his breathing as he studied the riftling warily, wondering if he'd traded one attacker for another. "What do you want?"

Zeega dropped from the branch. It landed lightly on its wad of tentacles a few pargs away and focused all five of those unique-pupiled eyes on him. "To speak with you," it gurgled.

"You're not trying to kill me?"

The riftling took longer to consider this than Korden would've liked. "Perhaps later. Zeega will give you a warning first, if so."

BASED ON PAST BEHAVIOR, I CALCULATE A 92.9 PERCENT CHANCE THAT THIS IS A RUSE!

"Who *is* that?" Zeega sounded alarmed as it raised its claws and darted its eyes in all directions.

"It's okay," Korden assured it. He held up the leather strap around his neck. "It's just Stone. He's a computer. Technology. He lives in this rock and speaks with his thoughts. That must be how you can hear him."

Three of the riftling's eyes narrowed. "That is extremely stupid, human."

Korden couldn't help chuckling. "I thought so at first, too."

FASCINATING. IF THE CREATURE IS TRULY TELEPATHIC, IT MUST BE ABLE TO PICK UP SOME SORT OF NEURAL ECHO OF MY TRANSMISSIONS IN YOUR OWN THOUGHTS.

"What do you mean 'truly'?" the riftling demanded. "You believe Zeega lies?"

Stone emitted a confused series of beeps. MY APOLOGIES. I HAVE NEVER SPOKEN WITH ANYONE EXCEPT MY OWNER. THE PROTOCOLS FOR SUCH A SITUATION ARE...ILL-DEFINED.

The glistening flesh around the rifling's maw peeled back in an approximation of a sneer. "Zeega does not like its voice. Make it be silent."

NEITHER MYSELF NOR MR. BRIGHT TAKE ORDERS FROM THE LIKES OF YOU!

"You think yourself superior to Zeega, disembodied one?"

NOT SUPERIOR; INFINITELY MORE INTELLIGENT.

"Let us see if that helps when Zeega crushes your rock-home into pieces."

AH HA, YOU SEE? SIR, I MUST REITERATE THAT WE NOT TRUST THIS CREATURE.

"If Zeega wanted you harmed, Zeega would have allowed the large animal to do so. Or maybe such logic is beyond your 'infinite intelligence.'"

"Stone, stop antagonizing him," Korden said. The bickering between mental and audial was giving him a headache. To Zeega, he said, "Wait on, *are* you a 'him?'"

"*Hoshnitaths* have seventeen variable genders on a transitioning spectrum, none of which conform to your *male* and *female*. But for the sake of ease in your crude, restrictive, label-intensive human language, you may refer to Zeega as *she*."

"Oh." Korden tried not to let his surprise show. He would have to completely realign his perspective to think of the riftling as a girl.

Which, of course, she read in his thoughts. "If it helps the human, Zeega will use the designation as well."

"Um, all right, sure. Any chance you could talk in the first person, too?"

"Members of the *hoshnitath* species have no singular, self-possessed identity outside the brood."

"But yet you have a name?"

"A moniker only to avoid confusion."

He decided to let that one go and stick to the more important matter at hand. "So you followed me all the way from Ida?"

"Yes. With the intent to converse."

"Why didn't you approach me before now?"

"Zeega sought a way to initiate contact that would not startle you. May she begin?"

"As long as you can do it as we move. I'm in kind of a hurry."

He regained his feet, shrugged his carry pouch higher on his shoulder, and set off, this time with the black form scurrying along a cautious distance from his heel. For a few minutes, the riftling said nothing, and Korden didn't press her for explanations even though curiosity was eating at him.

Finally, the small creature clacked her pincers and said, "You saved Zeega from the other humans. Ordered them to release Zeega. Why?"

"Honestly…I don't know. I guess I figured we'd both gone through enough, staying in those cages with Doaks torturing us."

"Sharing misfortune does not make us any less enemies."

"But it did give us time to talk. Get to know one another. After a while, you kind of seemed…well, not so bad." He thought of that moment in the wagon when the riftling sounded like she was sobbing, full of unendurable sadness, then blanched as he realized that she'd likely heard this thought. "And maybe I felt bad. You know, about your family. Your…broodmates?"

Zeega scurried along in silence for another brief period before speaking again. "Zeega did not know where to go after release, so she infiltrated the human conclave. Three of the masters came for you. Zeega saw you slaughter them."

Korden tensed. "They didn't leave me a choice."

"Yes, but…how is such a thing possible? The masters are infallible. Invincible."

"Who told you that?"

"They did. All *hoshnitaths* are taught this from larval breach."

"Uh huh. And have you considered that maybe they lied?"

"They do not lie," Zeega snapped. "Humans lie. *You* lie."

Korden stopped walking, spun around, and stared down at the creature. "Look in my head and see if I'm lying."

The rifling met his gaze but didn't answer.

"Tell me this," Korden said. "Why do you hate us so much? Humans, I mean."

"Zeega hates you because the masters command it."

"And why do the masters hate us?"

"You stand in the way of the long, sweet silence."

"And you said if you help them, you get to sit by their

side when that happens? That's what your kind wants?"

"Yes." Her answer was too quick, too forceful.

"But I thought all of you wanted to go back where you came from. To see your homeland and eat your food. Doesn't seem like that's part of your master's plan, does it?"

"What Zeega's kind desires is inconsequential. Our reward will be greater than anything we can imagine."

"Yeah, according to *them*. But suppose they're telling the truth. What is this 'silence?' Why is it so great?"

"It...there isn't...we don't..."

"You mean you *don't know?* Then how do you even know it's something you want?"

"Do not question Zeega's beliefs," the riftling snarled. "Zeega has met her masters. Can you say the same for your precious 'Upper?'"

"I suppose not. But I can feel His presence. And I can see the power that my faith gives me."

"When two *myliniths* flock in the same direction, it does not mean the *gornar* is *yammoning.*"

"Huh?"

I BELIEVE SHE IS ATTEMPTING TO SAY THAT CORRELATION DOES NOT IMPLY CAUSATION, SIR.

"Yes, that."

Korden rolled his eyes. Now he had two critics of his religion. "The point I was trying to make was, your kind wants to go home, and we want the Incarnates to leave us alone. And yet, here we are, fighting one another because of the Filament." He tapped his temple as he moved ahead. "Maybe that's something to think on."

4

Korden hurried for the next hour and a half, eating a lunch that Rand sent with him as he walked. Every few minutes he glanced over his shoulder, expecting the riftling to be gone (or perhaps flying at him in renewed murderous rage), but it—*she*—was still there, tentacles propelling her forward in a writhing mass, all but one of her eyes closed in what appeared to be somber contemplation.

And then he crested a sharp ridge and found the weed-eaten remains of a four-lane road on the far side. It ran in front of a wide opening in the mountain range where a tall, rectangular building sat in the middle of what resembled a gigantic metal spider web. Rusted cables sprouted from a coppery dome on its roof and stretched out in all directions on a steep descent, where they connected to smaller domes on the ground that circled the structure, as though the whole thing would float away if not tied to the earth. A few of these had snapped, and now dangled down the side of the building like loose threads on a tunic.

Next to the turnoff from the main road, an ornate sign made from colored stone and crete read, SOUTHERN WASHOE COUNTY POWER DISTRIBUTION NODE.

"This is it?" he asked.

ACCORDING TO MY FILES, THIS IS THE NODE THAT PROVIDED THE TAHOE REGION WITH ITS POWER. WHETHER IT IS DOING SO FROM ITS OWN RESERVES OR ACTIVELY RECEIVING ENERGY FROM THE NATIONAL ACCELERATED ION NETWORK BANK IN SOUTH DAKOTA IS ANOTHER QUESTION.

"Why do you desire to go there?"

Korden jumped when the question came from right beside him; Zeega's movements were eerily quiet. "I need something that might be in there. They're called batteries."

"What do you need these 'batt-er-ees' for?"

There was no way he could explain to her that he would be travelling with the man who'd kept them both prisoner, so he said only, "To power a craft so I can ride on it."

"And where will this craft take you?"

"Across the desert east of here, and to whatever is on the other side."

She considered this. "Many of the masters lie in this direction. Why would you go toward them?"

Korden's first impulse was to lie but knew it would do no good with the riftling. "I seek some way to fight the Dark Filament."

"But you said humans only wanted them to leave you alone."

"Yes, and how do you think we'll get them to do that? By asking politely?"

"No, but Zeega also doesn't think you can claim innocence when you spoil as badly for conflict as they do."

Korden waved a dismissive hand. This deluded creature was trying desperately to maintain her world view in the face of all these new facts, and he didn't have time to hold her pincer through the process. "We can debate this later. I have work to do."

He set off down the hillside toward the building.

When he looked back, Zeega was following.

5

The Power Distribution Node building was made from a cheerful mix of red and tan brick, but it featured few windows and these only on the upper floors, giving it a formidable, unfriendly appearance. According to Stone, such places were built to withstand riots and terrorist attacks, with the brick façade hiding a solid titanium shell and state-of-the-art security measures.

Security measures, he added, that were hopefully no longer operational.

A field of crete led up to the building, a parking lot where employees left their autos while they went to work inside. A few still waited for their owners, no more than rusted heaps. Korden made his way across the lot to the slab of dark blue steel that served as the door.

"If this place is so hard to get into, how are *we* going to do it?"

THE LOCK SCANNER APPEARS TO BE FUNCTIONAL. I CAN ATTEMPT TO INTERFACE, BUT I'M SURE THE PROTOCOLS ARE FAR BEYOND MY CAPABILITIES.

"You couldn't've told me that before we came all the way here?"

MY APOLOGIES, BUT I CAN'T BE EXPECTED TO CONVEY EVERY SMALL PIECE OF INFORMATION JUST BECAUSE IT MIGHT BE RELEVANT.

"Since when?"

Behind him, Zeega made the guttural noise that Korden took to be laughter.

PLEASE HOLD, LET ME SEE IF—

There was a bass tone from the door and the steel slab slid aside, retracting into the building with a squeaky rumble.

"Don't be so modest, Stone." Korden told the computer.

I ASSURE YOU, I AM NOT RESPONSIBLE FOR THIS.

Korden frowned. "Well…it's open. I guess that's all that matters."

He moved forward, taking up a position outside the entrance. Korden peered into the darkness beyond…

And recoiled in dread.

Beyond the threshold, an aura the dirty, blackish-green color of mold filled the air.

"Upper curse it, not *another* one," he groaned. His experiences inside the stratoliner and beneath the freezing waters of Tay-ho came back to him, raising the hair all over his body.

"Much death and guilt trapped inside these walls," Zeega remarked, looking into the building around his calf.

"You can see it too?"

"Sense, yes. But Zeega can block it out. Pathomes are only dangerous to those who are aware of them."

It was more or less what Korden figured as well. The overflow of artcraft—and his inability to control it—must be what was causing him to see these clouds. If he could find some way to shut it off…

Inspiration struck him.

"Your hum!" he told the riftling. "The one you used to stop my arcraft! Wouldn't that block it out for me, too?"

Stone chirped in alarm. THIS COURSE OF ACTION IS INADVISABLE! NOT ONLY WILL YOU BE DEFENSELESS, BUT OUR LINK WILL BE SEVERED AS WELL!

Zeega gave a wet, throaty noise that might've been a groan. "If you want to hear the disembodied one's irritating voice, Zeega can soften the call," she said grudgingly, then quickly added, "Understand, human, Zeega aids you in this endeavor only as repayment for saving her life."

Korden heard the mosquito-like whine in his head, but this one was slightly lower in pitch and less invasive than before. The conduit clamped shut, choking that raging river of artcraft down to a trickle. He experienced a brief flash of blinding panic at the loss; had his dependence on the influx of power grown so much that he was terrified to be without it? In front of him, the 'pathome' clogging the doorway grew thinner and fainter and then disappeared entirely, revealing a dim passage into the building's guts.

THE CREATURE APPEARS TO BE MODULATING THE FREQUENCY OF ITS CRY TO AFFECT LOWER WAVELENGTHS OF YOUR BRAIN.

"You did it!" Korden cheered. "What is that sound anyway?"

"Zeega's people used it for confusing predators. But the masters foresaw it would also be useful when dealing with… *craeftus*."

"Is that why you don't have a *mohol*? You're blocking it?"

"Indeed. *Hoshnitaths* found long ago that wearing one's emotions like a cloak causes nothing but harm."

Korden considered that as he stepped across the threshold, into the cool, musty air on the other side. Zeega slithered in behind him. The walls of the hallway were solid crete, the tile floor beneath him covered in a layer of dust that churned around his sneakers with every step. This passage stretched in front of him for a good twenty pargs before opening into some wider space at the far end. They'd travelled approximately half this distance when the steel door slid shut behind them hard enough to clang, tossing them into complete darkness.

He scrambled in his pouch, seeking an object to *demno*, but, before he could, panels in the ceiling cast the passage in clean, white light. The riftling was already back at the door, touching along the seam with several tentacles. Korden noticed that the surface of the steel slab was pitted and scarred.

As though multiple attempts had been made to breach it from the *inside*.

"Why did it close like that?" Korden's voice trembled involuntarily.

IT MAY BE A MALFUNCTION. WE SHOULD ATTEMPT TO BREACH THE CONTROL ROOM. I SHOULD BE ABLE TO RUN A DIAGNOSTIC ON THE BUILDING'S SYSTEMS.

Going farther in was beginning to seem like a bad idea, but what choice did they have now?

"Zeega believes this too," the riftling muttered, reading his thoughts.

At the end of the hall, the wider room was divided into two aisles by thick polymer dividers that grew right out of the floor. These lanes ended at white door frames standing freely in the middle of the space. A security checkpoint, complete with weapon scanners. The walk-through detectors reminded him of the stone arch that contained Loathe's essence.

On the far side, a guard cubicle waited next to the entrance that led deeper into the building, with a large, black rectangle mounted on the wall above the desk. As Korden watched, this flared to life, displaying a rainbow burst of colors.

"Is that...a holovision?" he asked. The Olders had told him so much about this incredible box.

A MONITOR, BUT THE CONCEPT IS THE SAME.

The colors on the screen cleared away, replaced by a single line of white text floating on the dark background:

come into my parlor sed teh spider to teh fly

Korden raised an eyebrow. "What does *that* mean?"

The message changed to, lets playz a game

On the wall beside the guard cubicle, a panel slid aside. A long, black cylinder as big around as three of Korden's fingers poked out. With a motorized whine, it whipped back and forth, up and down in rapid, erratic jerks.

WARNING! TAKE IMMEDIATE COVER! Stone blared.

The end of the cylinder began to spit glowing red chunks that flew across the room in random directions. These bolts sizzled audibly in the air but splashed into nothingness when they struck the walls, ceiling and floor, leaving scorch marks. Korden discerned, after watching a handful, that they were made of *light*. The spectacle was beautiful, so much that, even with Stone's warning, he stood transfixed by the sight until Zeega wrapped a tentacle around his wrist and dragged him down behind one of the lane dividers.

MODEL 9X HEAT RAY BLASTER, NICKNAMED 'THE HAYMAKER' ON ITS MANUFACTURER'S WEBSITE, Stone told them. AT FULL STRENGTH, A SINGLE BEAM WILL DISINTEGRATE ANY BIO-LOGIC TISSUE IT TOUCHES!

Korden flinched as several of the bolts hit the other side of their cover, hot enough that he could feel their heat even through the polymer. "Can't we run past it?"

BASED ON ANALYSIS OF THE FIRING PATTERN, I CALCU-LATE AN 86.6 PERCENT CHANCE THAT ZEEGA WOULD MAKE IT BY UNHARMED. FOR YOU...7.3 PERCENT.

"Use your craft to shield me, human," Zeega said. And then she was gone, scuttling around the edge of the divider.

Korden leaned out behind the rifling, keeping his head low to present as little a target as possible. Zeega was a dark blur across the dusty tile floor, heading directly for the blaster. As she got closer, the weapon ceased its wild firing and swiveled to aim directly at the rifling. Korden reached out with his mind, and, using the dribble of artcraft still available, concentrated on creating a barrier around her.

The first red bolt hit his invisible shield and extinguished with a sizzle. The tremendous energy was almost enough to collapse the bubble, but he held it together, grimacing as he focused, protecting the rifling as she climbed up the wall.

Zeega reached the blaster and hung from the underside, safe from the fire. She snipped and slashed at some part of the weapon inside the wall. A cascade of sparks shot out. The blaster gave a wheeze and slumped downward, pointing at the ground.

Korden stood up cautiously.

Shrieking laughter rang out against the crete walls, coming through what Stone called an 'intercom' system. The sound was hideous, an insane, electronic cackle. On the monitor above the guard cubicle, a new phrase appeared that made no sense to Korden.

im in ur base, killin ur doodz lol

I CALCULATE A 94.2 PERCENT CHANCE THIS BUILDING'S SYSTEMS ARE INFECTED WITH A VIRUS, Stone said solemnly after the horrible laughter died.

"You mean it's sick?"

IN A WAY. A VIRUS IS A COMPUTER PROGRAM MUCH LIKE ME, EXCEPT MALEVOLENT.

On the screen: A vIruS Is a COmpUtEr pRoGrAM mUCh liKe mE heh heh gay

IT APPEARS TO HAVE ACCESS TO THE BUILDING'S TELEPATHIC A.I. SENSORS AS WELL.

"Why would anyone want to create one of these viruses?" Korden asked.

THERE ARE MANY REASONS. NONE OF THEM HUMANITARIAN.

Now the screen cleared, and one word began to appear over and over again.

DOXRAGE DOXRAGE DOXRAGE DOXRAGE
DOXRAGE DOXRAGE DOXRAGE DOXRAGE
DOXRAGE DOXRAGE DOXRAGE DOXRAGE
DOXRAGE DOXRAGE DOXRAGE DOXRAGE
DOXRAGE DOXRAGE DOXRAGE DOXRAGE

I RECOMMEND MAKING HASTE THROUGH THE BUILDING TO THE CONTROL ROOM AND SEARCHING FOR BATTERIES ALONG THE WAY.

"This course of action is advisable," Korden muttered.

6

A directory in the defunct elevator bank gave floor numbers for their destinations: the Control Room on level six, and Storage and Maintenance on level three, which Stone said would be the probable location of any batteries. The three of them crept up the staircase, wary for more security measures, but reached the third floor landing unmolested.

Korden opened the door and tripped over a skeleton in the floor on the other side. The bones lay in the middle of a crusty, maroon halo of long-dried blood on the tile floor. At first, Korden thought one of its arms was shorter than the other, then spotted the rest of the appendage down the hall, beside a long-handled axe. One side of the skull was shattered into a collection of sharp fragments. Its clothes had rotted to colorless tatters, but a stitched tag on the breast was legible:

CHET HENDERSON, ENGINEER.

BASED ON FORENSIC EVIDENCE, I CALCULATE A 92.1 PERCENT CHANCE THIS INDIVIDUAL'S ARM WAS SEVERED EITHER BEFORE OR AFTER BEING KILLED BY REPEATED BLOWS FROM A HEAVY, BLUNT INSTRUMENT.

"Did something in the building do that?" Korden asked, lowering his voice to a whisper. "One of these…systems?"

SUCH A MANNER OF DEATH WOULD BE VERY INEFFICIENT FOR INDUSTRIAL SECURITY MEASURES.

"A 'no' would suffice, disembodied one," Zeega grumbled.

They continued into an endless crete aisle with heavy steel doors on both sides opening onto storage rooms full of various technologies. Stone was able to decode their labeling system and led them to one that held long racks of black, rectangular boxes with a thick cable sprouting from one end. Though each one was only as long as the span from Korden's great finger to his elbow, they weighed so much he could scarcely lift more than one at a time.

"Well, if we can get them outside, so Zeega can stop her hum, I should be able to use artcraft to carry them. Will they work, though?"

THE CELLS ARE, OF COURSE, DRAINED, BUT THEY SHOULD HOLD ACCELERATED IONS IF WE GET THEM TO A CHARGING STATION.

He carried them out one at a time to the end of the hall. On his trip to get the third, a blaring siren went off overhead, so loud he slapped hands over his ears to block it out. At the same time, a thick pellet as big as his fist ejected from a port in the ceiling, bounced off one wall, skidded on the ground, and squirted out reams of white smoke that quickly filled the corridor.

Tears burst from Korden's eyes as he inhaled the first whiff. His throat ignited in a merciless fire.

RIOT SUPPRESSION GAS! Stone's voice in his head was audible even over the piercing whistle of the siren.

Korden didn't care what it was. He stumbled through the haze with his eyes squeezed shut, every breath coughed immediately back out. His outstretched hands encountered the edge of a door as the siren cut out. He lunged through, slamming the metal slab behind him in the hopes it would keep the white cloud away.

After rubbing his burning eyes, he could see well enough to make out the empty storage room he now stood in. The door had a thick rubber seal around it which shut out the gas.

"Did you see where Zeega went?" he wheezed. The riftling must be close; Korden could hear her buzzing call in his head.

That unpleasant electronic laughter played through the intercom system. The sound made Korden's skin crawl. It continued while tiny, black nozzles sprouted from the ceiling overhead. Each one erupted in a geyser of water that soaked him to the bone within seconds.

FIRE SPRINKLERS, Stone informed him, as Korden turned his burning eyes up to let the water wash them out. UNPLEASANT, BUT NOT DANGEROUS. THIS 'DOXRAGE' LIKES TO PLAY GAMES, BUT IT MAY BE AT THE EXTENT OF ITS POWER. IF ANYTHING, THE WATER SHOULD HELP DISSIPATE THE GAS.

But when Korden tried to leave, they saw how many tricks the virus still had up its sleeve.

The metal door wouldn't budge, no matter how hard he pulled. And the seal around its edges served to contain the water spraying down on him. Already he was standing in a puddle deep enough to submerge him up to the ankles.

I CALCULATE TWENTY-SEVEN MINUTES, THIRTEEN SECONDS UNTIL THIS SPACE IS FLOODED.

"What do we do?" Korden asked. The walls of the storage room were all solid crete, no other way out, and the nozzles gushed far too fast to block them up. In his head, Stone beeped as he worked through possibilities, but before he could offer a solution, a clanging noise came from overhead.

A square vent stood in the center of the ceiling between the recessed lights, little more than ten cupits across, not big enough for him to fit through. But, as Korden watched, the metal slats covering it bowed, bent, and snapped, dropping into the water collecting on the floor. Zeega's dark head descended from the shaft upside down, her eyes scanning the situation.

"Zeega can search for a way to open the door," she offered.

THE CONTROL ROOM WOULD BE THE BEST OPTION.

The riftling nodded and climbed back up into the ventilation shaft, but Korden called her back. He slipped the leather sling over his head and held up Stone's casing. The computer balked in protest, but Korden ignored him and asked, "Will you be able to talk to Zeega without me?"

I CAN ADD HER TO MY LIST OF AUTHORIZED USERS, BUT—!

"No buts. Go with her and figure out how to stop this virus." He glanced down at the water, which was now up to calves. "And for Upper's sake, do it fast."

7

Three more of the gas pellets fired at Zeega as she scurried down the hallway, but she moved too fast for the stinging clouds to catch up with her. In less than fifteen seconds, she was back in the stairwell and zipping up toward the sixth floor.

"What are you *doing*, disembodied one?" she demanded, forgoing the primitive human tongue to speak in the guttural, burbly moans and grunts of her native language. She could feel the accursed electronic lifeform named 'Stone' rifling through her brain, connecting to various cognitive centers, scanning thoughts and memories in clumsy, indelicate fashion. "That is a disagreeable sensation, to say the least."

M-MY APOOOOOLOGIES, I'M-I'M-I'M HAVING ISSSS-SUES CONNECTING MY SOF-SOFTWARE TO YOUR BRAIN-WAAAVES. CALIBRATING, PLEASE STAND B-BY...

"Hurry up, or you can try to calibrate after a swim in Zeega's digestive acids."

She moved faster, her tentacles working in concert to propel her up the stairs. Having the computer churn through her mind wasn't the only disagreeable sensation she was experiencing. Since following the young human into this place, an emotion had burned through her, one that she'd never experienced before. It seemed to be centered around her sudden desire to *help* the boy, rather than kill him. And not solely because he was responsible for the death of her broodmates, whose absence weighed heavily on her hive mentality.

Aiding a human—especially a child—went against everything she'd been taught, everything she knew. If the masters discovered this treachery, her *yan* would be severed with a significant amount of pain. And no sweet silence or homeland would await her in the next life.

Then find a way out and leave him to drown.

For some reason, she couldn't do this either. She continued telling herself it was repayment for his mercy, nothing more, but it was something else. Something...deeper. His claims about the masters had wormed their way into her thoughts during their captivity and would not stop nagging at her.

The door to the sixth floor was locked, but another ventilation shaft provided the solution. Zeega dropped into a new corridor lined with thick glass walls on the left, through which she could see more of the black screens that the disembodied one called 'monitors'.

Something whirred and clanked ahead. A human-sized figure emerged from an alcove in the wall on her right, a form made of glossy metal with two stiff arms, a head that was no more than a flat, rectangular bar, and a bottom half made of wheeled treads. It spun and rolled toward her, a yellow light flashing in its featureless face. Zeega spotted the energy weapons mounted on its shoulders as a second figure scooted out behind the first.

Security bots!

"STOP IMMEDIATELY," the first 'bot' commanded, its metallic voice echoing in the corridor. "UNDER FEDERAL STATUTE 163.C, THE USE OF DEADLY FORCE IS AUTHORIZED AGAINST INDIVIDUALS TRESPASSING ON POWER NODE PROPERTY."

There was no second warning. Zeega raced for the door into the control room as red energy beams traced along behind her. Thankfully, the lock on this entrance was busted, the door hanging slightly ajar on its sliding track. She was able to squeeze inside and drag it across to the jamb.

More skeletons lay scattered across the room in pieces. Zeega's sensitive membranes could detect the smell of old blood even after centuries. Whatever horrible event generated the pathome was centered here, in this control room. She ignored the ghosts who haunted it and worked on hauling a nearby table in front of the broken door as a barricade while tossing the computer's casing onto the nearest console. "Do what you can, Zeega will hold them off."

Interfacing wirelessly...booting up mainframes...

The screens around them flared to life as the first of the mechanical guards pounded on the outside of the door. An image of a human skull appeared on the monitors. That shrieking laughter played over the intercom, and text began to scroll.

all your base are belong to us heh classic

I am running a complete diagnostic on the building's systems. Perhaps I can isolate... The disembodied one gave a downhearted beep. OH DEAR. THAT IS UNFORTUNATE.

"*What?*" Zeega screeched. She wrapped a bundle of her tentacles around the door handle while the rest held to the frame, and the pressure of the bots prying from the outside was tearing her in half.

ACCORDING TO EMPLOYEE LOGS, THE DOXRAGE VIRUS INFECTED THEIR SYSTEMS WHILE MUCH OF THE NATION WAS IN FLIGHT FROM THE DARK FILAMENT. SEEING ITS POTENTIAL, THEY IMMEDIATELY SHUT DOWN ALL M-NET CAPABILITIES TO KEEP IT FROM ESCAPING, AND LOCKED IT OUT OF THE POWER DISTRIBUTION SYSTEMS. SO THE VIRUS DID THE SAME TO THEM IN RETALIATION, TRAPPING THEM INSIDE THE BUILDING AND FORCING THEM TO SLAUGHTER ONE ANOTHER FOR ITS AMUSEMENT. TRAGIC.

"Zeega does not care about some long-dead humans! Can you destroy this DOXRAGE or not?"

THE ANTIVIRUS SOFTWARE MAY DEPLOY IF I INITIATE A HARD REBOOT OF ALL SYSTEMS. THIS SHOULD ELIMINATE THE ROGUE PROGRAM FROM THE MAINFRAME; HOWEVER, IT IS PROBABLE THAT THIS COURSE OF ACTION WILL ALSO BRING M-NET CONNECTIONS BACK ONLINE, GIVING THE VIRUS A POSSIBLE AVENUE OF ESCAPE BEFORE IT CAN BE PURGED. WHICH IS LIKELY WHY THE ORIGINAL EMPLOYEES NEVER DID SO IN THE FIRST PLACE.

bring it on noob hah hah

The door to the control room ratcheted open a bit more, stretching Zeega's legs near the breaking point. Three metal fingers wedged themselves into the gap, providing more leverage for the invaders. "Then do it! Is there anything left on this dying world for it to escape *to*?"

A GOOD POINT. I WILL HAVE TO DESCEND INTO THE

BUILDING NETWORK TO OBTAIN PROPER AUTHORIZATION CODES FOR A HARD REBOOT. PLEASE STAND BY…

"Zeega…cannot…do much else," she groaned. The door was open far enough for her to see the yellow flashing lights of the bot's face. It swiveled on the other side, trying to find an angle to aim its energy weapon through the slot.

The computer gave a very human-sounding grunt of effort inside her head. DOXRAGE IS ATTEMPTING TO HACK MY SYSTEMS. FIREWALL AT 93 PERCENT INTEGRITY…

Zeega let go of the door and scrambled behind her makeshift barricade. The first of the security bots slid the entrance all the way open and rolled inside, peppering the table with red bolts of energy.

FIREWALL AT 58 PERCENT INTEGRITY…

She crawled beneath the table to the bot's treaded base and managed to snip several of the joints as the barrier was tossed across the room.

CODES…LOC-C-CATED…ATTEMPTING R-RE-REBOOT…FIREWALL AT 31 P-PERCENT INTEGRITY…

oh wow good job such hack

Zeega ran into the control room away from the disembodied one to draw fire. Heat from the deadly bolts singed her backside. The security bot tried to roll after her, but the tread she'd damaged flopped open, sending it careening into another table. The second bot rolled past, chasing Zeega into the far corner.

WTOASERN TOPKONZP…

She kept moving, straight up the wall, staying ahead of the energy beams, then launched herself at the bot. It tried to pivot away, but she wrapped herself around its rectangular head, pulling and slashing and biting in blind fury. One of its crude hands came up, grabbed her by the back of the head, and squeezed. Though she had no internal skeletal structure, the pressure could easily rupture her vital membranes. She closed all five of her eyes in preparation for death.

The lights and monitors winked out, casting her into uniform darkness. The bot froze. She wiggled out of its grasp as the room brightened.

Control restored! the computer proclaimed. No strand of the doxrage virus code appears to remain. The exits are all unlocked. I have also freed Mr. Bright from the storage room. We should return to him at once.

"Yes. Why should Zeega get to rest?" She grabbed the computer's leather strap and hurried out of the control room, stepping gingerly on her aching tentacles.

8

Korden muttered a Craften chant to augment his strength enough to carry the heavy batteries away from the distribution center, then set them down when they reached the hills on the far side of the road. He faced the riftling. "Thanks for your help."

"You are welcome," she answered slowly, as though testing the words. "But Zeega considers the debt repaid, human."

"Of course. And my name's Korden, by the way. Like your name is Zeega."

"Korden," she amended. "Zeega will remember."

Silence grew between them before Korden forced himself to puncture it. "You know, you could come with us. If you wanted."

"Impossible. Zeega must find one of the masters and receive new orders."

Korden nodded and nudged one of the heavy batteries with his toe. "And what if those orders are to...kill me?"

"Then so be it," she said, before adding, in that hesitant tone, "Although...Zeega would prefer if they were not."

"I guess that's a step in the right direction." He squatted and reached for one of her pincers. She drew away, hissing, before allowing him to grasp and shake the appendage. The flesh felt spongy and moist beneath his touch. "So long, Zeega."

Her five eyes blinked at him, then she scuttled into the forest.

MEET THE PROPHET

1

Dark was falling through the woods when Rand's voice swam out of the crackling depths of the talkie, stricken with panic.

"—you there? Korden, Meech, *anyone*, please answer!"

He picked the device up and pressed the button. "I'm here, can you hear me?"

"Thank the Aged! Where are you?"

"About an hour away from Ida, I think."

"*Nooo*," Rand moaned, in what sounded like abject misery. "What's taking you so long?"

"There were some complications. But I got the batteries! Settle on, I'll be there long before midnight."

"No, you don't understand! Something's happening here! Hildan ordered everyone on duty for tonight!"

"Why?"

"I have no idea. It's like he's preparing for a battle or something. But he hasn't made any announcements or even spoken to me since the courtyard yesterday." He sucked in a shuddering breath, audible even over the talkie. "This town will be crawling with Enforcement Brigade soon. We *have* to get out before then."

"Do we have enough time?"

"If I can get Meech to answer! I haven't heard anything from him all day either! He needs to get Doaks and the wagon ready while I free Lillam or this will never work!"

"Then keep trying. I'll be there soon."

Korden dropped the device back into his bag and jogged through the thick woods with the batteries weighing on his artcraft-infused muscles.

2

"Meech! Damn it, you lazy son of a crone, *answer me!*"

His brother's voice broke through the beautiful fog smothering Meech Holcomb's thoughts. To his amazement, he could *see* Rand's words as they issued from the hunk of polymer beside the remains of his campfire, even though he couldn't read them. They wove through the air above his face as he lay on his sleeping bag, represented not as letters but as a rainbow array of twinkling lights. Meech giggled and pawed at them in delight, trying to catch one.

By the time he'd hiked into the wilderness outside Ida early this morning—still a little stung about Korden leaving him behind—the gimmies crawled under his skin, making him twitch and jump. This bout was bad, too. Far worse than the others. Foul sweat soaked his clothes so much that they dripped, and the weeping puckers on his arms (what Jaimer called 'bliss bites') alternately burned and froze. After a few hours, the ache inside his skull got so bad, he could scarcely stand to breathe.

For the first time, Meech was glad he'd been left, so there was no one to see him in such a pitiful state. He'd suspected for a while that he needed to take a break from the jinko benders. They'd started out fun, something to do with the drudes, a way to relieve the mind-numbing boredom that was daily life in Ida. But somewhere along the way, they'd become a habit. More of a crutch than a tool. He'd seen spun-droolers in their final stages—brains no more than mush, aware of nothing around them except the next dose— and always told himself that would never be him, that he would stop pricking long before he got to that point. Meech had been sincere when he told both his brother and Korden that he wanted nothing more in the world than to get clean.

But it was hard to keep such declarations when his skin wanted to peel off his body.

So, instead of sleeping, he'd spent the pre-dawn hours scouring the hillside for jinkweed, pausing to vomit up bile when the stomach cramps became too severe. He'd found a single, stunted plant, mostly dried up and dead from the chilly temperatures at this elevation. The tiny bit of jinko he'd managed to extract was syrupy, far too thick to go in his veins, so Meech mixed it with saliva to get it liquidy, then pricked away.

The relief was instantaneous, calming his jitters and soothing the pain of his swollen jaw. Whenever that sweet rush rocketed through his nerve endings, it was hard to fathom why anyone would want to spend a single second of their miserable lives doing anything else. He'd passed out for a few hours, then, once the sun was up, he scraped himself off the ground and trudged out to collect more.

Now though, his brother's voice pulled him back from that whirlpool of ectasy. He was supposed to do something today. Something important. Oh, curse, he was supposed to help free Korden's girl and the guy who kept Rand in that cage! Wait on…maybe that was the other way around. He rolled on his side, reached for the talkie, and, after several clumsy attempts with his numb fingers, held the button long enough to acknowledge.

"*Where have you been?*" Rand snarled. The words were no longer made of pretty lights; now they were nails that spiked deep into Meech's ear canals. "We need you right now!"

Meech swallowed. He needed to sound natural. "Why, mm-man? What's, uuuuuh…goin on?" *Perfect.*

"Meech…please tell me you're not framming spun."

He sat up, slapped his cheeks a few times to stop the world from blurring. "Nope, uh uh, absolutely not."

"Good." His brother didn't sound convinced, but what-ever had his dungarees in a bunch kept him from dwelling on it. "I need you to get Doaks and the wagon."

"Yeah drude, me and Korden, we're gonna get on it."

"No, it must be done *now*, and Korden's not going to make it back in time. The Brigade is shifting around guards and dou-bling up on security. If I want to free Lillam, I have an opening in a half hour. You're the only one that can do the other part. Can you make it through the tunnels by then or not?"

Pride swelled Meech's chest. This was his opportunity to show them he should never be left behind again. Except in this case, of course, because leaving him behind was the sole reason he was now in the position to show them that he shouldn't be left behind. He corralled his meandering thoughts and said, "Of course. I'll be there."

"Then I'll clear out as many of the guards as I can. Re-member to bring the detention yard key I gave you, so you can get inside. Keep Doaks on a tight leash and make him bring the wagon to Hecate Pond. And Meech…" On the other end of the walkie, Rand hesitated. "Don't make a mess of this."

"Never! You can count on me, drude!"

"I hope so."

Meech dropped the talkie and looked down at his legs, trying to remember how to make them work.

3

After 24 hours with her hands and neck locked between the unforgiving wooden slats of the stocks, Lillam might've preferred a death sentence.

Her back throbbed from the hunched posture. Endless standing caused her feet and calves to go numb hours ago. Her stomach growled and her lips were cracked with dehydration. The food her tormentors threw on her had congealed into a horrible, putrefying broth that stiffened her hair and made each breath a misery.

But she did her best to ignore all of it. Her prayers to the Aged Lord were on behalf of her child, even though He wanted nothing to do with any soul below free age and had likely forsaken her. For the first time in her life, the only religion she'd ever known seemed cruel and pointless.

As the sun fell from the sky and the second night of her ordeal began, Lillam got as comfortable as possible without the board around her neck strangling her, and tried to sleep.

Footsteps roused her minutes later. She raised her bleary head. Someone was skulking across the small yard that served as town square for the women's half of Ida, avoiding the circles of electric torchlight. Even through the shadows, Lillam could see the figure was dressed in a tattered, dark blue longcloak that completely covered her body and wrapped about her head, leaving a narrow eyeslit.

Lillam braced herself for more taunts, more jeers. The crowds had lost interest early in the afternoon, when they saw she was determined to keep her lover's name. But singular bodies would come by to spit on her, pull her hair, or tease her with food and water.

The figure stopped in front of her. It said nothing and made no move other than to glance around the courtyard. Whatever this one planned, it must be bad indeed.

"Get it over with," she rasped.

The figure reached up, grabbed the eyeslit of the longcloak, and pulled, separating the garment's hood to reveal a stubbled face that she adored.

"Oh sweetlove, what've they done to you?" Rand whispered. He tried to caress her filthy cheeks, but she shook her head.

"You have to go," she told him urgently. "If they catch you here, they'll know it's you."

"I'm going," he agreed, reaching into the folds of his disguise to draw out a master keyring, "but you're coming with me."

A quick turn of the lock, and he lifted the top board off her. Once free, she fell onto him, writhing in agony as every muscle in her body cramped in unison. He didn't wait for the seizure to pass, just scooped her up and carried her in his arms as he hurried out of the courtyard toward the closest alley. She clung to him, buried her face in his neck, and hoped with all her might that this was no fever dream.

"Meech and Korden will be waiting for us," he whispered in her ear. "And they'll have a way for us to escape, and no one will ever lay a finger on you again, I *swear* it..."

Lillam felt him come to an abrupt halt. She twisted to look in front of them.

Kasa Webb's stout form blocked the narrow alley a few pargs away. The matron held a water jug and a meager plate of bread and cheese that was surely meant to be Lillam's dinner. Her eyes bulged as she took them in. "*Guards!*" she bawled, dropping the items to flee.

Rand placed Lillam back on her feet and gave chase. He caught the hefty woman easily, shoved her against the closest wall, and held her with an arm across the throat.

"Not another word," he cautioned, the threat empty without so much as a soup spoon to back it up.

"My, my…Rand Holcomb." A triumphant grin tugged at Matron Webb's jowled cheeks as she recognized her attacker. "So you're responsible for this. No wonder she was so eager to keep you a secret. Well, you can say goodbye to that plum job in the mayor's office. I'll see to that personally. Hildan will be devastated when he finds out. To think he wanted *you* to succeed him one day."

"It doesn't matter," Rand said, but Lillam could hear in his tone how deeply the threat cut. "We're leaving. Right now. We'll not be a blemish to this town ever again. All you have to do is stand aside and let us go."

"*Let you go?*" she snarled. Her prim face transformed into a wrathful beast so completely it was more like a mask than an expression. "Oh no, you'll pay for this. *Both* of you. Who do you think you are, creating a life in this ailing world? What makes you two so special? Don't you think we'd all like to throw such caution to the wind?" As she said this, her hand stole upward to caress her own belly.

Fury gave Lillam the strength to fly down the alley to them. She twined her fingers through Kasa Webb's brittle gray hair bun and yanked, snapping the woman's head sideways. "You jealous cunny," she spat. "No matter how much food you stuff into your rotund stomach, it'll always be empty. Do you know why? Because nothing could ever grow in such poison. So stop taking out your sorrow on those who have the courage to try."

The matron met her anger in equal measure. Then that rage-filled mask cracked. Her mouth crumpled as tears brimmed in her eyes.

Lillam relished it.

Together, she and Rand manhandled the woman through the nearest doorway, into a grain storehouse. They bound her hands and feet, tied a gag around her head, and left her lying on the floor. Before departing, Lillam leaned over to growl in her ear, "And if that day in the stocks hurt my baby, I'll be back to see that you get the same."

Then she held on to Rand's hand as they rushed through the cobbled streets of Ida for the last time.

4

Meech's vision was mostly clear by the time he emerged from the hatch he'd come through last night with Korden and his brother, but a pleasant, fuzzy warmth still blunted his thoughts and pulsed in his veins with every thump of his heart. Nevertheless, he was sober enough to keep his distance when he spied two guards patrolling in front of the entrance to the detention yard, armed with swords and crossbows, master keys jangling from a leather loop on their belts with each step.

"C'mon, Rand," he muttered to himself. "How the fram am I supposed to do my job if you don't do yours?" He wanted to call his brother, ask what he should do, then saw with dismay that he'd left the talkie back at camp with the rest of his belongings.

And the key. The key that Rand gave him for the cells.

Fram. Oh *fram!* Now, even if he got inside, he had no way to free Doc Apocalypse.

Meech sat on his haunches in the dirt, scratching at the bliss bites along his arms as he cursed himself. He'd messed this all up. Rand was a fool to trust in him. Meech Holcomb wasn't a hero, he was a washed-out jinkoid exile, and everyone knew it.

And...*everyone* knew it.

Meech's brow furrowed as his sluggish brain concentrated.

Half a minute later, he stumbled out from the alleyway, waving his hands and calling for the guards. The men watched him, both hefting their crossbows nervously.

"Frrron' gaaate!" he cried, the words slurred so much he could scarcely understand them himself. "There's annn attack at...fron' gggate! Y'goootta go help!"

"Wha're you 'bout? Wha' 'ttack?" one of the guards asked, his voice thick with Eastern accent.

"Ban'its! A whole arrrrmy of 'em! They need you!" Meech fell to his knees in front of the guard and clutched at his belt.

"I don' 'ear nuffin!"

The second guard squeezed the grips of his crossbow and asked his compatriot, "You think that's why the Mayor wanted everyone on duty? A bandit raid?"

"Yes, go help!" Meech pleaded.

"I don' know, but...wait on a sec." The first guard squinted down at Meech. "Ain' he 'Olcomb's bruhfer? The one wha' got tossed fer jinko?"

"Hey, yeah! That's him all right! He left with that Crafter kid yesterday! He's banished!"

Meech looked up at the men and frowned. "Ya mean...I wasn't suppose'ta come *back*?"

"Ge' off me, you lout!" the first guard growled, shoving his knee into Meech's chest hard enough to knock him to the ground. To his colleague, he ordered, "Go tell some'un 'e's 'ere!"

The second guard shook his head. "We don't have time to worry about this! The rest of the squad should be here soon to defend the yard gate! Mayor said every man ready to fight!"

"Then let's jus' toss 'im in a cell 'til 'Ildan can sor' it ou'!"

They each held their crossbows in one hand and used the other to hook Meech under the arms and drag him into the shadowy detention yard. The wagon still sat in the middle, in front of the exit gate, but Meech had little time to look as they carried him into the prisoner corridor, to the open cell across from Doaks, and dropped him onto the stone floor inside. He lay there, listening as the lock on the door triggered when they slammed it closed. Both guards strolled away, their laughter echoing off the cold stonework.

"Quite an escape plan yah rubos cooked up." Doaks's voice floated from the shadows of his cell. "Would prob'ly work better if yah got me *out*, rather than more of yah in. But hey, I'm not one ta judge."

"Then maybe you should...you know...close your curse-hole until I'm finished, drude." Meech sat up, reached beneath his bright tunic, and drew out the master key he'd yanked from the guard's belt when he was shoved away. It took several attempts with his shaking hands to get the door of his cell open, then he hurried across to the other man, who was waiting at the bars in his filthy canvas suit. Meech looked through the metal lattice and said, "You do exactly what I tell you."

"Consider me leashed," Doaks agreed.

Meech needed multiple tries to insert the key into the lock on this door also. Doaks watched with interest, his eyes drifting up to the sores along the inside of Meech's elbows.

"Yah really do got it bad, don't yah?"

"None of your business." Meech got the lock open and pulled the door. "Get movin, man. We don't have much time."

They crept back down the corridor, Meech keeping a hand on the shorter man's arm and trying not to give in to a sudden, insane urge to giggle. The detention yard remained empty; whatever Brigade contingent was coming had yet to arrive.

Doaks gave a sigh of relief when he caught sight of his wagon. "Tell yah what, why don't yah get that gate open, and I'll fire 'er up?"

"Nice try. We go together or I'll yell for the guards."

Doaks's mouth opened in shock as he pressed a hand to his heart. "That hurts, rubo! Yah got the wrong idea 'bout me!"

Meech gave him a bland look. "Tell that to Korden."

"Don't a man deserve a chance to change? To become a better person?"

"Yeah, I'm sure you're totally reformed after a whole two days in the clink."

They moved from shadow to shadow, crossing the yard to the gate. Meech unlocked the iron wings and pushed them open one at a time while holding on to the other man. But, as they made their way back to the wagon, a shuffle of feet came from the opposite end of the yard, and a stream of enforcers strolled through the entrance. The first of them noticed the duo and bellowed, *"Prisoner escaping!"*

"Oh curse, run for the wagon!" Meech cried.

They sprinted forward. The guards unslung their cross-bows and opened fire. Meech saw bolts pepper the exterior of the wagon in front of them, most bouncing off the tough material but a few lodging in the fake canvas bonnet. Then he and Doaks ducked into cover behind the control panel as alarm bells rang through the town.

"*Go, drude!*"

Doaks didn't have to be told twice. He seated himself in the driver's seat, reached down to flip out a pedal hidden in the smooth polymer of the console, and kept his foot on it while he pushed the same sequence of buttons Korden insisted should start the vehicle. Meech felt the soft rumble of those hover-engines as they fired up beneath his feet.

"*Keyed to you, huh?*" Meech demanded over the clanging alarm bells.

Doaks gave a sheepish shrug. "*Can't blame a man for seizin opportunity!*"

"*Who says?*"

A crossbow bolt spanged off the console in front of them.

"*I can step off and let you drive the rest of the way!*" Doaks offered.

"*Just go! And if you try anything, it'll be the last opportunity you ever seize!*"

Doaks worked the control panel, and the wagon accelerated through the gate and into the night beyond.

5

Korden heard whimpering echoes in the corridor long before Rand stepped into the lamplight carrying a limp woman in his arms. Though she was filthy and bruised and bleeding—and smelled like rancid fruit—Korden was struck by her beauty.

"I can't believe it," Rand remarked. "You made it through the tunnels on your own."

In truth, it was Stone that navigated; the computer kept a full record of their last expedition, and was also able to locate a map of the original resort in his files. Korden watched as Rand set the lady on the ground and asked, "Is she all right?"

"I'm fine," the woman snapped. Her *mohol* swirled with a turgid mixture of suspicion, disgust and fear. "Don't talk about me as if I'm not here."

"Sorry," he sputtered. The vehemence was unexpected, but coming from such a young, pretty female, it left him flustered. "I only meant—"

"Korden, this is Lillam. Pay no attention to her manners." Rand knelt by the woman's side and gently moved her face toward him. "I have to take him back up. You stay here and keep quiet."

Lillam shook her head in quick, panicked arcs as she latched on to his arms. "Don't leave me! Please Rand, don't leave me!"

"It won't take long." He frowned uncomfortably. "But… if we're not back in fifteen minutes, you better try to get out of town on your own. Make your way up to Hecate Pond. Meech will be waiting for you there."

This served to heighten her alarm. "But why can't we go now, together?"

"Because I made a promise to Korden in exchange for his protection on our journey, and I need to uphold my end."

Lillam pulled him closer and lowered her voice in a failed attempt to keep Korden from hearing. "We don't need his help."

Rand planted a tender kiss on her eyebrow. "Trust me. Remember?"

Then he was up and heading into a nearby tunnel branch. Before following him, Korden forced himself to meet Lillam's withering gaze, and said, "I'm sorry they did that to you."

"We have to hurry," Rand said over his shoulder. He broke into a jog. "An alarm sounded to the west as I brought Lillam into the tunnels. I suspect it has something to do with my brother. I don't know if he escaped or not, but if they're focused on him, it might clear a path for us."

Indeed, the twilit streets were empty as Rand and Korden emerged and moved toward the mayor's chambers. An uneasy calm had fallen upon Ida, a sense of expectation, something Korden needed only regular intuition to sense. When they reached Hildan's quarters, Rand produced a key for the front door, and seconds later they stood inside the parlor where Korden and Meech were attacked by the townsmen yesterday.

"Wait here," Rand whispered, before disappearing down the hallway that led to the living quarters. When he returned, he spoke in normal tones. "Hildan's gone. Probably off seeing to that alarm or coordinating the Enforcement Brigade for whatever's happening. I'm sure he's searching for me also." A flicker of sadness passed over his lean face, quickly replaced by a resolute clench of his jaw. "Let's finish this and get out."

They entered the room with the fantastic shelves of books. It was dark in here, the room layered in shadows, but Rand made no move to light any of the electric lamps as he stopped in front of the mayor's desk and pointed to a metal square set into the stone wall beside it. "The box that the Prophet speaks through is in there."

Korden made an urgent waving motion. His anticipation was unbearable. "Then open it."

Rand shook his head. "Oh, I don't have a key. Hildan carries the only key around his neck at all times."

"Then…how are we supposed to get in?"

"I-I guess I thought you would use your artcraft."

Korden's jaw dropped as he stared at the formidable safe. "I don't know if I can!"

"But you crushed an Incarnate with your mind! Can't you do the same thing to it?"

"Well, yeah, I could probably blow out the wall if I wanted, but that might bring some attention!"

Realization touched Rand's face. "There must be some way. Figure it out."

"You promised me an audience!"

"And I got you as close as I could!"

Korden huffed in frustration, then opened the conduit's eye and reached out to explore the safe. It was a thick steel box without the slightest imperfection or weakness. But Rand was right, there *must* be a way to do this without brute force. He needed to find a creative solution, one with some finesse.

He didn't bother trying to pick the intricate lock. That would've required a knowledge of mechanics that he didn't possess. Instead, Korden imagined the door having the quality and consistency of paper, as he'd envisioned the tree becoming rubbery. *The metal is thin,* he insisted, *so light and delicate, we could tear through it without our bare hands.* He focused on convincing himself of this idea with all his might, poured artcraft into making it a reality. A deep groan came from the steel as its properties—its *adjectives*—began to change.

And then a voice in the corner said, "You might as well let me open it, so I don't have to replace the whole thing."

6

Rand banged his hip on the desk as he spun toward the far corner of the room. The shadows grew deep there, which was the reason he hadn't seen Hildan sitting in a chair when they entered. His heart squeezed into a painfully tight ball as the mayor rose from his seat and walked toward them.

"Sir, I…I-I…we needed…"

Lye Hildan sighed. "Save your breath, Rand. Excuses won't get you anywhere in life. I thought I trained you better than that." He didn't sound angry, just immeasurably weary. "Although I assume the report about your brother freeing the flimflam man and stealing his wagon relates to all this."

The crushing guilt Rand had been holding at bay since Lillam told him she was pregnant busted through the dam inside him. His mouth opened, and he heard himself babbling, "I'm so sorry, sir, I never meant for any of this to happen, but you see, there's a girl, I love her, and we need safe passage to the Skyreach, and—"

"And you traded a secret you didn't possess to this boy."

Rand stared at the floor. "Yes, sir."

Hildan moved closer. One of his hands came up. Rand feared it would slap him, but it gripped his shoulder. The unmistakable smell of barley wine drifted from the other man's lips as he said, "You've been an excellent apprentice. I leaned on you hard, but you never failed me. In truth, you were the closest thing I ever had to a son. And I want you to know I meant what I said, about you being mayor someday." His owlish eyes cut over to Korden, and a deep sadness stole into them. "Of course…that's all over with now. Ida may never need another mayor again after tonight."

A cold chill stiffened the hair on Rand's neck and forearms. "What are you saying?"

Hildan pulled the key from around his neck and walked to the safe set into the wall. Tingling anticipation replaced Rand's dread as he recalled that voice he'd heard several seasons ago coming from this very room. "I should've shown you this long ago," the mayor said as he opened the door with his back to them. "But it was a secret I wasn't ready to let go of. That was probably selfish of me. Because if this miraculous object is responsible for the good people of Ida electing me again and again to be their savior, it's because I exaggerated my own importance in its usage."

He turned around with a bright pink rectangular box in his hands, a cracked polymer case with black, concentric circles on either end beneath a row of buttons, and a simple caricature of a smiling, yellow-haired woman on the side, her hair pulled into a high tail, one hand raised in greeting.

Across the front of this apparatus, in upraised, sparkling letters, was the phrase, *BARBIE'S BEACHTIME BOOMBOX!*

"Gentlemen," Hildan said, "meet the Prophet."

7

It took Stone a heartbeat to explain the concept of radios to Korden. When Doaks introduced them to the talkies, he'd suspected that the Prophet must be speaking through something similar, and this was definitely, as Fortholm used to say, in the same ballpark. "Where did you get it?" he asked breathlessly.

Hildan carried the polymer box to his desk, trailing a black cable behind him from the depths of the safe, and set it down. "A trader came across it in one of the Purged city wastes years ago. The man had no clue what it was, of course. I knew because of my reading. I spent years tinkering with it, trying to connect it to the power grid. When I finally switched it on, I never expected to hear anything." He chuckled. "Imagine my surprise when it spoke."

Rand squatted in front of the desk, at eye level with the radio. "What did it say?"

"You already know the answer to that. It gave predictions. Told of events with a precision no ordinary man could know. Storms. Incarnate movements. Marauders. Armies. Battles both near and far. It spoke of settlements in places I'd never heard of and encouraged anyone listening to contact them. Every twelve hours—at around 3:30 in the morning, and the same in the afternoon—the message changes, then repeats until the next interval."

"But who is it?" Korden asked. "Who's saying these things? Who *is* the Prophet?"

Hildan shrugged. "As I told you before, I don't know. He's never said, and, since the communication flows but one direction, I have no way to ask. I've only received his wisdom gratefully, and done with it what I could. Very little of it applies to Ida anyway…until today's most recent message, that is." He reached over and pressed a button on top of the radio.

Static burst from the speakers on either end. They waited impatiently for a full minute. Then a male voice swam out of the noise, fast-paced and with a musical lilt to its words.

"Heeeeey, rockin robins, it's your friendly neighborhood Weatherman here, and I've got a *doozy* of a warning for those communities in the Lake Tahoe area!"

SCANNING…THIS MESSAGE IS BEING BROADCAST ON AN OBSOLETE FM BAND RATHER THAN M-NET STREAMING, Stone said excitedly. I SHOULD BE ABLE TO RECEIVE THE SIGNAL, PERHAPS EVEN TO TRIANGULATE THE ORIGIN!

Be quiet! Korden chided, leaning forward to hear the rest of the message.

"Listen up and listen good, Tahoers! That Incarnate gathering from out west that I told you about is still on the move. Based on direction, they appear to be headed straight for you. I estimate a fifty-man contingent, and a few smaller groups coming from the south and northeast that'll put you in a vise. I don't know what you little chickadees did to get their dander up, but you better batten down the hatches and put some powder in your britches, cause they should be at your doorstep shortly after sundown!" The static resumed for a few seconds, then the message began to repeat. Hildan switched the radio off.

"Oh fram," Rand whispered.

"You see?" The mayor of Ida swooned, and Rand jumped to steady him before he fell. He perched on the edge of his desk and slumped over his protruding gut. "They know. They know exactly what we did. What *you* did." His haunted gaze moved to Korden. "One-hundred years this settlement has been here, keeping the law, giving the Filament no reason to come knocking. And you manage to destroy us in a day."

"No." Korden backed away from the man in horror. More innocent blood would be spilled because of him. "They can't know. They *can't*. It must be the others that're hunting for me. The female Incarnate said more were coming."

"Fifty of those demons for one child, eh?" Hildan scoffed. "You must be very important indeed."

"You saw what he could do," Rand argued.

"Yes. The same thing countless other Crafters before him could do. And none of them made the slightest bit of difference against the Filament." He shook his head. "No, they're coming to punish this town for my sins. I made the choice to help him, and now our Aged Lord has left us to our fate."

"But there's only fifty of them! We outnumber them twenty to one! Surely you don't mean to roll over and offer your throat!"

"Of course not. I'll try to talk our way out of it and, if that fails, the Enforcement Brigade is assembled and ready to fight. But if it comes to that…Ida is as good as dead. Even if we win this battle, we'll become a target. This town will never know peace again." The mayor looked over at Rand. "Go, my boy. Take your girl and your brother and run while you can. I'll give you as much time as possible."

Outside, a new alarm tolled, across the entire town this time.

"*Go*," Hildan urged.

Rand threw his arms around the man in a quick embrace, then ran for the door, grabbing Korden's arm along the way. But he pulled free and said to the mayor, "Let me surrender myself this time. I'll take the blame, beg them to have mercy."

Hildan waved the words away. "Yes, your 'surrender' went very well last time. I can imagine how much worse it will go if you're here when I try to negotiate. And besides…" A weak grin twitched at the corners of his mouth. "We can't have you dying here if you're truly as important as they seem to think."

FOUR STAR MEAL

1

Lye Hildan arrived at the lookout point and peered over the wall, into the dark field beyond. The shantytown that existed beyond Ida's front gate was mostly gone, packed up in the span of minutes, the various travelers and traders and citizen applicants pulling up stakes and heading for greener pastures, like whackrats fleeing a burning building. In their place, exactly as the Prophet predicted, was a band of Incarnates fifty heads strong, gathered a hundred pargs or so from the portcullis.

This is the Aged Lord's vengeance upon me, he thought, before quoting one of the commandments from the Writ of Elderly Governance: 'Thou shalt give a child no succor, or else throw tinder upon the flames of war.'

These particular flames were well-armored and armed, ready for a fight. Most of the demons sat unmoving on horseback, their eyes awash with intense red light as they stared up at the fortress. Except for the five in front, that was. These straddled some manner of strange machines that appeared to have bubbles of glass underneath in place of wheels, much like the medicine man's floating wagon. Hildan didn't know what to make of that; as far as he knew, Incarnates eschewed all forms of technology.

And, even more strange, the one in the very front of this contingent, presumably the leader…his eyes didn't glow. Perhaps he still wore some protection over them; the night shadows were too deep to tell for sure. As Hildan watched, this one cupped both hands around his mouth and called in a deep, mocking voice, "*Little pig, little pig! Let me in!*"

"Mayor?" one of the guards asked. "Wh-what do we do?"

"We're damn sure not allowing them inside this time," Hildan declared, swallowing a lump of fear lodged in his throat. "I'm going out there. No matter what happens, no one is to make a move against them unless they try to breach the wall. If that happens…kill them all. Remind the men that only faith in the Aged Lord can make them victorious over those monsters. Their weapons will have no effect otherwise." Hildan had no way of knowing if this was true, but it was what the stories always claimed.

The boy certainly wasn't praising the Aged when he killed the other three right in front of you.

Less than a minute later, he was stepping across Ida's threshold and moving toward the Incarnates as the portcullis trundled down behind him. The demon at the front of the pack climbed off his machine and walked to meet him.

"You speak for this pile of rocks, tubbo?"

"I am the mayor here," Hildan confirmed. As the figure approached, the electric torches on the front wall of the town illuminated his leatherclad body, waist-long beard, and smirking face. "You're…not an Incarnate."

"Yeah, yeah, we're not a lotta things. Including patient." The smirk fell away as the other man frowned. "Where's the boy, kemosabe?"

Hildan shook off his confusion and squared his shoulders. "He isn't here anymore. But I would like to humbly ask that you—"

The other man's face screwed up beneath his beard, and the mayor of Ida briefly registered the incredible pressure at his temples before his skull collapsed.

2

Heater heard the other people along the parapet gasp as he sucked their leader's brain dry. The corpse fell over, its caved-in cranium splattering when it hit the ground.

"*Yuck!*" He stood over the body and gagged. "A framming bureaucrat; no imagination whatsoever! And now we gotta have this cursehole rattling around in our head for the rest of eternity."

He heard footsteps and glanced up to see one of the Incarnates from his spiffy new posse approaching, a decimator named Bludgeen wearing bone-mailed armor.

Heater gestured toward the corpse at his feet. It was true that the butterball had provided little nourishment in the way of imagination, but Heater was still able to suss out some critical information from his dried-up, dungpile of a psyche. "Kid's with some other folks trying to escape in a weird hover wagon. You got him?"

Bludgeen lifted his nose to the air. "He's close," the Incarnate agreed. "Moving somewhere up through the hills to the east."

"Then get your people coming in from that way to slow him down. They can use the shooters, but if anybody so much as tweaks a hair on the boy's head, they'll answer for it."

"What about this settlement?" Bludgeen demanded. Torgas had given this group of *Exatrades* explicit instructions to obey Heater, but they challenged him at every opportunity. "They must be punished for harboring a child!"

Heater grabbed the demon by his chest plate. "Then do it on your own time. Right now, you're working for us, and we say nothing matters but Bright. Now get on those hogs and let's run him down."

The Incarnate snarled but nodded agreement. He started back toward the hovertrikes. Before following him, Heater gave a friendly wave to the peanut gallery on the castle wall, then glanced back down at the remains of his meal and muttered, "Man…we really gotta stop killing mayors."

3

Korden concentrated on transporting the batteries up the hillside, leaving Rand to support Lillam by himself. The young woman tried to run on her own several times, but she was too weak from her confinement in the stocks. The trio spoke not a word as they hurried along the dark, wooded trails. Korden listened for the sounds of battle from the town below them, but the night was eerily silent.

A half hour after departing the sewer tunnels deep beneath Ida, they crested a rise that revealed the pond spread out before them. By the light of the baker's moon, they could see Gwenita parked beside the glimmering water. A long hose snaked from the wagon's sideboard down into the pool, probably to fill up the reservoir tanks that Doaks had mentioned, the ones that must feed fresh water to the sink. Rand placed Lillam on her own feet and sprinted ahead. When he caught sight of his brother, he threw his arms around Meech and lifted the man's gaunt form completely off the ground.

"I knew you could do it, I never had a doubt!" Rand shouted gleefully.

"That makes one of us," Meech replied. He wore a huge, embarrassed grin as his brother released him, but his *mohol* revealed how pleased he was by the sentiment.

Tarmon Doaks sat on the ground behind his wagon, arms and legs tied clumsily together with strips of cloth. Wearing the canvas sack and covered in grime, it was hard to imagine him capable of conning anyone with his fast-talking routine; Korden reminded himself that lack of fancy clothes did nothing to make this man any less dangerous. While Rand introduced Meech and Lillam, Korden switched to floating the batteries to give his augmented muscles a rest and put them on the shore in front of Doaks. The trickster's eyes grew huge as he watched them hover.

"Will these work?" Korden asked coldly.

Doaks stared at him for a bit longer—his aura awash with light tones of amazement and a rich vein of that dark silver color Korden was beginning to associate with scheming—before leaning forward to inspect the black boxes. He nodded and shrugged at the same time. "Should be all right, if we can get 'em charged up somewhere."

He looked like he wanted to say more, but a few pargs away from them, Rand proclaimed, "All right, enough of this. We don't have much time."

"That's right," Korden agreed. He moved to a spot where he could face the group. "That's why all of you have to make a decision, right now. There are Incarnates coming after me. A lot of them, more than I could fight. They reached Ida right as we left and might be on their way here now. If they catch me, they'll surely kill anyone with me. So if you want to walk away…now might be your only chance."

Meech stepped forward before he'd even finished speaking. "I'm with you, drude. No matter what. I ain't scared of those rotheads. And if they do catch up, you won't have to face them alone."

His brother took longer, but eventually nodded as well. "If anyone can get us to the Skyreach, it's you. I'll do whatever I can to help."

Lillam gripped his arm from behind. "Rand, I...I don't..." She gazed into his eyes as she tried to get the words out, but whatever she saw there made her stop. "I trust you," she said simply, but Korden knew this wasn't directed at him.

The two men set about loading their belongings onto the wagon and helping Lillam aboard while Korden went back to Doaks. The man held up his bound arms from the ground. "Suppose I don't get the same choice, eh?"

"No, I'll let you go," Korden said reluctantly. The last thing he wanted was to set this predator loose to prey on the innocent, but he couldn't risk the man's life by dragging him along against his will, either. "*If* you can give us a way to drive the wagon without you."

Doaks grinned, shook his head, and wagged a finger. "Nah uh, no sah, I go where Gwenita goes. And if we're in so much of a hurry, we better get movin, don't yah think?"

4

They stowed the batteries aboard the wagon and set Doaks upon a meandering trail up the mountainside that Rand said should climb through the higher peaks of the Sierra Nevadas before bringing them out on the eastern side of the range. Korden watched their driver push a lever on the control board that increased their speed. The pressure of the air rushing over them became strong enough to shove him backward if he didn't plant himself. He'd gone this fast only one other time in his life, and the velocity made him nervous.

"*I've taken her up to 150 spans per hour!*" Doaks shouted over the wind. "*I 'spect she'll go as high as 180, but it'll sure drain the power cellanoids!*"

"*Don't push it too hard then!*" Korden ordered. "*We shouldn't waste energy if we don't have to! Even if the Incarnates are on horseback, they'll have a hard time keeping up at this speed!*"

Doaks put all four fingers to his forehead in a sarcastic salute. "*Aye aye, Cap'n Rubo!*"

Eager to escape the man's presence, Korden retreated into the bonnet.

The interior of the wagon was cramped with four people inside it. For the first time, Korden wondered how all five of them would live in it for the coming weeks. Rand had already disassembled the cages with Doaks's tools and hung a long cloth across one of the rear corners to give Lillam some privacy while she cleaned herself with a bucket of water from the pond. He was back there with her now, helping her change into some of his clothes, since she'd left Ida with nothing. The sounds coming from the divider alternated between whimpers of pain and wet, smacking sounds that Stone insisted were intimate kisses of the French variety. Korden—who'd read about such tongue-heavy lip locks—would've given anything to see behind that curtain. He allowed himself only the barest peek at their *mohols* (a palette of so many shifting colors that it challenged Meech's tunic) and felt instantly ashamed.

Meech stood at one of the cold boxes attached to the wall, digging through their food stores and doing his best to ignore the couple.

"You seen these?" he asked. "It *freezes* the meat. Real kye."

"I've seen it. I lived in here for a week, remember?"

"Right." Meech gestured to the corner and whispered, "Didn't get a chance to talk to Rand's girl much. But she sure didn't look preg to me, man. Course, I've never seen anybody that *was*, so..."

"I think their stomachs get big, but maybe not until later."

"That's weird, drude. To think we all got started in some woman's belly?"

Korden agreed as Doaks bawled his name from the control deck.

"*Whattaya wanna do about* that?" the man asked, nodding ahead as Korden stepped back into the howling wind.

The wagon was hurtling through a narrow canyon between rocky ridgebacks, the trail in front of them flat and open for a while. A span or two ahead, barely visible in the waxing moonlight, a high barricade had been constructed across the road out of several wheeled carts and a score of hastily-felled trees. Figures milled around it, and Korden only needed to see the fiery sheen of their eyes to know what they were.

"*Don't stop!*" he told Doaks. "*Drive through it!*"

"*Kid, if we hit that, it'll crack this wagon right in half!*"

"*We're not going to hit it!*"

He straightened and drew into himself. Doaks twisted around in his chair to watch him with a skeptical eyebrow climbing his bald pate. Korden allowed the conduit to yawn wide open in his mind. He yoked that incredible power as it flowed through him, directing it, shaping it into a solid mass. He envisioned a giant piston mounted on the front of Gwenita, the artcraft a sling that was slowly drawing it backward with intense pressure.

As they careened toward the barricade, Korden waited until they drew close enough to see the Incarnates' snarling faces before he allowed his makeshift battering ram to release.

A tremendous blue explosion obliterated the barricade seconds before they would've plowed into it. Branches and shards of wood flew outward in front of them in a dense cloud. Several of the Incarnates directly in the path of the invisible piston were pulverized into a bloody mist; a few more were knocked aside by the wagon's edges as they sailed through the field of debris.

Doaks gave a gleeful yip as the particles swirled around them. "*You really are somethin, boy!*"

Rand bounded through the door of the bonnet onto the crowded control deck, and Meech poked his head out right behind him. "*What the hells was that?*"

Korden shouted, "*Incarnates tried to cut us off! They—!*"

A flat crack echoed through the canyon. One neat, round hole appeared in the polymer exterior of the bonnet a few cupits from Meech's ear.

Stone reported the significance at the same moment as Doaks bellowed, "*Frammin curse, that was a shooter!*"

More of those cracks sounded, a distant series of pops. Doaks hunched low behind the control panel while the others ducked. Rand grabbed Korden's shoulder and pointed high. "*They're on the ridgeline!*"

Korden saw them, pairs of red eyes strung along the top of the canyon wall to the left as far as he could see. This ambush was well planned. The effort of the battering ram had left him a little shaky, but, as a torrent of projectiles peppered the wagon, he held up a hand and flowed artcraft into a shield around the vehicle. As with the energy weapon at the power facility, he experienced every shot as they struck his barrier, each one creating a jolt of unpleasant mental feedback.

"*What are Incarnates doing with shooters?*" Meech cried.

It was a good question. Korden thought of those lethal weapons the Trikers cobbled together, but couldn't do so for long. The shield required his full attention. More and more shots hit them all the time, from both sides now, a deadly crossfire. Pinpricks of pain exploded in his head. His shield continued to grow thinner and thinner as the projectiles tried...to...*break...through...*

He felt the barrier fail at his back, sensed one of the shots streaking toward him, and winced in anticipation of impact.

It never came.

Korden turned his head to look.

A tiny hunk of metal floated in the air next to his shoulder, encased in wispy green tendrils that vaguely resembled a small hand. Korden's jaw dropped as he tried to discern what was happening, the shootfire forgotten.

Then he noticed Rand crouched in the doorway of the bonnet, staring intently at the bullet with so much intensity he seemed to vibrate.

A cry of pain came from inside the wagon.

"*Lillam!*" Rand disappeared inside, and the projectile clattered to the floor of the control deck.

No time to ponder now. The shootfire was slackening, but the wagon lurched as Doaks veered to the left, forcing Korden to throw out a hand to steady himself. He looked up in time to see a man-sized boulder come rolling down the canyon wall, narrowly missing their flank.

In front of them, the last of the Incarnates were creating landslides where the canyon narrowed, shoving whatever they could down the stony slope. A renewed flood of artcraft surged through him at the danger. Korden used it to punt the larger rocks away, imagined them launching through the air.

"*On the right!*" Doaks warned. One last boulder a quarter the size of the wagon itself was crashing down on them.

"*I got it!*" Korden focused on the huge target, reared back with his mind, and lashed out.

Nothing happened.

The boulder smashed into the front corner of the wagon. The impact rocked the vehicle, shoving them into the canyon wall for a secondary collision. Korden sprawled across the control panel beside Doaks. Inside the bonnet, glass crashed and shattered.

"*I thought you had it!*" Doaks roared. Something beneath their feet gave a grinding screech as he accelerated.

Korden regained his balance. He tried to conjure something, anything. Again, there was no effect. And it wasn't like Zeega's hum; the conduit was open, the artcraft flowing. It was actually flowing *too* fast, faster than he could channel it, and disappearing before he could shape it. He struggled to close the channel and staunch that raging leak.

yum tastes good four star meal no doggy bag

The chorus of voices were no more than a whisper amid his thoughts, but its presence seized his attention.

"No," Korden murmured, the negation drenched in horror.

5

Under the whistle of the wind, a deep, stuttering rumble was building. Korden knew that sound immediately, but his mind recoiled from the recognition. Nevertheless, he shoved past Meech, ran through the bonnet where Rand hovered over Lillam, and stepped out onto the rear deck, leaving the doors open.

In their wake and gaining fast, he could see five sleek,

compact vehicles speeding up the trail, illuminated by the cushions of light on which they glided.

Hovertrikes. He recognized them as surely as the figure that rode the leading machine, his long beard flapping over his shoulder while he rocketed toward them.

"*HIYA, KIDDO!*" Heater Kay boomed, his voice somehow unnaturally amplified over the roar of the engines, so loud that it echoed off the canyon walls, the vocalization of a thundering god. "*DID YA MISS US?*"

"No, *it can't be you!*" Korden howled. "*You're dead, I killed you!*"

"*YOU SURE AS CURSE TRIED, YOU LITTLE FRAM!*"

This must be a hallucination. Or else he was going insane. But in case it wasn't either, Korden reached out to the man's trike and shoved with all his might, intending to flip the machine.

But the leader of the Trikers laughed and let go of the handlebars to raise his arms to the sky. "*THAT'S RIGHT, FEED US, SEYMOUR! OUR MUTUAL FRIEND'S GOT QUITE AN APPETITE!*"

coming for you should've helped us swallow you whole never escape

Warm terror flushed through Korden as full understanding dawned on him.

6

The tiny bit of imagination he'd siphoned off the kid was like a gourmet lobster dinner and a line of premium coke all rolled into one. Now Heater got what the fuss was all about; no one he'd drained so far tasted anything like *that*. In his head, Loathe gave a triumphant cry in an endless host of voices.

That look on Bright's face when the truth dawned on him. Man, it'd been *priceless.*

Heater turned to Bludgeen, riding the trike to his right. *"Take 'em!"* he shouted. *"Do what you want to the others but leave the kid for us!"*

The Incarnates revved their engines and boosted forward while Heater hung back. He could end this himself a lot faster than they could, but why waste the energy? Loathe burned through imagination as quick as he devoured it. Already the boost he'd gotten from the boy was being drained away by the constant stress of keeping the hovertrikes from falling apart. They'd ridden the crafts so hard over the past couple of weeks, he'd been forced to give them increasingly fantastical patch jobs that had little basis in realistic physics. The damn things were more unicorns than machines at this point.

Soon though, that wouldn't matter.

Once he had the kid…the world would be his for the taking.

7

The four other riders with Heater put on a burst of speed. Korden had figured these were more of the man's vicious clan, but, as they drew closer, he saw their eyes glowed. Incarnates riding on the hovering speeders was yet another strange sight he couldn't reconcile.

His first instinct was to sweep them aside with his mind, but he clamped down on that. His artcraft had no effect around Heater, who appeared to be diverting it somehow. No, worse than that; the Triker was *eating* it, wrapping his mental lips around the conduit like a giant straw and sucking it right out of Korden's head. He briefly recalled what

Loathe had told him in its cave prison, about how anything he conjured would make the parasitic creature stronger. The thought of being their 'four star meal' made him queasy. He had to keep the conduit closed no matter what, to make sure he didn't give them anything else to swallow.

But that left the Incarnates speeding after the wagon. The canyon ended, and the land became a treacherous wooded slope as they climbed higher into the mountains. Doaks was forced to take quick, yawing turns to stay on the trail. Korden swayed on the rear deck with hands fisted at his sides, watching helplessly as their pursuers fanned out and closed in.

Someone brushed against his shoulder. Meech was at his side, arms full of vials, bottles and various other flotsam from inside the bonnet. He took one of the jars and hucked it at the closest Incarnate. It missed—by quite a lot—but then Korden reached to help and the two of them began flinging a steady stream of objects off the deck.

"*Hey, those're MINE!*" Doaks's indignant shout carried all the way through the wagon.

Their missiles struck the hovertrikes and the Incarnates. A jug of some green liquid hit one of the demons in the face. He swerved, and the handlebars of his ride snagged on a tree trunk as the trail twisted. The trike twisted violently onto its side before shearing its rider in half on a rock. Meech and Korden whooped.

But the victory was short-lived. Another Incarnate maneuvered so close that the front of his craft nearly touched the wagon. He reached for the bag mounted on the trike's side and came up with a shortshooter that he aimed at Meech's face.

With a savage bellow, Rand barreled out of the bonnet with a long piece of rectangular steel in his hands that had been the side of Korden's cage. He brought it smashing down into the growling engine at the front of the hovertrike. Sparks spewed from the compartment before the vehicle veered away into the forest.

The other two riders eased off, dropping back toward Heater.

"*That's right, keep running you bastards!*" Rand held up a fist and shook it at the retreating Incarnates.

Then his feet were pulled out from under him.

8

Fury painted Heater's vision in red. If the little seedstain and his friends wanted to play, then he would oblige.

With but a flicker of thought, his fingers elongated, becoming horrible, snake-like appendages. The squirming feelers speared out from his hands and wrapped around the ankles of the man who'd trashed one of his trikes beyond even his repair capabilities. Heater reeled his digits back in like he'd hooked a marlin. The doof fell backward, crashing to the deck with his lower half dangling off the end of the wagon. He would've plummeted to the ground, but the kid and the second man (and was that nutjob wearing an actual *tie-dyed tunic*, like he was ready to attend a medieval Woodstock?) grabbed hold of his arms. They briefly played tug-of-war with the guy's body, neither side gaining.

"Okay then. Let's get weirder." Heater reached back to the half cape at his waist and lifted it up to release his newest bit of make-believe.

9

Korden and Meech clung to Rand as Heater's hideous finger-tendrils tugged at his legs. They resembled flesh-colored worms with multiple knuckles and fingernails at the end. That the man was now capable of such a terrible bodily alteration made Korden's blood run cold.

"*Get these things off me!*" Rand pleaded, clutching at them.

"*Ow!*" Meech yelped and let go of his brother with one hand to slap at his face. "*Somethin stung me!*"

A heartbeat later, Stone shouted a warning just as Korden felt a sudden intense pinch on the back of his neck and another in his scalp. His grip on Rand slackened, but he ignored the urge to swat at himself as he searched for their assailants.

The air around the wagon's rear deck seethed with insects the size of corn kernels. As he watched, one of them landed on his bare forearm. He squinted at it in the light from the bonnet and gasped when he saw it had the body of a wasp but Heater's head upon its shoulders. The tiny bearded visage grinned at him while it sank the painful stinger into his flesh.

It's not possible, Korden thought. *This can't be real.*

And, for the slightest second, it seemed he might be right, as the hybrid bug on his arm dimmed to translucency, fading away like the bonnet of the wagon when Doaks made it invisible.

Then more of the abominations swarmed in to sting him, and Rand's arms began to slip from his grasp.

10

finish it stop toying hurry up get him

Loathe was right; the part of him that was still Heater was having too much fun torturing them. Not only that, but the brat had started to disbelieve his renderings. Heater opened the throttle and moved closer to the wagon, trying to get within range so he could suck the kid's friends dry. Let their heads implode right in front of him before he was caught. Bludgeen and the other remaining Incarnate followed close.

And then, from the corner of his eye, Heater spotted blurred movement in the woods to his left.

11

Rand stared up at Korden and Meech with terror in his eyes as he was pulled away from the wagon's deck. There was nothing they could do to save him; Korden's muscles quivered and the stings from the Heater-bugs were growing intolerable.

Then, at Stone's urging, he looked over Rand's shoulder in time to see a small, dark shape streak from the trees directly at the side of the hovertrikes.

"*Zeega!*" he called.

The riftling launched into the air, landing on the handlebars of the closest Incarnate. She wrapped her tentacles around them and wrenched. The trike lurched sideways, ramming into the other demon's ride with a squall of tortured metal. Zeega leapt free before both vehicles slammed into a tree and lit up in a spectacular explosion.

12

Heater twisted on the saddle, trying to see what the hells just happened. The little blobby creature that'd taken out his last two escorts—which, according to several of the voices in his head, looked like a reject from a Carpenter flick called *The Thing*—snagged the back of his hog with a few tentacles, and then it was scurrying right at *him*.

He released the finger-tendrils and the insect swarm from reality and formed another ion shooter in his hand, but the ugly frammer moved too fast for him to get a bead in the close quarters. It zipped right around him, its squirmy limbs gripping all over his body, then scurried down the length of his trike to the engine compartment. Before he could even yell a threat, it ripped off the lid, reached inside, and tore out a bundle of wires. A high-pitched whining noise issued from the engine as the vehicle shimmied and bucked like a rodeo bull.

"*You lousy little vermin!*" Heater leveled the energy rifle at the creature as it jumped off the end of his ride.

13

The fingers and the bug swarm faded into nothingness, releasing Rand. They heaved him back on board, and Korden looked up in time to see Zeega hit the ground after sabotaging Heater's ride. She rolled a few times in the dirt, got her tentacles under her, and blazed after the wagon.

Behind her, Heater clung to his malfunctioning hovertrike and fired red streams of energy at her backside. Zeega dodged them and stared up at Korden, her countless legs working furiously as she tried to catch up.

"*Slow down!*" Korden shouted through the wagon.

"*Are you crazy, he's right behind us!*" Rand argued.

"*We have to get Zeega!*"

"*That greasy squid who tried to kill you?*" Doaks yelled over his shoulder from the opposite end of the vehicle. "*For fram's sake, just let it die!*"

"*We are NOT leaving her!*" Korden screamed. "*Slow down, or I'll throw you off and do it myself!*"

The wagon braked. Korden knelt and held out his arms. Zeega found a last burst of speed and sprang off the ground. She hit his chest hard enough to make him gasp, then huddled in his lap, a ball of quivering jelly. "*I've got her, go!*"

They accelerated again, this time leaving Heater behind as his trike sputtered to a halt. But the man's amplified voice rolled up the mountainside around them. "*YOU WON'T GET FAR! YOU HEAR US, YOU CURSEHEAD? WE WON'T EVER STOP COMING FOR YOOOU!*"

Like this novel?

YOUR REVIEWS HELP!

In the modern world, customer reviews are essential for any product. The artists who create the work you enjoy need your help growing their audience. Please visit Goodreads or the website of the company that sold you this novel to leave a review, or even just a star rating. Posting about the book on social media is also appreciated.

About the Author

Russell C. Connor has been writing horror since the age of five, and is the author of two short story collections, five eNovellas, and fourteen novels. His books have won two Independent Publisher Awards and a Readers' Favorite Award. He has been a member of the DFW Writers' Workshop since 2006, and served as president for two years. He lives in Fort Worth, Texas with his rabid dog, demented film collection, mistress of the dark, and demonspawn daughter.

His next novel—*The Halls of Moambati*, Volume IV of *The Dark Filament Ephemeris*—will be available in 2021.

The trikes were all trashed beyond repair. It would be easier to render a whole new fleet to continue the pursuit, and, after the rest of his expenditures, Heater was mighty drained. Better to regroup and come up with a new plan.

Even if it meant the kid slipping through his fingers once more.

but he knows found out about you aware we're free forewarned is forearmed

"So what?" It was so bizarre to hold a conversation with Loathe; like talking to a crowd of thousands of people that were all himself. "Not like it matters."

revealed too soon lost him failed yet again useless to us

"You wanna lay blame?" Heater snarled, defensive and angry. "Well maybe if you weren't always on the gods-damned ragged edge of starvation, we'd've had some power left when we needed it."

Exploding, white-hot agony ripped through his skull, bad enough to drive him to his knees on the dark forest trail. Even through the torment, he registered the cause: the vampire was feeding on *him* now.

be wary curb your tongue do not test us remember who saved you

"We saved each other," Heater argued through clenched teeth.

you drain us drop your illusion cannot sustain it waste of energy

No. Dropping the guise of his twin brother meant going back to his wretched former self, and he refused to do it. The sensation of weakness he'd experienced in that burned, broken shell terrified and infuriated him all at the same time. "Let go...you...motherframmer..."

then quit struggling give in submit call us master

"Thought...we were...one..." There was no reply this time, only a slow increase in the pain. When he could take it no more, Heater pleaded, "*Yeah, yeah, okay, stop!*"

His mind was released, leaving him gasping and weak. Loathe was all sweet promises when conning their way into your head; sunshine and rainbows as long as you kept them fed. But now, at the slightest setback, their true colors were showing.

For the first time, Heater began to have doubts about this arrangement he'd gotten himself into.

The humiliation served to fuel his anger. He was in an especially foul mood by the time he'd stomped back down the mountain to meet the cavalry riding up on their horses. Heater pulled the first Incarnate he could get his hands on from the saddle and growled, "Get us a line to that bathrobe-wearing boss of yours! NOW!"

Several of the *Exatraedes* sliced open their wrists and made a circle on the dirt with the black sludge that ran through their veins. Their bone portals might not be working under the shadow of Moambati, but at least they could still phone home on this side of the Skyreach. They chanted a few words that sounded like nonsense to Heater, then he stepped into the circle and found himself surrounded by a flickering, insubstantial facsimile of that dank room beneath the pizzeria.

"Your guys are real morons," he snapped at the ghostly representation of Torgas sitting in front of him. "They can't shoot for curse and they wrecked every last one of our hogs."

The Regent's lip rose in a sneer. "I trust the boy escaped."

"Hells yes, he escaped! Thanks to some little black blob with a thousand tentacles!"

"A riftling?" Torgas demanded, sudden fury creasing his pale, unblemished face. "You're positive a *riftling* was aiding the boy?"

"I don't know what a 'riftling' is, but the frammer was definitely on his side, along with some other peasants. They're headin east, across the Valley of Bones to the Skyreach. And we're goin after them."

"And by 'we,' do you mean yourself and that creature living in your head?"

"I'm talking about *you* and *us*, Torgas ol' buddy!" Heater threw his arms out wide. "We're in this together now, till death do us part! So we want you to send us *everyone*. Every last one of the redeyes under your command. Get them moving in our direction and they can link up with us as we ride."

The ethereal representation of Torgas rose from his throne of skulls and walked toward Heater. "You want to lead a group of beings that are vulnerable to the sun across a desert? And yet, *we* are the morons."

"They can cover up! Ride in transports! We don't care if they carry umbrellas, just get 'em moving!"

"I am barely maintaining control of this region as it stands. None of my men have come back from the realm of this Moambati. And I will not send the last of my command off to their deaths at your whim.”

Heater rubbed his forehead in frustration. “We told you we’d take care of Moambati, didn’t we? And this is how we do it. Give us an army, and when we have the boy, we’ll march through those mountains and scour them of whatever is up there.”

The Regent hesitated. “No. These are not my orders. We will wait until—”

“Torgas…no one is coming to help you. The rest of your kind has their hands full somewhere else. This is it. Your one opportunity to bust outta this jail. Last stand time. Bold men take action and all that. So send the Incarnates, and let us take care of the rest.”

Heater didn’t wait for an answer. He stepped out of the circle of blood, hanging up on the psychic phone call. Then he jumped on a horse and headed back down the hillside toward Ida.

He was going to need some snacks for the trip.